THE HELL OF IT ALL

A T.J. PETERSON MYSTERY

BOB KROLL

PUBLISHED BY ECW PRESS
665 GERRARD STREET EAST
TORONTO, ONTARIO M4M 1Y2
416-694-3348 / INFO@ECWPRESS.COM

THIS IS A WORK OF FICTION. NAMES,
CHARACTERS, PLACES, AND INCIDENTS
EITHER ARE THE PRODUCT OF THE AUTHOR'S
IMAGINATION OR ARE USED FICTITIOUSLY,
AND ANY RESEMBLANCE TO ACTUAL
PERSONS, LIVING OR DEAD, BUSINESS
ESTABLISHMENTS, EVENTS, OR LOCALES
IS ENTIRELY COINCIDENTAL.

LIBRARY AND ARCHIVES CANADA
CATALOGUING IN PUBLICATION

KROLL, ROBERT E., 1947–, AUTHOR
THE HELL OF IT ALL : A T.J. PETERSON
MYSTERY / BOB KROLL.

ISSUED IN PRINT AND ELECTRONIC FORMATS.
ISBN 978-1-77041-338-2 (PAPERBACK)
ALSO ISSUED AS: 978-1-77090-982-3 (PDF)
978-1-77090-981-6 (EPUB)

I. TITLE.

PS8621.R644H45 2017   C813'.6
C2016-906339-9   C2016-906340-2

COVER DESIGN: CYANOTYPE
AUTHOR PHOTO: MARY REARDON

COVER IMAGES: STREET SCENE © DENISTANGNEYJR / GETTY IMAGES; MAN WALKING AWAY
ON AN EMPTY DESOLATE ROAD INTERNATIONAL © PETER WOLLINGA / SHUTTERSTOCK;
SNOWSTORM TEXTURE © KZWW / SHUTTERSTOCK

THE PUBLICATION OF **THE HELL OF IT ALL** HAS BEEN GENEROUSLY SUPPORTED BY THE
CANADA COUNCIL FOR THE ARTS, WHICH LAST YEAR INVESTED $153 MILLION TO BRING
THE ARTS TO CANADIANS THROUGHOUT THE COUNTRY, AND BY THE GOVERNMENT OF
CANADA THROUGH THE CANADA BOOK FUND. *NOUS REMERCIONS LE CONSEIL DES ARTS DU
CANADA DE SON SOUTIEN. L'AN DERNIER, LE CONSEIL A INVESTI 153 MILLIONS DE DOLLARS
POUR METTRE DE L'ART DANS LA VIE DES CANADIENNES ET DES CANADIENS DE TOUT LE
PAYS. CE LIVRE EST FINANCÉ EN PARTIE PAR LE GOUVERNEMENT DU CANADA.* WE ALSO
ACKNOWLEDGE THE SUPPORT OF THE ONTARIO ARTS COUNCIL (OAC), AN AGENCY OF THE
GOVERNMENT OF ONTARIO, WHICH LAST YEAR FUNDED 1,737 INDIVIDUAL ARTISTS AND 1,095
ORGANIZATIONS IN 223 COMMUNITIES ACROSS ONTARIO FOR A TOTAL OF $52.1 MILLION, AND
THE CONTRIBUTION OF THE GOVERNMENT OF ONTARIO THROUGH THE ONTARIO BOOK
PUBLISHING TAX CREDIT AND THE ONTARIO MEDIA DEVELOPMENT CORPORATION.

ONTARIO ARTS COUNCIL
CONSEIL DES ARTS DE L'ONTARIO
an Ontario government agency
un organisme du gouvernement de l'Ontario

RECYCLED
Paper made from
recycled material
FSC® C103567

Canada Council
for the Arts

Conseil des Arts
du Canada

Canadä

PRINTED AND BOUND IN CANADA

TO JULIA, ELLERY, SARAH,
VIOLA, XAVIER, AND REBECCA

CHAPTER
ONE

Peterson swung the black Jetta onto the shoulder of the narrow coastal road, grabbed the cell phone from the shotgun seat, and caught the call on the fourth ring.

"You're late," a man's voice said.

"I'm five minutes away."

"I don't like it, man."

"Just sit tight!"

"Five minutes, and I'm counting."

The phone went dead, and Peterson gunned it. In the darkness, he missed the snowed-in path to the beach and squealed to a stop. He scowled at his mistake, then popped the transmission into reverse, backed up, and made the turn into the icy snowmobile ruts.

Scrub spruce and alders raked both sides of the Jetta. The occasional frost-heaved boulder ground hard against the undercarriage. Peterson heard a snowmobile roar to life not far away. Then the path took a wide turn and abruptly ended in a small clearing surrounded by snow-matted grass. At the far end, a heavy-set man in a black snowmobile suit and black helmet stood beside his machine.

Peterson knew him as a low-level criminal with big dreams; the kind who talks speed but cruises twenty clicks under the limit. His name was Harvey Roop, but because of the way he hunched over, as though he were carrying a heavy shell on his back, everyone called him Turtle.

Peterson reached for the .38 Ruger in the glove box and climbed from his car. He shoved the gun into the right-hand pocket of his brown field coat. He could taste the salt air in the cold wind off the ocean and looked over to where he heard waves breaking against the rocky shore. In the moonlight, he saw their crests bright with foam and the dark shapes of wild pea and rose bushes poking through the snow.

Then Turtle snapped on a heavy-duty flashlight and blasted the beam into Peterson's eyes. Peterson hollered for him to aim it somewhere else.

"I don't like being here with you," Turtle said, his voice muffled through the helmet. He crossbeamed the path Peterson had driven down.

"You're the one dressed like Darth Vader," Peterson said.

Turtle shut the flashlight, then leaned over the snowmobile and killed the motor. He removed the helmet and set it on the seat. He worked a wad of gum in his mouth.

"They dump you from the payroll, so how come you still doing them favours?" he said.

Peterson didn't answer.

"Pensioned off for head games, right? That's what I heard. You seeing a shrink?"

Peterson didn't answer.

"I mean what's with that?" Turtle said, talking with his gloved fingers as much as his mouth. "A girl cuts herself and bleeds to death, so what? I thought cops see it all the time. Car accidents and blood all over the goddamn road. Like that old guy the other day in a half-ton that took out a tollbooth on the bridge. I didn't see it, but I heard. The guy goes through the windshield. You see that shit a hundred times, you get used to it. Like doctors do. I don't mean the ones with the flu shot. I mean the ones who cut you open and fuck around with your insides."

"You got something to tell me?" Peterson said.

Turtle pushed his head forward and frowned. "You're the one begging for what I got."

"You called us."

"I called Danny, and Danny sends you."

"Danny didn't send me. We work together."

"That's not what I heard."

"What did you hear?" Peterson said, hiding the discontent he'd been feeling ever since administration had labelled him a psych case and shown him the door to early retirement. Now he was getting the same dismissal from the bottom.

"I heard Danny only feeds you table scraps," Turtle gloated. "And I heard you're working them hard to get back in the department."

Peterson took it on the chin.

"That puts you on the B-team," Turtle continued. "Danny sends *you*, maybe Danny don't think what I got is any good."

"What do you got?"

"Not how it's done. I get something before I give, a guarantee or something."

"No guarantee. First you give, and if what you give works out, then you get."

"Danny and me work it different. I'm talking favours, here. Only now I'm wondering if you can pull through on the favour I want."

"What favour's that?"

"Whatever favour I need."

"Like finagling the child abandonment charge against your old lady?"

That caught Turtle off guard. He shifted his weight.

"You think I'm an errand boy?" Peterson said. "You thought wrong. You're holding both ends of the same stick. Wrong word whispered in the wrong place, and someone opens you like a Ziploc. You're no undercover hero. You're a goddamn snitch!"

Turtle's mouth moved, but no words came out.

"So what's your bargaining chip?" Peterson pressed. "Otherwise I'm out of here, and your name gets scratched off the list. And you know what that means — you get no calls, no favours, and no insurance when the time comes and you need a good word for whatever charge comes your way. And if that's not enough, try this on for size: The nice-guy call to child services about your old lady, the call Danny was going to make, it doesn't happen."

Turtle swallowed his first few words, then tried again. "I overhear things, bits and pieces. I take what I get, you understand? I don't ask questions."

"What are you not asking questions about?"

"About rag asses jumping drug deals, you hear what I'm saying? Wearing masks and shit. Heavy duty. They're muscling hand to hand. Strictly petty cash. Pissing off a lot of people."

"Like who?"

"Like Sammy O."

"You brought me out here to talk about Sammy O pissed off at someone ripping off drug dealers? You got to be kidding, right?" Peterson knew Sammy O as a six-foot overweight slob who swaggered around the north end. Sammy and his boys casing the neighbourhood meant bad news for anyone getting in their way.

"There's a body too."

"What body?"

"Buried in Laurie Park, like thirty years ago."

"Whose body?"

"They didn't say."

"Who didn't say?"

"That's something I ain't giving right now."

"And when are you giving it?"

"After you find the body, and I get what I want."

"Where in the park?"

"In the campground."

"It must be forty acres under six inches of snow. You got a campsite number?"

Turtle shook his head.

"We're talking holes again, Turtle. The last time, you had us digging holes like we were gophers."

"The last time was on someone else's say-so," Turtle said. "This one I heard myself. And what are you griping about? The last time, you found the body."

"But not where you said it was."

"You never knew Jonah was missing. It was my heads-up that got the cops looking for Jonah. Same thing with what's buried in the park. So I put something on the table, and now it's your turn to put something up."

"For rag asses and a thirty-year-old body buried someplace you don't know."

"A campsite."

"But you don't know the number. There could be thirty, forty, maybe a hundred campsites in the park. You want us to dig up every one on your say-so?"

Turtle squirmed. He picked up the helmet from the snowmobile seat and put it back down. "The body's for real," he said. "I heard them talking."

"But you're not telling who you heard. Here's the thing, Turtle, it's not a meat sandwich if you leave out the meat."

Turtle's face went through ten shapes of anxiety. Then he said, "It stays with you, right?"

"Me and Danny."

"You and Danny, but nobody else."

"Cross my heart and hope to die."

"The hell with you and that kid stuff."

"Just tell me what you got."

"I heard Willie Blackwood say something to this other guy. I don't know who. I never got a good look."

"Where was that?"

"Willie has a camp upcountry, and he was there with his snowmobile pals."

"Not your kind of company. What are you doing there?"

"I'm not riding with them. I show an hour later. They have me packing the blow, so if they get stopped on the highway, they're clean. Then one of the machines goes down, and I'm outside pulling spark plugs and cleaning them. That's when I heard Willie talking."

"You heard what, exactly?"

"The guy said, 'We do the fucker and dump him where he can't be found.' Then Willie said, 'Try a campground.' He said, 'Who walks a campground looking for a grave?' The guy left and Willie said to that friend of his, you know, big fucking nose, Willie's muscle, the one they call Come On . . ."

"Cameron," Peterson said.

"Yeah. Willie said to him about burying one in Laurie Park thirty years ago. Nothing but bones now. Like a place that nobody finds."

"And that's all Willie said?"

"Yeah."

"When was this?"

"The day after it snowed."

"Two weeks and you're bringing it now?"

"I ain't the fucking mailman."

Peterson thought about it a moment. "Tell me more about the rag asses. Strictly low level?"

"Dollar store."

"They've got nothing to do with the body in the park?"

"You going deaf or something? The rag asses don't mean shit."

"You think Willie knows the campsite number?"

"How do I know what Willie knows? If he put it there he knows. But that ain't something he goes around talking about. And we don't shack together. If the man talks in his sleep, I ain't going there, I ain't hearing it."

CHAPTER
TWO

Peterson grabbed a red vinyl booth at the back of Reggie's Place, a downtown diner where eggs, bacon, pancakes, and hash browns flew off the black cast iron grill all morning. Office keeners lined up at the takeout bar, early birds eager to make an impression. Those working construction at the new Trade Centre, wearing jeans or canvas overalls, sat in booths along the walls or at tables covered with red-and-white checkered cloths. A forty-something waitress named Angie saw Peterson and brought his order without his asking: burnt toast and black coffee.

Danny showed up ten minutes later carrying a newspaper. Square face, tight lips, and brown hair tinted to leave just a little grey. He was dressed to kill, in a black leather car-coat, blue button-down, and yellow tie.

"Oscar de la Renta," Peterson kidded.

"Don't go there," Danny warned. "I don't need you busting my balls. I got enough hurt with Fultz wringing my ass in spin dry."

Peterson knew all about Fultz, the deputy chief, suck-holing his way to the top and shafting the lower ranks to get there.

Danny signalled Angie for a number three on the chalkboard hanging behind the counter. He leaned toward Peterson. "Did you go home last night or walk the streets?"

"You checking up?"

Danny scowled and looked at the table of construction workers. He looked back. "Maybe I know what's in the back of your mind."

"You going to tell me what it is?"

"No. I'll let you figure out. Tell me about Turtle. What'd he have?"

"Not much. Rag asses muscling the blow trade."

"That's drug squad," Danny said. "I'm homicide. They don't share. Why should I? Anything else?"

Peterson held back a grin. "Get a shovel!"

"Not again?"

"Thirty-year-old body in Laurie Park. Don't know who, don't know where."

"What *does* he know?"

"That Willie Blackwood or someone Willie knows put it there."

Angie delivered Danny's scrambled eggs, hash browns, and whole wheat toast. She stood at the booth with her weight on one leg, coffee pot in hand.

"Busy this morning," Danny said to her.

"Busy every morning," she complained. Her cheeks

were rouged like ripe apples. "Short staffed. You'd think Reggie would cough up the bucks and hire someone. But no way. He says busy gets more coming. Like we need more? Pretty soon he'll be setting tables on the sidewalk."

"Not in this weather," Danny said.

"Yeah," she said, "who can get warm? Not like those guys." She gestured over her shoulder at the table of construction workers. "Two of them off to Florida next week. Me? I stay home and freeze. And you know what my husband says? He says, 'You want to get warm, Angie? Go to hell.'"

One of the construction workers held up his mug and drew the waitress away.

Danny chewed and swallowed. He reached for the newspaper beside him and showed it to Peterson. "City Council is pushing Fultz's buttons, and Fultz is pushing on every cop in the building."

Peterson glanced at the editorial about the sudden increase in violent crime in the city.

"Last night's drive-by didn't make the morning news," Danny said. "Someone blew out a picture window. Nobody hurt." He dug for another forkful.

"Where?" Peterson asked.

"C'mon, they shit in their own bed. All for a piece of turf. More action, more money, more greed, more bodies."

"Something's stirring the pot."

"That last drug bust the Mounties made," Danny said. "Coke goes short, the dealers get restless. Little turf wars. Dominoes falling. He took my corner, so I'll take yours. Bullets fly and people get hurt. Then two days ago, Sammy O, someone put a bullet through his car window, and that has Sammy shitting bricks. Why the attempt? We don't know."

Peterson waited for Danny to say more, but Danny just dug into his eggs and hash browns.

"You investigating the Sammy O shooting?" Peterson pried.

"We're keeping the public out," Danny said between mouthfuls.

"And I'm now the public?"

"I didn't say that."

"Implied."

Danny set down his knife and fork. He reached for a paper napkin and wiped his mouth. "Some things I can't talk about. It involves the Mounties and us, joint task-force investigation. You know the drill."

"Yeah, I know the drill, trust only people you can trust." Danny cringed.

"After twenty-three years, I thought I deserved—"

"There's a protocol," Danny insisted. "I buck that, and I'm bucking the department."

"And any chance of climbing the ladder."

"That's not what this is about."

"Then what's it about?"

Danny drank some coffee. "Don't look so pissed. We keep doing what we're doing. We work together on what we can work together on."

"Table scraps."

Danny rolled his eyes. "What's going on? You feeling hurt all of a sudden, left out?"

Peterson didn't answer.

"We both know why," Danny said. "You're a time bomb. I bring you in on something sensitive, and what if the same thing happens again like what happened six months ago?

Things get tight, the stress goes up, the flashbacks start, and you're looking for a corner to scramble to, or worse you come out like Dirty Harry. Then I'm the one who wears it. I'm the one called on the carpet for you being involved. Well, I'm not wearing it. I'm not taking chances with what goes on inside your head."

"So, I'm a liability," Peterson said and got up to go.

"C'mon, sit down. We've been friends too long for you to walk away like this."

Peterson remained standing.

"Christ almighty, Peterson. How many examples do you want?"

Peterson turned to walk away.

"All right!" Danny said. "It's not all you. I have my eye on something. Ambition. About time, don't you think? I'm toeing the line, for Christ's sake. I got something here, a woman I care about. You know how long it's been since I could say that? She wants more for me. Is that so bad?"

Peterson looked at the clock above the takeout counter. "I got to go."

Danny held up his hands in peace. "What time's the funeral?"

"Memorial service."

"You know what I mean."

"Ten o'clock."

"I won't make it, you know that?"

"I didn't expect you to."

Danny waved a hand to change the subject. "How you coming on the Rafferty case?"

"Frozen solid," Peterson said.

Danny thought for a moment. "Let it go and I'll see what else I can pass your way."

"Another table scrap."

"You don't give up, do you? If Fultz found out about us working together — and it don't matter what we're working on — if he found out, he'd have a shit fit."

Peterson was expressionless. Danny dug another forkful of hash browns. He talked and chewed at the same time. "Turtle calls, says it's important, then hands over drug squad info they should be carving off their own snitches. What does he think I am? He knows I don't trade favours for rag asses busting drug deals."

"And a body," Peterson said.

Danny frowned. "Thirty years old and he don't know where it's buried. Did he ask for something?"

"He wanted you to ease up on his old lady."

Danny swallowed. "If he doesn't come across with something we can use, he goes back inside and his wife loses custody. It's time I told him that. Light a match under his ass."

CHAPTER
THREE

Peterson didn't have much in the way of memories of Michelle MacKinnon, a seventeen-year-old runaway from St. Thomas, Ontario, with a crush on whatever would keep her feet from touching down. It didn't matter what. Pop, blow, or honeydew, if it exploded her mind in a fountain of sunsets, it was up her nose or in her arm.

The street had called her Mickey Mac, like she still had some innocence left after being trucked east by a gang of pimps, screwed over in less than a year, and tossed out to the low-life for ten bucks a throw in the back seat of a junked out Chevy Impala. Now she was dead from an armload of over the top. Found on the shower floor in the Valley View Women's Correctional Facility. Two guards had smuggled the stuff inside while admin operated with its head up its ass. Pointing fingers.

Her parents had written her off from day one. They had hung up on the social worker who called them to report their daughter was dead. They refused to claim the body. Word had reached Peterson, and he posted the cash to have Mickey Mac cremated and a memorial service held.

He had enlarged the only photo he had of her, a mug shot that Billy Bagnall, the communications specialist at police headquarters, had doctored by darkening her emaciated skin tones and brightening her raccoon eyes. A wooden frame gave the photo a homey look on the dark oak table. Beside it was the ceramic urn that held her ashes. Peterson had picked it up at Value Village for seven bucks.

He had met her only three times: the first time when she was working the corner, hustling johns outside a north-end pub. Spiked black hair, eyeballs wide and rattling, tight red bondage pants, and a blue boat-neck sweater worn off one shoulder and showing off tattoos of vines and foliage twisting up both arms. The second time had been when she showed up at his front door with her born-to-bleed face hidden inside a grey hoodie and a .22 Smith & Wesson pointed his way. The third time had been when he had sat behind her at her short and simple trial. Guilty plea. No negotiated settlement and not a whole lot of remorse. He remembered staring at the back of her neck with the tattooed phrase in quotation marks, "God Gave the World To the Wicked."

There were no strings for her memorial service, and no pipe organ. There was just the awkward rustle of five mourners in the United Church hall in the north end. Yellow painted walls, hardwood floor. Two dozen stackable chairs looked all the more uncomfortable for staying empty. He had put the word out about the memorial service, and was not surprised at the no-shows. It wasn't like he had offered the head cleaners and gum chewers coloured poppy seeds as giveaways.

A teenage girl with iridescent blue hair, pencil-thin legs, and red warm-ups sat in the first row. Two guys with heavy eyes and mopey grins hunkered in the back, angling for an early exit. One of them had a voice like a morning hangover. A woman in her late forties, wearing a tan sheepskin coat, brown skirt, and high leather boots, sat in the middle of the hall and stared at Peterson's lined and expressionless face. He stood beside the oak table and sneaked a glance her way a couple of times. She was unembarrassed to be caught staring.

Mid-morning sunlight pouring in through gothic style windows spotlit Eleanor Lively, the United Church minister, as she stepped behind the white podium and loudly addressed the five. Her deep voice did not match her spindly shape, but it did wonders at quickly bringing the two guys sitting in the back to silence.

"I did not know Michelle MacKinnon," the minister said, "but you did. You knew the tormented life she led. You knew her sadness and how tragically she suffered both mentally and physically. In John's Gospel, Jesus said: 'Peace I leave with you, my peace I give to you. I do not give it to you as the world gives. Let not your heart be troubled, neither let it be afraid.' Let us be thankful that Michelle MacKinnon has found peace in the arms of the Lord, that she is no longer troubled, that she is unafraid. Let us be thankful that she has been rescued from her suffering and her enemies. Let us give thanks that our Heavenly Father is now her shield and her fortress. Like the sheep wandering alone in the wild wood, Michelle was lost but now is found. The trumpet has sounded for Michelle MacKinnon. Her mortal nature has put on immortality. The peace Christ promised is now hers. It is an eternal peace. In the words of Our Lord, let us pray."

She said an Our Father and then another prayer, a long one that Peterson figured nobody listened to. Then she asked, "Does anyone wish to say something on her behalf? Something to share, something to help each of us remember her?"

No one did. And that was it for Mickey Mac. A whore strung out on drugs and dead before she was twenty.

Reverend Lively shook hands with everyone, expressed her sympathy, and left. Then the two guys left, followed by the girl with blue hair. The woman approached Peterson and offered her hand.

"Patty Creaser," she said.

"Peterson."

"I know. We worked together a couple of years ago."

"Worked?"

"I had a client you arrested."

She turned to the urn on the oak table. "What's next?"

"Dump the ashes, I guess."

"Scatter, you mean."

"Yeah, scatter."

"You want help?"

They drove to the waterfront in two cars, Patty in her red Corolla and Peterson in his black Jetta. They parked near the ferry terminal and walked to the end of the jetty. March sunlight hinted at warmth, but so far it had delivered nothing above minus five Celsius. A light wind from the north smoothed the water into a sheet of blue steel. He popped the top off the urn and looked at the water and then at the urn. Lost in thought. She stepped forward and placed her hands over his.

"Two years ago I saved her life," Patty said. "I wish it had turned out better." She shifted her eyes from the urn to Peterson. "Do you have something to say?"

He shook his head. Carrying the urn together, they shuffled to the edge of the jetty and emptied Mickey Mac's five pounds of ashes and powdered bone to the outgoing tide. A clump became instantly waterlogged and sank. The rest floated for a moment or two, then dissolved away.

"Bounded into the bonds of life," Peterson said, and pulled a hapless grin. "A rabbi said that at a burial I went to years ago. It's stuck with me."

On their way back along the jetty, Patty asked, "Now what?"

Peterson was confused by the question until he realized Patty was asking if he had something else planned by way of ceremony. "Nothing else," he said. "Unless you'd like a coffee."

They walked over to the coffee shop nearest the ferry terminal and sat at a table beside the window overlooking the harbour. Sunlight filled their faces. Peterson watched a pilot boat guide an outbound container ship, and Patty watched him. He felt her gaze and turned her way. He liked her bobbed brown hair and the confidence he saw in the way she flattered her looks with minimal makeup.

"How did you know her?" he asked.

"I'm a social worker, and Mickey Mac was something of a hopeless case. It was difficult not to bury her file under

18

a stack of others more worthwhile. But that wasn't what I was paid to do."

"You wouldn't be here if concern was nothing more than a job," Peterson said. "How did you save her life?"

"She partied too hard one night, and I just happened to be on my way to another client, in the same building. Mickey was lying in the hallway with a needle stuck in her arm. Ten o'clock in the morning. Like nobody noticed?"

Peterson thought about how many of those he had seen. He tried for a smile, but it didn't happen.

"Your turn," Patty said. "Why a memorial service for Mickey Mac?"

Peterson looked at the container ship and pilot boat. Then back. "It was the least I could do. A life ruined with drugs. Whoring herself to buy more. Vicious circle"

"She shot you in the chest. It was all over the news."

"And the knee."

"Because of that, you claim the body and scatter her remains?"

"Mickey Mac only pulled the trigger. Someone else put the gun in her hand."

Patty studied him. Then her look suggested an implicit connection. "Do you drink wine?"

He shook his head.

She was enjoying herself. "I didn't think so. Beer?"

He again shook his head.

She nodded at the coffee cup. "But you do drink coffee."

"I drink coffee," Peterson said. "I drink lots of coffee. But you should know I'm not a long-distance runner. I'm not even a good sprinter."

Patty laughed. "Who said I want to race?"

"I'm just telling what I'm not."

"I'm more interested in what you are." She pulled a napkin from the dispenser, then reached for the pen in his shirt pocket, and wrote something on the napkin. She slipped it into his hand.

They walked to the parking lot in awkward silence, Peterson still holding the napkin. He spotted a street punk in baggy-ass jeans and sporting a head of Jheri curls leaning against the passenger side of his Jetta. Peterson knew the guy. He stuffed the napkin into his jacket pocket.

She had parked two cars away from Peterson and heard every word of the exchange.

"Peterson," the punk said. Brazen smile and dropping a half dip as he stepped away from the car.

"Why soil this side of town, Cory?"

"Business trip," Cory said, and smiled.

"You still working the order desk, or you out here scouting home alones?" Cory Ferris was the front man for a back-door body shop. He took the orders for stolen cars and made deliveries. A sweet talker with a mean streak, but nowhere near as mean as his brother, Leon. Leon the Neon was always on the muscle, a hired enforcer eager to play with guns.

"You got me wrong, Mister Police," Cory whined. "I'm an auto trader. I'll fix you up with a change of wheels." He pointed at Peterson's Jetta. "I'm driving by and see this shit box and I know this got to be a man that's light for cash, a man picking lint from his pocket. Then I look up and see you, and I know this is the man that belongs to this car. Who else would roll around in something with a hole in the roof?"

20

Peterson didn't look at the ragged hole in the car's roof. He knew all about it.

"I mean, what's with that?" Cory continued. "It's a fucking bullet hole, Peterson. Somebody try to pop you off?"

Peterson sidled to the driver's side and watched Cory across the roof, the bullet hole between them. "You didn't just show up. You got a reason for being here, say it."

"Yeah, I got a reason, but I'm worried about someone messing up your car."

"Say it!"

"My brother says hi. That's all. He just wants you to know he's thinking of you. All the time, man. He does nothing else but think about you. He said maybe you and him should get together. Old times. Sooner the better, that's what he said."

"You make another visit, you tell Leon I said hi right back."

"Yeah. The thing is, I don't got to make no visit. I don't know if you heard, but Leon made parole."

Peterson's body tightened, stopped a feeling that tried to escape. Cory saw it and grinned. With that he shoved off with another half dip and strutted across the street to a late model black Cadillac Escalade.

Peterson watched him get into the SUV then looked over at Patty, and Patty looked at him.

"Bullet hole?" she said.

Peterson let it go.

CHAPTER
FOUR

Six of them sat in a circle in various positions of defiance and regret in the sunlit classroom of a school that now served as a community services building. Peterson was hunched forward as though guarding a secret, elbows over his knees, his face expressionless, listening.

"Orders come down," the bearded guy said, his voice croaky. "They wanted proof, like a village with no men wasn't enough."

The man lifted his head to gaze at the rack of windows high up the east-facing wall, as if searching for an answer to a frightening question.

There was no discomfort with the long silence. All six of them were used to unwelcomed thoughts and unfiltered memories. Then the bearded guy said, "What happens after? I wanted to know. We tag the bodies, then what? Who do we nail for doing it?"

Peterson regarded him. War zone, city streets, same concern, same need to punish the cruelty someone did to someone else.

Dr. Beatrice Heaney, the retired psychiatrist in a grey turtleneck and jeans, was a volunteer with the underfunded self-help program for vets and first responders. She stirred in her seat enough to get the bearded guy's attention and nodded by way of encouragement.

The man looked at Peterson and shuffled his hands like they needed something to do. "You work the city, you ever see shit like that?"

Peterson stared at the guy without seeing him. His eyes were focused on something inside his own head.

"Yeah," said a middle-ager, his face jutting from a blue hoodie. "Try driving ambulance for ten years."

The bearded man clenched his hands. "We got what they sent us for," he said. "Jackpot in a ditch the Serbs covered over. Twenty, thirty. Arms and legs tangled up. I don't know. We kept losing count."

The woman with the shaved head jumped up and sat back down. She wore a heavy grey coat that she never took off.

"Wanda?" Dr. Heaney said.

"Same thing, different war," Wanda said. She shook her head and waved her arms. "Talking's just bullshit!" She pointed at Dr. Heaney. "You don't live it, you don't know. Write it down, like that makes it fucking go away. Twenty-four seven. That's what it is. Day and fucking night."

Wanda had exploded before. Each one of them had. They all had misgivings that talking didn't help, that nothing did. Not the one-on-one sessions, not the group therapy, not the booze, the drugs, or the runaway nights curled up in a corner chasing sleep with every light, radio, laptop, and TV spinning the meter.

"It's all the time," the bearded guy said. "In your face, all the time."

"It's like it's inside your eyes," Peterson said to the space between his feet. "You look away but it's still there. You still see it."

Dr. Heaney leaned forward. "What do you see?"

Peterson lifted his head. "You don't have to go to war to see bodies so mangled you don't recognize them as people. You don't have to leave this city."

CHAPTER
FIVE

Peterson was into his second cup of black coffee, using the mirror behind the bar in The Office to cover the door.

Dave Cotter, a jumbo who filled a lot of space behind the bar, pulled a couple of drafts for the middle-aged waitress standing at the far end. Despite its name, The Office was a pub that had working stiff written all over it. Dark wood chairs and tables, a stand-up bar, two dartboards, VLTs along one wall, four ceiling-mounted televisions, a pool table, and a hideaway corner where there used to be a platform for musicians who'd play on Friday and Saturday nights. Cotter, a retired cop, owned the place, worked it, and, since his second wife had caught a red-eye to Toronto and left him a note saying she wasn't coming back, he'd lived in it. He had named the place as a joke, so his regulars could say for the fun of it, "I'm going to The Office."

Cotter mouthed something to the bus driver sitting in front of him, then took the beers over to the waitress and came back to Peterson. He nodded at Peterson's coffee. "You want something to eat with that?"

Peterson grimaced. "Low-fat diet."

Cotter reached under the bar for a bowl of peanuts and set them in front of Peterson.

"They make me fart," Peterson said.

"Nobody sits with you anyway," Cotter said and popped a few into his mouth.

"You sure about this kid?" Peterson asked, picking up the conversation where he and Cotter had left off.

"I wouldn't bet my life on it, but he poked his head in three times like he was looking for someone. The last time about an hour ago."

"No idea who he is?"

Cotter shook his head. "Twenty-something. Had that 'fuck you' look, you know, like everybody owed him something. I thought with this Ferris thing, I ought to tell you."

A guy with a bulldog face sitting at the bar raised his glass for a refill. Cotter pulled him a draft.

The waitress, Janice Doyle, returned to the bar and hiked her left buttock onto the stool beside Peterson. She had a spiritless face, droopy lips, and heavily veined legs that always swelled at the ankles two hours into her shift. She gestured toward his coffee.

"You're holding up pretty good," she said. "But drinking black coffee all day, I don't know how you sleep."

He flashed a smile. "I don't sleep, Janice. I just lie there thinking of you."

"About the same way I lie there wishing for another

26

husband. No way. After working here, all I want are empty rooms and quiet."

"I like quiet."

"But you don't like empty rooms."

"It's hard to find yourself in a house full of empty rooms."

"Like you're looking," Janice said. A customer at a nearby table caught her eye and she gestured that she'd be right there. "You want the latest on my sister's kid?"

Peterson let his eyes tell her that he knew the latest about her nephew.

"So what does she do?" Janice asked.

"Anything that keeps her son from learning life lessons on the inside. Does the kid have a lawyer?"

She rolled her eyes. "Collins."

Peterson coughed a laugh. "A legal aid with more hope than common sense," he said.

Cotter had been listening in and now leaned over from the tap to offer his two cents' worth. "The kid sold M&Ms to an undercover. I said he should play it as entrapment. Fifteen, not knowing any better."

"Yeah, like he didn't know Oxy was illegal," Peterson scoffed. He reached for a coaster and pulled a pen from his jacket pocket. He wrote down a name and number.

"He's a good kid, Peterson," Janice said, the hitch in her voice giving away her flagging spirit.

"They all are, until they start respecting the knuckleheads that do time."

"Role models," Cotter chimed in. "Bitch-slapping in their videos. Asses out. Street whores pawing all over them. Who tells them different? Doesn't matter if someone does, because they ain't listening. Not to anyone, and not to the judge who warned the kid two years ago not to come back. So he goes up on charges and then what? I don't know. I mean, who does?"

No answer. Peterson slid Janet the coaster.

She looked at it and then at him. "How far can I take this?"

"As far as it has to go," he said.

"Do I mention your name?"

"You don't get past reception if you don't."

She slipped the coaster into her apron pocket, eased off the stool, and returned to taking and filling orders.

Cotter leaned over the bar. "The Mink don't do pro bono."

Peterson allowed a faint smile. "He will for me."

Cotter inched closer. "Who doesn't owe you a favour in this city?"

Peterson ignored the question. "How good's your memory?"

"Is this a game?"

"Thirty years ago, a missing person."

"You expect me to remember something like that?"

"Carlisle Martin?"

"Him, you don't forget," Cotter said. "Thirty years? Jesus, I would have guessed fifteen, maybe twenty. I hate when time goes by faster than you think. Like the other day a guy mentions Rolly Sullivan. A forty-goal scorer in college, thirty at least. Anyway he takes a heart attack and drops dead on the ice in front of maybe five thousand fans. I figured he died maybe forty years ago. The guy says sixty. Sixty! I was seven years old, and I remember it like it was yesterday. It goes by fast and there's nothing we can do about it. Thirty years, huh? Jesus, I was still married to my first wife and . . . Where the fuck was I working then? I would've been mid-thirties, so it was after that kid ran a red eye and I piled into the corner of St. Joe's. Fucking desk jockey after that. I met you around then, right?"

"A few years later. I had the Central beat."

"You had a warrant I had to help you with. See, the ol' brain comes back when you prod it a little. Thirty years, huh? It doesn't seem that long ago. Back then Martin was running the show in town. Big time connections in Montreal. That's when Robbie Yorke was undercover and comes out a hero. A good fucking cop."

"Best I ever knew," Peterson said.

"You and him were tight, like father and son."

Peterson shrugged.

"When did he retire?" Cotter asked. "It must be . . . Here we go again."

"Twelve years ago."

"Twelve? He must be soaking up the sun this time of year."

"Pretty much stays put and lives where he always did."

"Wife still alive?"

"She died a year after he retired."

"You still see him?"

"Off and on. More off than on."

"The next time you see Robbie, tell him I was asking."

"I will. How about Carlisle Martin?"

"I'm trying to remember, but I was working a desk back then."

"A lot of paper crossed that desk," Peterson said.

"Too much to remember all of it. What are you scrounging for?"

"Whatever you know about Carlisle Martin."

"Thirty years later?"

"Does that make a difference?"

Cotter shook his head. "He had out-of-town connections."

"Montreal?"

"They kept him supplied. I mean not for nothing. Martin was tough. Mangy too. He had notches in his reputation that made him top dog in the drug trade down here. But he wasn't smart. Every once in while we'd get tips from Yorke and a warrant would go out. A lot of times it would stick. Possession. Gun violation. Chump change, but it shows the guy was careless. Willie Blackwood isn't like that." Cotter thought for a moment. "You almost had him once though, didn't you?"

"I couldn't make it stick," Peterson said. "The man had enough rock candy to go up for ten big ones. But Blackwood's lawyer got it thrown out of court, made a big thing about me not reading him his rights."

"Right. After you threw him down a flight of stairs?"

"He deserved every step he hit."

"You almost lost your badge. Must have been twenty years ago. You grew up near him, didn't you?"

"My father's family did. I'm a city boy. Visited there a lot of summers."

"Did you know him?"

"I knew of him. He was older by twelve, fifteen years."

"Was he hustling drugs then?"

"Let's say he was no son of a fisherman," Peterson said.

"He always had money in his pocket, and a lot to throw around."

"Still does from what I hear," Cotter said. "Worked his way up to running the show. Retired to a little island near that fishing village, but that holds no weight, right? The man's sitting back and still pulling all the strings."

"Maybe someday it catches up," Peterson said.

"It hasn't yet, and the guy's sixty-something. Big house on the water. Whoever said crime doesn't pay was a goddamn liar. He came in here once. That big needle hanging around his neck, like him saying, 'Don't fuck with me or this is what you get.'"

"What about Carlisle Martin?"

"Like I said, he ran things before Blackwood took over, and Martin worked the Montreal connection, but more than that, I don't know. Robbie Yorke's the man to talk to, undercover like he was. He'd know a hell of a lot more than me. Jimmy Stiles would know a lot too. Him and Yorke worked together back then. Good friends. Hung out. Partners for a while after Yorke came out from undercover. But Stiles fell apart." Cotter made a drinking gesture. "He lives with the pissy-pants gang in that rooming house near the flour mill. Him and Yorke, that's who you should talk to."

• • •

Peterson nursed a black coffee at a table in a corner of The Office, far enough from the bar to be alone, but close enough not to miss the action at the front end. He saw Tanya Colpitts come in and went hollow inside.

"Don't jack me around, Cotter," she said and brushed

the big man's hand off her arm. "I don't work shit holes like this, and I don't work standing up or sitting down."

She was fortyish and had the racked look of a user and the spike-heeled strut of a working girl. She dressed that way too: black stretch pants and, despite the cold outside, a black leather jacket open to a low-cut blouse that showed off everything she wanted to show.

Cotter tried to use his size to back her out of the pub, but she wasn't budging. "The sign says 'No Soliciting,'" he said, pointing at the sign on the pegboard inside the door. "It ain't for salesmen."

"I came to see *him*," she said and looked over at Peterson.

"But does he want to see you?"

"You know what this is?" she said, raising both hands to frame her once pretty face. "This is my sweet way of telling you to fuck off." She barrelled past him and swung her ass as she made her way to Peterson, who sat with his feet on the chair beside him.

She stopped in front of him, and he lifted his hazel eyes to her hardened face. Her mouth was set in a straight-edge smile, and her body rippled with sex. He made no bones about seeing it. He saw something else too — her sitting on the rickety front porch of a crack house and fuck pad off the Bay Road, her arms slung over her knees, teary eyes, strung out with worry at being rounded up with half a dozen crackheads and whores. "I need help, Peterson," she had begged. He remembered having dropped down on the porch beside her. "I can try, but no promises." And her pulling away, eyes flashing. "Promises are what I need!"

Now he saw Cotter watching them and signalled to him that all was fine. He looked at her. "It's been a while," he said.

She sat down in the chair across the table from him and pasted on another smile, this one menacing. "Two years, eight months, and two weeks. I could nail the day and hour, but who counts every drop of water?"

He took a sip of coffee to avoid the awkward moment. "We both knew it was over before it started," he said, thinking that loss and abandonment were the same thing.

"Is that what you tell yourself? Easier that way? You reached into the gutter and came away patting yourself on the back."

"We started something we never should've started," he said. "But it was more than just a moment of weakness. It got too complicated to go on."

"For you, maybe. You weren't on the receiving end." Tanya held up her hands and arms as though playing a violin. "Yeah I know. You had a rough time. I understand. Sad eyes, hurt feelings, so you change the rules to work better for you."

He folded his arms. His strained look gave away the hurt and dark inside. "There's a price paid for everything," he said.

"What'd it cost you?"

He said nothing.

"Your wife dies," she said, "you walk, and I'm in rehab dreaming of a house and white picket fence."

"You were dreaming something that wasn't going to be. I reached out, and I reached too far, but helping you get straight was—"

She wrestled him with her eyes. He held firm. Then he said, "We needed each other. You needed me, and after that thing in the container terminal and my life going to hell, I needed you."

"And then you didn't," she said.

"It wasn't that simple. I couldn't go on like that. Not after what had happened."

"When I found out another guy was in the car with your wife when she died, I didn't say 'Serves him right.' I cried, Peterson, because I knew you were never coming back." She leaned forward. "But that's not why I'm here. My daughter's missing."

"Daughter?"

"Daughter. Her name's Cassie."

"I didn't know . . ."

"Foster homes. When she got older she came by sometimes. She had a baby and didn't know what to do. She couldn't keep it. And then . . . What was I supposed to do? I couldn't take care of my own."

"She's been missing since when?"

The confidence that had her smiling moments before had drained from her. "A week ago, eight days. We'd text sometimes. Now there's nothing, no texts, and none of the other girls has seen her. She's involved in something, and I don't know where she is. I don't even know if I should be telling you this, but you're the only one I trust."

Tanya saw his surprise. "It wasn't just you failing me. I know what I was, what I am."

He watched her thinking it through.

"You said there's a price paid for everything," she said. "This is what I'm paying for being a whore."

He swung his feet off the chair. "I'm listening."

She looked over both shoulders to ensure no one was near enough to hear. Her hands were trembling, and she folded them to keep them quiet. "She saw someone killed."

"Did she say that, those words?"

Tanya shook her head. "She said there was a gun, and she had blood on her clothes."

"Did she say who?"

Tanya shook her head.

"Did she say where?"

"She was talking nonsense. She said something about the empty building on Canal Street."

"Which one?"

"I think the one across from where the girls take their johns."

He looked past her to where Cotter stood at the bar looking their way. No one else was within earshot.

She clutched her shoulders, struggling to hold herself together. Her voice went from street smart to stringy. "Just say you'll find her."

"Tell me what she saw."

"Goddamn you, Peterson!" Her shout drew the attention of two pub lizards working the VLTs. She pulled a deep breath and let go of her shoulders. "Please say it."

He reached across the table and gripped her hands to stop them from shaking. "I'll try, but the police would do a better job."

She searched his eyes. "No cops," she said. "If she did something, I don't want her going down. She does time, she'll come out worse than she is. Please. Find her and get her out of it."

He thought of his own daughter, who ran away almost three years ago. Working the streets. Shooting up. He knew where she was, but he never reached out, for reasons he didn't understand himself.

She slipped one hand free and pressed it over his. "I never came back and asked you for anything. Not once."

He nodded. "Tell me about your daughter. How old?"

"Fifteen."

Four years younger than his daughter. He couldn't help feeling their hope had been squandered.

"Trouble since day one," Tanya said. "But what chance did she have with a whore for a mother?"

"Don't do it to yourself."

"See! You still care." She pulled her hands back. "It wasn't just you walking away. I never would've made it through rehab. Hopeless, right?"

"Not hopeless. I gave you a reason to get clean, then I took it away. I'm sorry."

"That's why I can't hate you. You tried to help. You tried a lot harder than me."

He heard the dryness in her voice. "You want a beer?"

She shook her head.

"I've been clean and dirty, on and off," she said. "I'm working it through but I can't get anywhere."

He saw in her eyes how much she hungered for a nickel of something sweet.

"You won't make it without help," he said. "I can put in a word."

"I've heard that before."

"I know."

"They don't want losers in rehab," she said. "Anyway, I can't do it. A straight whore's a liability."

He saw what hadn't been there three years ago: the hardness in her. The backhands, the knuckles on her jaw, the scarred lip. He saw her whore's life of buckle and bend. It ripped him to see it.

"She ran with the wrong crowd," Tanya said and faked a laugh. "What mother doesn't make that excuse? Then she got mixed up with that bastard."

"What bastard's that?"

"The Needle."

His eyes flew up. "What was she doing with Willie Blackwood?"

"What do you think she was doing? I found that out from someone who knew Cassie was my daughter. Then I didn't hear a thing for I don't know how long, until one day she shows up with her baby, and there was nothing I could do. Then I hear she gave it up and now she's with another bastard."

"Which one?"

"Logan Morehouse."

Peterson shrugged. The name meant nothing.

"She got sucked in. You know how. You know about falling for promises men make."

Peterson let it go.

"He had her hustling smokes in the high schools," Tanya continued. "Morehouse and his Indian friend, Kenny Paul. Selling out of parking lots and schoolyards."

"Just smokes?"

"Where have you been, Peterson?"

"Just tell me."

"Smokes, drugs — same players." She looked away, momentarily locked into a three-foot stare of thought or memories. She continued. "He made Cassie go along, tied to his hip. Pimping her out to help him make deals. Then she bragged about him scoring big. New friends. No Kenny Paul no more, too big a mouth."

"When was that?"

"A while back."

"When?"

"Three months."

"What was the big money?"

"I don't know. Cassie didn't say, and I didn't push it. He's a bastard, Peterson. The Needle too. They both are. Blackwood got her shooting up. All fucked up, spazzing from one fix to another. Now it's Morehouse who keeps her supplied."

Peterson held her eyes to keep from thinking of his daughter living on the streets and flophouses on the east side of Vancouver. He knew what Tanya was talking about. He watched her squeeze down what needed to get out, the same way he suppressed what was eating away his guts. The days, nights, especially nights, when he sat alone in his den in the dark and thought about having nothing to show for fifty years of living. He reached again for her hand and held it.

"Tell me what Cassie saw."

Tanya shook her head, holding back a sob. "I got it in pieces, Peterson, not straight out like we sat down to chat. She was sick about it, throwing up. I told her to get away from it, to put some money up and go somewhere."

Peterson waited a moment, thinking about how many times he'd heard that one.

"She said a taxi dropped off this guy and drove away. Makes you wonder, a guy that sparkles in that neighbour-hood, letting the cab drive off."

"Meeting someone?"

"I don't know. Just the way she said it."

"A guy that sparkles?"

"Well dressed. They went behind the building."

"Who did?"

"Cassie and the guy."

"Was he there to meet her?"

Tanya shrugged and ran a hand through her hair.

"Was he the hit?"

"I don't know. I don't know! She was crying. A gun, she kept saying. And there was blood on her clothes."

"Where are the clothes now?"

Her head sunk into her shoulders. She was still shaking. "In a plastic bag, a Sobey's bag. She changed and left, took the bag with her." Tanya started sobbing.

Peterson saw the strain. He saw the failure, the guilt, the white powder and the way it dragged her days under a remorseless drive for more.

"That was last week," he said. "Why now?"

"Why now what?"

"You said you and Cassie texted back and forth. Then she comes by and tells you she saw someone shot. Then you don't hear from her. No texts. So why does it take eight days for you to know something's wrong?"

Tanya spoke to her hands on the table. "I was trying to get straight. I was really trying. Then I get a call. Party time. A regular and two guys from out of town. They'll double the rate for me if I bring two more girls."

She lifted her head. Her eyes were full. "We were doing lines, and I was backing them up with a needle. Balling whoever. Talking about what Cassie said but too stoned to

39

do something. I got so messed up, Peterson." She started to sob again.

He waited for her to stop. Then he said, "I'm straightening out my own life. I should walk away from this. It scares me. But I won't. I'll find her. If she's in trouble, I'll do what I can. But what I find may not be what you want." He let that sink in. "You at the same address?"

She nodded.

He pulled a dog-eared business card from his back pocket and slid it and his pen to her. "Write down where Cassie and Morehouse are living."

"With his sister in The Tower," she said.

"Write it down."

She reached for the pen and card and touched his hand. "I have a photo." She went into her jacket pocket and pulled out a phone. She tapped the screen a couple of times then showed him a photo of her daughter. A pretty girl, rake thin, brown hair to her shoulders, and a good-time smile showing a small gap between her front teeth.

"Send it to me."

She took her time tapping in his email address. Then she wrote what he wanted on the business card. She wrote something else. She got up to leave.

"You buried yourself when you buried your wife," she said. "Maybe you buried a lot more than that." She left without giving him the chance to respond.

CHAPTER
SIX

Peterson drove down the main drag on the east side of the harbour, past a couple of boarded up businesses, and slowed past the auto-body shop with the lights still on. It was after 1 a.m., and the boys inside were hard at it. He knew they were doing what they had been doing for years, chopping down a late-night score that would be gone before morning to a parts dealer somewhere else in the province. They sold the leftovers through the salvage yard next door. He remembered once climbing the yard's high grey fence and hiding behind piles of junk. When was that? Seventeen, eighteen years ago. In uniform, him and Danny, chasing down a petty thief who had boosted a gas bar for a couple of bills. A sixteen-year-old scaling the fence then curling up in the back seat of a junked out '85 Ford Taurus. A .22 Colt automatic tucked under his chin. Threatening to shoot himself. Then doing it.

Bad memory. The entire neighbourhood was a bad memory. It was difficult for him not to judge the people who lived in it, harder to separate himself from what he went through patrolling these streets.

He scanned the take-outs lining the drag. Burger joints and pizza by the slice. A Payday Loan on one side, a Money Mart on the other. Then another boarded-up building next door to a twenty-four seven convenience store with riot gates on the door and windows. In front of two rundown apartment buildings, half a dozen guys hung out in the light spilling from both vestibules. Black leather bombers over black hoodies. Arms slapping the cold. Jiving one another, waiting on sugar cubes delivered from the passenger-side window of a dark blue Beemer. Upscale selling to the low down, he thought. Who the hell cares? Not the downtown suits wheeling and dealing under the table, not the movers and shakers juking the public for re-election.

At a Robin's coffee shop, he turned down Canal Street and cruised through a neighbourhood that could have been rummaged from a trash heap. There were three eight-unit apartment buildings on this dead end, along with a handful of poorly kept single houses. All of them backed onto a power generating station, an ugly monstrosity of blue-painted concrete surrounded by transmission towers and an aerial maze of high-tension power lines.

He parked under a streetlight beside a snowy field of scrub bushes and the dry stalks of Japanese knotweed. The scorched remains of a wood-framed waterfront business poked through the snow. Across the street was the abandoned single-storey building Tanya had told him about. It had boarded windows, a sagging roof, and its clapboard had silvered.

He pulled a Maglite from a duffle bag in the back seat and walked down a stony lane, past the broken relics of boat cradles, to a wide gravel turnaround at the water's edge. Spent rubbers and used syringes testified to its steady use.

He picked up a handful of pebbles and skipped them one at a time across the rippled black water. Then he walked back up the lane and stood beside the weathered boat cradles. He faced the abandoned building and thought through what he knew. A well-dressed guy took a taxi. Meeting someone, probably expecting to get his knob polished. Cassie was the set-up and was more than likely decked out as bait.

He saw how the front door of the abandoned building was lit by two streetlights. Cassie in the limelight, he thought, picturing how it might have happened. Flashing what the guy needed to see, then leading him around the back.

He crossed the street and tried the front door. Locked. Then he followed the tramped snow to the back of the building. He tried the back door. It was not locked, but it was swollen tight in the frame. He shouldered it open, turned on the flashlight, and went inside.

He was in a large empty room that took up the ground floor except for two smaller rooms leading off, one on each side. He had been in this building ten years ago when it had been the office for an oil delivery and furnace repair business, which had since relocated to an industrial park. Two other businesses had taken its place, one after the other, and both had failed. The building had stood empty for at least five years, and that had him wondering about the guy who sparkled coming here.

The plastered walls bulged and the ceiling drooped from the leaky roof. Some floorboards were spongy. Door and window frames as well as baseboards had been scavenged long ago. In the centre of the main room was a folding table and two kitchen chairs, one with broken rungs and the other missing the right arm. A battery-powered Coleman lantern hung from the dead wires of a ceiling fixture. He turned it on, revealing the years of dust and grime that had gathered over the floor and up the walls. There were empty food cans, a coil of something rotten in a far corner, and two rolled sleeping bags in another corner. The sight of them stung his nerves. He muttered something to help hold it together.

Then he turned and saw a door off its hinges and a stairway to the cellar. He was slow going down, playing the light ahead of him and testing each tread before giving it his full weight.

Dirt floor. Stone foundation. Graffiti on the joists. Dirty words and dirty sketches carved into them. The signs of pubescents. There were pieces of charred wood in a shallow firepit in the dirt, a pile of driftwood beside it. The cellar stank of dampness and furnace oil. He smelled something else. He sprayed the beam around the room and saw it in the far corner — a shithole dug into the dirt floor.

He turned from the stink and spotted two figures huddled tight under the stairs. The light beam caught their teenage faces. He lowered the flashlight.

"Come on out," he said. His voice soft to calm them down.

The first out was a beanpole. He must have been eating his knees to ball up the way he had. Late teens, scuffed face in a halo of black hair. Camouflage pants. Doc Martens.

Then the girl lined up beside him. She wore a knee-length black coat cinched with a long chain. Her brown hair fell straight to the shoulder. She had scraping-by eyes set deep in a thin face, like she was feeding on nothing but Hamburger Helper. A face set in a perpetual scowl.

"Are you living the dream," Peterson asked, "or just out for a night on the town?"

They shuffled in place.

"I don't bite, if that makes a difference. I'm an ex-cop, and I'm just curious. How long have you been living here?"

"Two weeks," the boy said. Breath like a flamethrower's. "We sleep here, that's all."

"It must be cold."

"We start a fire."

Peterson looked at the dead fire in the pit.

"I didn't start it yet," beanpole said.

"Not a good idea in a trap like this. Keep it going all night?"

"We take turns," beanpole said.

"Him mostly," the girl said.

Peterson was amused. "Sir Galahad in dirty clothes," he said. "Let's go upstairs."

The teens followed him up and sat down at the folding table. Peterson stood.

"How long did you say you've been living here?"

45

"A few weeks," the beanpole said.

Peterson noted the difference between a couple of weeks and a few. He said, "Last week, eight days ago maybe, did you hear a scuffle outside, like someone getting roughed up?"

They didn't answer, but the girl glanced at her boyfriend and gave it away.

"It was a cold night," Peterson said. "The two of you snuggled in one sleeping bag. Sir Galahad here crawling down to the cellar to throw on another log. A car pulls up. Doors open and close. Then loud voices. Maybe a fight. Maybe a gun goes off. Am I half right?"

They didn't answer.

"I know you heard something," Peterson said. He stepped over to one of the boarded-up front windows and tried to look through a crack. He could make out the street, just barely, and lights in a neighbouring apartment building. He turned to the teens. "I was a homicide detective. A cop for over twenty years. What comes with all that time on the job is instinct. You get a feeling about what people know and what they don't know. Now I'm retired. I have nowhere to go and nothing to do. I'm not leaving until you tell me what you heard and what you saw."

They looked at each other again, then Sir Galahad said, "We didn't see nothing. We heard them outside and shut off the light and went downstairs. We hid like we did with you."

"What did you hear?"

"No gunshot," he said. "Just talking."

"Arguing," the girl said.

"How many were there?"

"I don't know," she said. "Like, we were trying not to listen. There was a lot of yelling."

"One was a girl," he said. "She screamed something."

"What did she scream?"

He closed his eyes to remember. "They were yelling for someone to get in the car. The guy kept asking where they were going. Then she screamed, like *no* or *go* or something. I don't know." He opened his eyes and grimaced. "We were scared, man."

"Then what?"

"They got in the car. Like, we heard it drive away and then we heard nothing."

Peterson knew he had all they had to give. He opened his wallet and pulled two twenties. He laid the bills on the table. "Spend it on food."

He went back to the Jetta and took notes on which units in the neighbouring apartment buildings had their lights on.

Night owls were night owls most every night. Some were insomniacs pacing the rooms, peeking out the window at every car that drove by. Others were glued to their computers or phones or to late-night TV. Some with the volume cranked, others more respectful of their neighbours. The respectful ones and the insomniacs would have heard a few people yelling outside. They would have looked. But they never would have called the cops, not in this neighbourhood, and they probably won't tell him a thing when he comes back tomorrow to canvass for information. They'll go tight lipped, street wise. Whatever you say, say nothing. The way they always do when a cop, or a cop look-alike, comes knocking. All with the same story: saw nothing, heard nothing.

CHAPTER
SEVEN

The look-off on the east side of the harbour was a refuge for Peterson, a place he went to think and to rummage through memories that sometimes brought him comfort, but mostly did not. He lowered the Jetta's windows despite the cold and listened to the traffic crossing the older of the two bridges spanning the harbour, listened to voices that the water carried from the dockyard, listened to sounds from the houses on the street below.

He had parked with the Jetta aimed at the harbour mouth, giving himself a postcard perspective of the naval base, two islands, and the concrete and glass of downtown. He looked without seeing Halifax as the "vibrant and safe capital city by the sea" promoted by the tourist board. He saw something else. He saw what cops see: the hard side, the ugly side, the side unreported in the press.

The rising sun ricocheted off the rearview and had him angling to avoid it. He reached into the glove box for the spiral scribbler and the pen clipped to the first few pages and settled behind the wheel to write down thoughts and feelings. Dr. Heaney had suggested it, and a few of the others in the therapy session had been doing it. But instead of words, he drew a large question mark. He traced it over and over, until the pen cut through the page.

He closed the scribbler and watched a ferry cross the harbour. He remembered the day he'd taken it back and forth several times with his daughter. It was a sunny winter day like this one. He remembered laughing with her. He could not remember laughing with her many times after.

He thought about Cassie, and her face and his daughter's blurred into one. He remembered Katy's last words to him: "Fuck You." He shifted uncomfortably and felt something in his coat pocket. The Ruger. He set it on the passenger seat. There was something else in the pocket. He pulled out the napkin with Patty Creaser's phone number and then his business card with Tanya's number and the address of Logan's sister where Cassie might still live. Tanya had written something else: "The sudden loss of you left me hopeless."

He closed his eyes, opened them. He looked at the Ruger and then at the sealed mickey in the open glove box. An uncontrolled breath escaped, and he rubbed his face. He shoved the Ruger back into his coat pocket and the spiral notebook back into the glove box.

• • •

Tanya had said no cops, but he knew better. He needed them for their database and fast access to the whereabouts of the people he wanted to find.

He waited for Bernie outside the police station in the employee parking lot. He knew she'd be in an hour ahead of the morning shift. She parked her car, slid out, and zipped up her down jacket. Detective Grace Bernard, who insisted on being called Bernie.

He got out of the Jetta and intercepted her before she got to the front door.

"Have you been ducking me these last few weeks?" she asked. Her grin said she was glad to see him.

"That goes both ways."

She pretended to juggle.

"You don't look overworked," he said, breaking out a weary smile.

"A comment like that means you're looking for something."

"Something like that."

"The deputy chief know you're coming in?"

"I doubt Fultz wants to see me," Peterson said, holding open the door. "Not enough time between us."

"You know he's up for chief as soon as Menard retires."

"Peter Principle in action," Peterson said.

"We could do worse than Fultz."

"Not by much."

Bernie led the way upstairs to the Investigation Unit. Peterson's gunshot knee hurt on the climb. He was tired too, from walking the downtown streets all night. Bernie saw he wasn't keeping up.

"You still living at The Office?" she said

"I don't change much."

"Except for trading your desk for a barstool."

"Better company than listening to old men complain at a coffee shop."

"You could go home," she said.

"The walls and furniture talk too much."

Two drug-squad cops in civvies came through the double doors and started down the stairs. One of them, Ryan Lewis, a giant of a man but a gutless wonder, the kind of cop who cuffed a suspect first and muscled him later, recognized Peterson and stopped.

"I thought this place kissed you goodbye," he snarled.

"Bad penny," Peterson said.

"Good thing the government is flushing them," said Eddie Bigger, the other drug-squad cop. He was the opposite of Lewis in size, mouth, and attitude. Like most little guys, Bigger was always looking for a scrap.

Peterson took it in stride and faked a smile. "Yeah, but a lot of people are saving them. Pennies will be worth millions someday."

Lewis wanted the last word but couldn't think of anything to say. He turned to go, but not before giving Bernie a quick nod.

"What was that about?" Bernie asked. She was holding one of the double doors open for Peterson.

"He misses me," Peterson said.

"They all do," Bernie said. Wry smile. "You want coffee?"

Jamie Gould, gelled hair, late thirties, held down the coffee room. Newspaper opened to the crossword page on the Formica table. He saw Peterson, rose, threw out his hand, and said, "Have you been forgiven, or am I just wishing it?"

"I doubt I'll get off the shelf," Peterson responded, shaking Jamie's hand.

"I should've known better," Jamie said. "Fultz would never take you back when he's bucking for chief."

They laughed as Bernie pulled two coffees and passed one to Peterson.

"You remember Billy Moran?" Jamie asked Peterson.

"I punched his ticket," Peterson said. "He backed over his mother and said it was an accident."

"Know what he's doing now?"

"He's out?"

"He did four out of ten," Jamie said. "Good behaviour."

"I'll bite."

"He goes door to door selling chairs in heaven."

You could've hung clothes off Jamie's grin.

"I got it straight from his parole officer," Jamie continued. "Moran targets seniors and quotes them chapter and verse, you know, Jesus telling his disciples he was off to prepare a room for them in heaven. Then Moran feeds the seniors some shit about charitable gifts and buying themselves a chair. I mean who wants to go through eternity standing up."

"People are buying them?" Bernie asked.

"A hundred bucks a chair," Jamie said. "The parole officer said Moran sold eight."

"What?"

"Discount anything fifteen percent and old people'll buy it," Jamie said. "Double the price and call the sale two for one, and seniors can't give you the money fast enough."

Peterson started for the door.

"Moran's lawyer is Lester Arnold," Jamie continued. "He's

arguing all religions take down payments on eternal happiness. So what's the difference, huh? The Catholic Church, the Prods, they're the ones selling the rooms in the first place."

Bernie was still laughing.

"Leon Ferris was another one of yours, wasn't he?" Jamie said.

That stopped Peterson.

"He's out, too," Jamie added.

"I heard," Peterson said.

"Fourteen shaved down to seven and out in five, double credit for time served. Like what's going on, right! The guy attempts a hit and the parole board goes short time on his candy-land smile."

Peterson didn't answer. Thinking.

Jamie shook his head. "Swinging door, know what I mean? It makes you wonder why we bust them in the first place."

Jamie had a fresh thought. "You and Leon had a thing together, right?"

Peterson feigned nonchalance. "A dust-up that didn't go his way."

He and Bernie carried their coffees down the hall past half a dozen early birds who waved or nodded to Peterson.

"Dust-up?" she said. "That's what you call it?" They entered the cupboard-sized room that a few detectives liked to use for private meetings. "I heard you broke his arm."

Danny was inside waiting. His legs shifted uneasily under the wooden table, and his fingers drummed the half-dozen case files on top of it.

"Whose arm?" Danny asked.

"Leon Ferris," Peterson said.

Danny's smile faded. "You heard."

"Little bird." Peterson leaned down to straighten Danny's tie. "It's amazing how a good woman can change a man." He winked at Bernie. "He never dressed this way for me."

"Not for me, either," Bernie said. "Danny has a steady girlfriend."

Peterson smoothed a hand over the tie. "She must dress him in the morning."

Danny slapped his hand away and tapped the files on the table. "You can see how busy we are. We got forms up to here." He slashed a hand across his throat. "And reports like you wouldn't believe. You jumped at the right time."

"Pushed was more like it."

"Either way, you miss out on all this paperwork. So, how about we close the Ferris file and call it past tense?"

"Not if it's happening now."

Bernie saw the strained look exchanged between the former partners, Danny's more drawn than Peterson's. They had a twenty-three-year history together. Uniform cops sharing a car and half their lives. Peterson stealing time from his wife and daughter and making detective first. Danny three years later. Partnered again. Covering each other's ass. Good cop, bad cop, with Peterson mostly coming off as Sir Lancelot with a grudge.

"Leon made a threat five years ago," Danny said, punching each word to sound convincing. "That doesn't mean—"

"Yes, it does," Peterson said. "I talked to Cory yesterday. Leon wants a reunion."

Danny straightened the stack of files, lining them up with the table edge. Jaw set. Voice insistent. "You're not the only cop on a nutso's hate list."

"Former cop. That means no badge."

"Which means what?"

"I keep an eye over my shoulder. Right hand hanging free."

"That's the part I'm worried about."

"That he might get hurt?"

"Straight-up fight, you come out on the short end."

"Leon Ferris doesn't go straight up," Peterson corrected. "He works the shadows with a sawed-off or a Glock."

Danny leaned toward Bernie. "Leon Ferris was . . . is—"

"I know all about Leon Ferris," Bernie said. "I helped work the crime scene when I was in uniform. He shot Serge LeBlanc point-blank with a Glock. Paralyzed him. There was something about a favour he owed."

"Drug debt," Peterson added. "Not his. Serge owed Sammy O'Brien big time, and O'Brien asked Leon Ferris to collect the bill."

"Sammy O is Blackwood's delivery boy," Danny said to Bernie. "But you're right about the favour. No money changed hands, but the word was that Sammy O had a small-time retail licence for sale, which Ferris wanted to tap." He nodded to Peterson. "His nibs had an inside source about the hit on Serge LeBlanc. A warrant turned up the gun, ballistics matched, and two witnesses put Ferris on location in a starring role."

"I made the arrest," Peterson said.

Danny nodded at Peterson. "He can't just read Leon his rights and arrest the shit like everybody else," he said. "No! He has to bust Leon's arm with that claw hammer he carries—"

"Cat's paw. It's a nail puller."

"Whatever." Danny waved a hand and said to Bernie, "It turned out Ferris had himself a real bad day."

"And you think he'll come for you?" Bernie said to Peterson.

Peterson nodded.

Danny tapped the case files again. "We'll do what we can to keep tabs on him, but more than that . . ."

"I'm not asking for police protection," Peterson insisted. "There's something else." He inched forward in his chair. "A woman corners me in The Office and says her fifteen-year-old daughter is missing."

"Different department," Danny said. "Down the hall, second left."

"You going to listen or not?"

"I'm listening."

"The mother thinks the girl witnessed a shooting nine days ago. The girl said something about a gun and had blood on her clothes."

"Did she say where?" Bernie asked.

"Near the abandoned building on Canal Street, where that oil business used to be. That's where the vic was grabbed."

"We've had no complaints from that neighbourhood." Danny said, a hint of scepticism in his voice. "Every other neighbourhood, but not that one."

Peterson let it go. "A well-dressed man arrived in a taxi. The cab drives off, and the girl shows up and takes the guy to the back of the building."

"Accomplice?" Bernie said.

Peterson nodded. "The girl has a pimp, boyfriend, whatever. His name is Logan Morehouse. She does whatever he tells her to do. He played the girl as the set-up, that's how I figure it. All I have is what the mother told me, which isn't a hell of a lot. I checked the building last night. Two street kids are living inside. They didn't see much, if they saw anything, but they heard someone being hustled into a car."

"Who's the girl?" Bernie asked.

"Cassie Colpitts."

"And the mother?" Danny added.

"Tanya Colpitts," Peterson said, and the name was no sooner out of his mouth than he regretted having said it.

"That's a name I remember," Danny said, watching for Peterson's reaction. "Why did she come to you and not the police?"

Peterson hesitated, but there was no way to backpedal, not now. "She knew I'd help," he said.

"Like you owe her," Danny said. "Past service or something like that?"

They locked eyes.

"I'm not opening a file on Tanya Colpitts's say-so," Danny said.

"Because she's a prostitute and a junkie?"

"Yes on both counts."

Peterson's face went stony. "This is going nowhere, Dan. I thought I had something important. But you're right. It's only a rumour. No body. No complaints of gunshots in a neighbourhood where people wouldn't call the cops if it was the O.K. Corral." He pushed his chair from the table and stood.

"I see it different," Danny said. "Her daughter runs off and she makes up a good story to yank your chain, get you sniffing around again. For Christ's sake, you pulled her from the garbage, and what happened? She shook her ass twice and wrecked your marriage."

"I was missing from my marriage long before that, and you know it. What's with you? We used to work up a file on less than this."

Danny pounced. "Is that what you're doing? You working up a file? Not satisfied with what you help us with?"

"Leave it alone, Dan."

"Yeah, I'll leave it alone. You want to know why? Because we're spinning plates," he said. "You know how many we got spinning at the same time? Bernie, tell him how many plates we got in the air."

Bernie made no effort to answer.

"Sammy O gets shot at, and every two-bit dealer is reaching for a piece of the pie," Danny said, his voice climbing. "Drive-bys. One outside the children's hospital. The media calls us up on it. They're having a field day with what's going on. Drugs and drug money has this city out of control. Statistics have us in first place for unsolved homicides in the goddamn country, and the mayor and council want to know how come. Like they didn't cut the budget. No new hires and two detectives sidelined. What the hell are we supposed to do? Tell me that! No, don't tell me, tell Fultz, tell the ones that have the whole department on a short chain. We're leaving more criminals on the street than we lock up. We can't handle the bodies already in the morgue, and you waltz in here with a hearsay hit because you're working up a file."

Peterson shut out Danny's voice. He heard hall traffic instead. Voices jabbering, catching up on last night's TV shows and sports scores; laughter that trailed off toward the coffee room and the Investigation Unit, with its grid of narrow paths and crowded desks. This building had been

58

his home. The job had been his life. And now he felt like a has-been looking for a place to hang his hat. He wondered if he'd been doing what Danny had just suggested. He wondered if he had been listening to Tanya and hearing what he wanted to hear, believing it because it worked up a file that could reopen a door into this building, into the life he once had.

"If it makes you feel better," Danny was saying, "I can get a car over there to ask around, something turns up, we'll do what we can."

"Yeah, you do that," Peterson grumbled. "And anything else comes my way, I'll keep it to myself."

"Don't be an asshole."

Bernie threw up both hands. "Maybe you're both assholes," she said. "A well-dressed guy gets shot . . ."

"We don't know that," Danny insisted.

"No," Bernie snapped, "but a corpse doesn't show up at home or at work the next day, and sooner or later someone will report him missing. I'll pull the list and see what matches."

She looked from one embarrassed face to the other. "I don't know what's going on," she said, "but good police work doesn't ignore a lead no matter where it comes from and no matter how many plates we're spinning. A girl says she saw a guy get shot, maybe helped in the shooting, I want to talk to that girl." She faced Danny. "Don't you?"

CHAPTER
EIGHT

The night owls had all denied hearing or seeing anything that night, but he was sure three of them were lying. They had answered his questions too fast or shrugged them off. One, a man, early middle-age, with a gut like a basketball, claimed he drank a six-pack and fell asleep on the couch, early. Another, a bearded guy wearing a skirt, smiled and said, "I don't hear nothing outside, and when I do, I still don't hear nothing." The third was an old woman who admitted she seldom slept at night and watched TV with the lights off instead. She often heard a lot of things outside, she said, "and when I do, I mind my own business," which meant she sneaked a peek through the blinds.

He couldn't coax her to say more than that, but, as he left the building, he marked her down for a return visit.

Danny was waiting for him across the street, leaning against his Malibu, his face deliberately expressionless.

"I said I'd send a car around, but then I thought I should come around myself," he said.

"Bernie find a match on a missing person?"

"She has lots of other things to do first."

"And you don't." Peterson gave him a sly smile.

"Bernie made a good point," Danny said. "We have an obligation."

"How'd you know I'd be here?"

Danny shrugged. "So, what do we have? A well-dressed guy in this neighbourhood, how come? On the make for what, company or drugs?"

"Why shoot him?"

"We don't know he's been shot. You said two street kids heard someone hustled into a car."

"And Cassie Colpitts told her mother she saw a gun, and there was blood on her clothes."

"You know what I think about what Tanya Colpitts has to say. Convince me otherwise."

"A guy shows up in a taxi and lets it go," Peterson started. "He's meeting someone."

"You know that how?"

"I chased down the taxi driver," Peterson said. "He picked the guy up downtown at the taxi stand on Duke. The guy had a street address."

"Did the driver describe the guy?"

Peterson shook his head. "No better than Tanya did."

"And I'm still doubting everything she said."

Peterson's phone signalled a Skype call. His daughter.

He answered it. He had to. As much as it hurt, her calls were the only contact he had with her. He looked at the image. Fleabag room. Rust-stained sink in the far corner. Grimy window pane. Nothing said.

Danny watched him shrink inside himself then slowly come back when the screen went white. "You should do something for her," Danny said.

Peterson closed his eyes and slowly shook his head. "Can't."

"Can't or won't?"

Peterson opened his eyes. "Don't ask."

"Yeah," Danny shrugged. "I know too much. I know you're afraid of what you'll do to the ones she's with." He changed the channel. "Suppose Bernie gets a missing person, we get a body, and it all holds up; the girl, the shooting, the whole ball of wax. We find the Colpitts girl, we find her pimp, and we notch one up for the good guys. Shouldn't be too hard."

"It could be harder than you think," Peterson said and drew a deep breath. "Tanya was high-beaming at a party, a free for all. She's splitting the night between rock salt and whatever else was on the table. Telling tales out of school."

"Jesus Christ." Danny threw up his hands. "If there was a shooting, and this Logan shit and whoever else find out she was talking, there's a problem." He walked away frustrated, thought for a moment, and walked back. He scrutinized Peterson. "Anything else you're holding back? I mean anything else that turns this circus act into more of a sideshow than it is?"

Peterson thought about his promise to Tanya that he'd

find and protect her daughter. "The girl once lived with Willie Blackwood," he said. "She had his baby."

"And that has you thinking what, that Blackwood's involved?"

"I've no idea how it stacks up. I'm just laying out facts, the way we always did."

"Or throwing in a name to raise eyebrows."

Peterson riveted him with a look that was anger laced with hurt.

"You don't think I know how much you miss it," Danny said. "You get dumped from the department because you're a drunk and out of control. PTSD, whatever. So you go off the sauce, live like a goddamn monk to prove what? That you can get it together? That you can prove to yourself, maybe the department, that you're still the cop you used to be? Well, you're not. It caught up to you, the day-to-day of what we see and do. One day it'll catch up to me. You're not what you were, not anymore."

Peterson balled his fists and leaned over the Malibu. His throat was too tight to speak.

Danny leaned beside him on the Malibu. They stood there in silence, then Danny said, "We'll look into it. But it goes to the bottom of the pile. That doesn't mean we'll let it go. If Blackwood's name pops up, it goes on top. But that doesn't stop you from looking. Only I have a rulebook I have to play by. You don't. In the end, it comes down to evidence the Crown can use in court. So if I get complaints, you get disowned. Fair enough?"

Peterson nodded.

"Just keep Bernie and me in the picture," Danny added,

"and don't take chances. We'll do our thing. You do what you have to do. But we share and share alike."

They walked to the Jetta. When they reached it, Danny asked, "Will Tanya complicate it for you? I'm asking because you have more than enough complications to send you around the bend."

Peterson gave it a moment's thought and answered. "That's long past."

Danny opened the door for Peterson. "I asked around. It's like you said, Cory's bragging about his brother doing a cop. Be careful. Leon likes playing jack-in-the-box."

CHAPTER
NINE

An old man wearing a heavy coat over his pyjamas sat on a wooden bench outside the front doors to the seniors' complex. He was shivering and squinting through his smoky breath.

Peterson nodded. The old man nodded back, dragged deep, and flicked the butt to the sidewalk. The automatic doors slid open and Peterson entered.

Inside, two women as wizened as apple dolls sat in wingback chairs and scrutinized everyone who came through the lobby. Peterson nodded to them, but only one nodded back. The other glowered.

The lobby was all business, with people using walkers and wheelchairs piled up at the bank of elevators and the hale strutting back and forth to show off their good health. Peterson negotiated the geriatric rush and walked a breezeway to a large sunroom where a crowd of seniors, with stiff bodies and gnarled hands, sat four to a table playing cribbage and forty-fives. He caught the eye of one of the staff, a big man built like a shade tree, all body and no neck, sporting a Maltese beard and wary eyes that mapped the room and the location of everyone in it. His name was Alfred Toi, only everyone called him "Dinky" for the absurd contradiction between his size and his last name.

Dinky nodded at the coffee shop across the corridor. Peterson chose a table at the back and ordered coffee.

"Must be important," Dinky said minutes later, as he lowered his massive frame onto a spindly chair. Peterson couldn't help notice the stains on the big man's tent-sized blue uniform.

The place was mid-afternoon empty. A few seniors chased memories in a far corner, and three staff squeezed a five-minute break from a busy day.

Peterson worked on his coffee. "You want one?" he asked.

The big man shook away the offer.

"What's up?" he asked, sweeping small talk aside.

"Logan Morehouse and Kenny Paul."

"Morehouse I only heard about. Young punk coming in when I was getting out. I don't keep up no more. Too many good things going my way."

"What about number two?"

Toi rolled his tongue inside his lower lip, his veined eyes not letting Peterson go.

"The Indian I know. Feeds school kids smokes and drugs. Taps the Native pipe out of Quebec for whatever he can get. Thinks being Indian protects him. The man's full of bullshit and make-believe."

He pulled his head into his shoulders and played his eyes over the coffee shop and as much of the corridor as he could see. "Works from the reserve. Cutting out a market for himself. Making enemies. One day those with a lock on the Indian drug game will ream his ass."

Peterson nodded his thanks, then said, "Leon Ferris made parole."

"Early out means Leon was a good boy. Maybe he learned a lesson. Why bring it here?"

"Duck and cover," Peterson said.

"No blanket big enough to cover me. Anyway, Leon ain't my worry."

"You nailed him as the shooter."

"Not for nothing, man. Leon was a liability to a lot of people. I had the okay before I let it slip."

"From who?"

The big man bared his teeth. "Some things I don't talk about."

Peterson flashed a fair-enough smile.

"What else you after?" Toi asked.

"A possible hit on Canal Street. Well-dressed man got hustled into a car. A girl said there was a gun and blood. I'm looking for her."

Toi thought about it. The chair squeaked under his shifting weight. He looked around the room once more. He nodded. "Who is she?"

"Cassie Colpitts. Joined at the hip to the Morehouse dude. Missing for over eight days. I find him, I find her. Only, I don't want anyone knowing I'm looking."

"Tippy toes."

Peterson smiled at the image of Dinky Toi doing a pirouette.

"How much time?" Toi asked.

Peterson frowned. "I'm worried we're already too late."

CHAPTER
TEN

The Tower was an eight-storey concrete mass of architectural dreariness. It had loopholes for windows and narrow balconies that served as little more than platforms for smokers or spring boards for residents seeking quick freedom from their closed-in lives. When it was built, The Tower had tried for respectability, but it settled for being a tenement in a neighbourhood crippled by poverty and scarred by crime.

Peterson knew the ins and outs of The Tower and the surrounding neighbourhood. As a uniform cop and, later, detective, he had sorted through homicides in both. He had no preference. One was just as raw and on edge as the other. Both were well armed.

He entered The Tower and, out of habit, felt for latex gloves in his coat pocket. He came up empty. It was little things like this that reminded him he no longer carried a badge, at least not a legitimate one with the municipality's stamp of approval. The badge he now carried was the one he had before the city had amalgamated with neighbouring cities and towns into a sprawling, ungovernable, unmanageable, and less safe metropolis. It opened doors and made people talk, so long as he flashed it in a way that no one could read it. He didn't use it often, only when he needed to, because getting caught impersonating a police officer meant jail time.

The Tower's foyer served as entrance and garbage dump. The intercom didn't work, and the inside security door was unlocked. One of the two elevators was out of order. He listened to the operating one rattle down from an upper floor.

The windows at either end of the narrow hallway on the sixth floor let in light that spread only halfway down, leaving the doors to the six apartments in the middle in deep shadow. He knocked on 618 and waited. A guy from 620 stumbled out and made for the elevator. He snuck a glance at Peterson. Then Peterson heard a shuffle on the other side of the door. He felt the force of someone staring through the peephole.

"Yeah?" said a scrawny female voice through the closed door.

"You Tessa Morehouse?"

"Who wants to know?" Her voice shook, and Peterson recognized the iron grip of a user's need.

"My name's Peterson. I'm looking for Cassie Colpitts and your brother."

"Yeah, well if it's bad news they don't want to know."

"No bad news. I just want to talk to them."

"About what?"

"Look, Tessa, walls have ears. Open the door!"

He heard her turn and press her back against the door. He knew she was thinking about it. Nibbling the edges of the situation. Frightened.

"You look like a cop," she said.

"I was a cop."

There was another long silence. Then, her voice still trembling, she said: "I'm not talking to cops or ex-cops. I'm not talking to nobody."

"Tessa, please." Then he heard her turn from the door and shuffle away.

He waited a few minutes, hoping she would shuffle back and open the door. No luck.

He left The Tower and walked back to his parked car and leaned against the passenger side. He pulled out his phone and punched in the number Tanya had given him. He got her voicemail.

A thirty-something panhandler stopped in front of him. Street life and booze had given the guy's face a ruddy complexion. Peterson guessed his clothes were freebies from the Sally Ann or a neighbourhood church. He pegged him as the guy from 620.

"You got some change you don't need?" the panhandler asked.

Peterson put away the phone and looked him over. "You eating it or drinking it?"

The guy stared at Peterson, unsure how to answer.

Peterson smiled. "No reason you can't do both. What's your name?"

"That depends who's calling me," the man said. "Mostly it's asshole or hey you."

"Which one do you prefer?"

The guy looked up from his feet. "My name's Benny Stokes."

"You live around here, Benny Stokes?"

He pointed to The Tower. "With two other guys."

"They squeezing the street too?"

Benny didn't answer.

Peterson held up his hand. "No more questions, Benny Stokes."

Peterson led Benny to a smoked meat sandwich joint two blocks away in a strip of retail shops where the avant-garde and educated socialists slummed it as a sort of penance. Peterson tucked Benny into a booth near the front window. He stepped over to the 1950s counter with rotating vinyl stools, ordered a sandwich, a beer, and a black coffee. The waitress, a thin brunette with a has-been smile, rustled up the order. He joined Benny in the booth.

Benny went for the beer and drained it before taking a bite, and Peterson ordered him another.

"The beer's not going anywhere, Benny, so you might as well eat between sips."

Benny nodded and wiped his mouth, then dug into the sandwich. Peterson sipped the coffee. Then Benny asked, "What's in this for you?"

"It gets me a chair in heaven so I don't have to stand up," he said.

"I don't take you for a do-gooder. You got an angle? I mean, I don't care. If it gets me food and beer, I'll play along. Unless you're expecting me to follow you home. Then I just drink up and disappear."

Benny smiled and Peterson smiled back. Then Peterson

reached into his jacket pocket and came out with his phone and brought up the photo Tanya had emailed him.

"You know this kid?" Peterson asked.

"Seen her around."

"Recently?"

"How recent?"

"Last few days."

Benny handed back the phone. "What's she done?"

"Her mother asked me to find her."

"Her mother?"

"She knows she's hustling smokes. She's worried."

"Not just smokes," Benny said.

"Yeah, she knows about that too."

Benny drained his beer. "You a cop?"

"Was."

Benny rolled the empty glass in his hands. "She lives next to me."

Peterson nodded.

"A guy and another girl live there too," Benny said. "Fighting all the time. A man can't live with one, why live with two?"

"Pimping them both, maybe."

"That too."

"You mean beside dealing the street?"

Benny shrugged.

"Tell me about it."

Benny held up his glass. "For another one of these."

Peterson reached for his wallet, pulled a twenty, set it on the table, and held it with his fingertips. "Buy your own."

Benny grinned and said, "A couple of weeks ago, the

73

supply runs short. Mounties rolled on something, and it had the bed bugs biting themselves to get high, you know what I mean?"

Peterson nodded.

"Only this Logan, he's not short. He's selling. He's high. His girls are high. Had me wondering."

"Wondering what?"

Benny eyed the twenty. Shrugged. "How he comes up with his supply. Then I hear about a stick-up. Three guys with masks bust a dope deal not far from here. They walk with money and whatever's in a backpack. It just had me wondering."

Peterson sipped coffee. Thinking. Then he said, "Tell me about the girls."

Benny's eyes went to the twenty then back to Peterson. "Rock stars," Benny said. "You know, the kind that trades sex for drugs. But what the fuck, right? If I was built another way, I would too. This Logan keeps them up and at 'em. A few days ago him and the one in the photo skipped out. That's what I figure."

"Why's that?"

"I seen the guy and one of the girls, the one always tagging his ass, I see them every day, maybe, but not in the last week. And the one left inside, she's climbing the walls."

Peterson lifted his fingers from the twenty and Benny reached for it.

"I saw you upstairs outside her door," Benny said, big grin, dignity in his voice. "So, who conned who?"

He slid from the booth and out the door.

Peterson laughed to himself. Then he hailed the waitress

and ordered another smoked meat sandwich, this one for the road.

He returned to apartment 618 and hammered the door. Again he heard her shuffling and felt her eye through the peephole. He held up the brown bag with the smoked meat sandwich.

"Logan left you something," he said. "He knew you'd be antsy."

"Jesus Christ," Tessa crabbed.

"It didn't have your name on it." Peterson sounded sincere.

He heard the bolt slide and the chain slip free. The door opened. She held out her hand for the bag.

"Not until we talk," Peterson said.

She glared at him. Then she shuffled down the cluttered hallway in red sock-slippers and an oversized black housecoat.

He shut the door and followed her into the kitchen, where she sat down at a chrome and Formica table. She lit a cigarette. The white fridge had dents in the door and a calendar with a picture of a chocolate lab with a red ball in its mouth. The surrounding white cupboards were smudged from grimy hands. One door was missing and another was hanging by a single screw. The dishes in the sink hadn't been washed in days, maybe weeks.

The grey light from the window beside her confirmed what Benny Stokes had said. She was a "rock star," twenty going on forty, with sullen eyes, an unpainted face drawn and grey, and a thin mouth that hardly moved when she spoke. "So what do you want?"

He sat down across from her at the table. "I heard Logan

and Cassie are missing." He caught the ripple of concern that she tried to hide.

"He's not missing." Her eyes went to the bag. "He went away like he does."

"He tell you where he was going?"

Her headshake was hesitant. Careful. "I'm not talking to a cop."

"Ex-cop."

"Same difference."

"Big difference. No handcuffs. I just want to talk."

"About what?"

"Cassie Colpitts."

"What about her?" She blew smoke in his face, and he let it swirl around his head without waving it away. Holding her eyes with his. Seeing her chippiness as a mask for her inability to get out of the gutter. Seeing his daughter in the same way.

"Her mother asked me to help find her, and I said I'd do what I could."

"That doesn't make me want to tell you anything."

"But the bag does."

Peterson put on a choirboy face, the one he had used on reluctant witnesses during interrogations, the one that sometimes had them half believing it. But it was the sugar in his voice that had more often hooked them, the nonchalant way he had of making what he said sound on the up and up. "I'm not out to bust her or him, just find her. That's all I want to do."

"Yeah?"

"Yeah. I know about them hustling smokes, and I know about them hustling drugs. Her mother told me. I know he keeps everyone high. I know she does whatever he says, and that he doesn't go anywhere without her. So where's your brother?"

"Wherever he is."

"Where's that?"

She squeezed her eyes shut.

"If you can help, help," he said. "Otherwise I'll go somewhere else."

She popped open her eyes. "What about the bag?"

"The bag goes with me."

She took a long drag and this time blew smoke out the side of her mouth. "He had something going on."

Peterson nodded. "I heard it was a big payday."

She rolled her head and scowled. "He told me that too. Always bragging. Fucking world beater."

"Cassie thought it was big."

Tessa didn't answer, but her eyes did, with two quick blinks that told him Logan had gone off to score, and this one was indeed really big.

"He ever go away this long before?"

"No." Her feet were doing double time under the table.

He knew she was worried about Logan not coming home with her steady supply of biscuits.

"And he never said this deal might take longer than usual?" Peterson asked.

"No." Her eyes wandered the room.

Peterson waited.

She stubbed out the cigarette in a jar lid she used as an ashtray. Then she got up and crossed the kitchen to get her pack of smokes from the counter. She tapped one out and held it in her mouth as she sat back down across from him.

"The day before he left, a guy came by. I watched them from this window."

Peterson raised himself to see the concrete courtyard at the back of the building.

"Logan didn't like what he was hearing. Then, whatever it was, they settled it, and the guy left."

"Did you recognize this guy?"

"A guy. Big like you. What about the bag?"

"The bag's okay where it is. You think this guy was hustling him?"

She struck a match and lit the cigarette. Hand shaking. She inhaled deeply. "Don't know. The guy left and Logan came upstairs."

"He say anything?"

"Not about the guy. He was pissed off. He said something about being ready to do it and now he had to wait. Logan hates waiting. He hates waiting for anything."

"Did you ever see Logan with this guy before?"

"Not him."

"Someone else?"

"Another guy. Curly hair. Blond. Glasses. I saw them talking the same way I saw this guy."

"Same place?"

"Uh huh."

"When was this?"

"A couple of days later."

"Logan in business with these guys?"

"I know fuck all about his business."

"But you know he always had some pick-me-up when the street supply was low," Peterson said.

She stared out the window to avoid looking at him.

"Logan had reserves," he offered, making it sound as though he knew for sure.

"Rainy day shit," she said. "That's what he called it."

"Stuff he put away, stockpiled? Or was it shit that dropped in his lap?"

"I didn't ask."

"Payday," Peterson said, like he knew. "He'd come home with a score and call it payday."

"It was stuff he didn't have to sell. He fucks me up with it. Her too. Couple of dimes on the fucking table. Then he takes it back. A motherfucker when he does that. Ringing us up. And I'm his sister. The fuck he cares about me."

"And Cassie?"

"So long as he can ride her how he likes it. Except when she can't. Then he goes out for what he can't get here. Once he got even for her bleeding when it wasn't her time."

"How?"

"How does any man get even? Then he threw her out. But she came back. She had something."

"Like what?"

"I don't know, something that'd make him money."

"Like those two guys who came around," he said. "The guys with the big payday."

She grunted and shrugged. Eyes on the bag. Fingers scrabbling under her chin. "I only saw them that once, like I said."

"That was when?"

"Couple weeks ago."

"Then a few days later, Logan and Cassie walked out?"

She nodded.

"And you're climbing the walls," Peterson added.

She gave him the finger.

"One more time, where'd they go?"

"I said I don't know, not for sure. Could be a fuck pad he has over there, maybe."

"Over where?"

"The bridge," she shouted. Losing it. Her nerves firing for a taste.

Peterson held up the bag. "Bag's yours if you just name the place."

"North end."

"Still not seeing it."

She locked her hands together and tightened her jaw. Spurted a breath through her nose. Ferocity in her eyes. "Albro Road."

"Number?"

She violently shook her head.

"Name?"

"Diddy Parks."

Peterson got up, set the bag on the table, and pushed it her way.

She grabbed for it and tore it open to get inside. Her hand came out with the smoked meat sandwich. "What the . . . !"

"Lunch," Peterson said, and closed the door.

CHAPTER
ELEVEN

Bernie had picked the spot, the food court in a west end shopping mall. Peterson was early. He toyed with a black coffee and watched people, sizing them up. Post-Christmas shoppers, loafers feeding off the free heat, a steady stream of teens, some of them scoring from the jugglers swapping foil-wrapped cubes for folded ten-dollar bills. Mall security hadn't caught on to the hand-to-hand transactions, or they didn't care.

Two teenage girls exited the washroom. Blank faced. Wasted. He swivelled their way and watched them shed their hooded polar jackets and expose arms heavily inked to hide the tracks.

He frowned at the sight of them, and his right hand fidgeted with his phone. Seeing them and seeing his daughter. And seeing the other girls he had failed, the ones who had worked the streets and stroke clubs with ten-cent smiles for a habit they couldn't shake.

Bernie caught him looking at the two girls. She saw his face scoured with regret. Saw him draw a deep breath and nod to himself in recognition of something painfully true. Then she drew up beside him.

"I always thought bag ladies were more your speed," she kidded to break the ice that spread around him.

Peterson turned to face her. "What speed is that?"

"Old and slow."

Peterson smiled. "Slow maybe, but my knee's the only joint not working right."

Bernie chuckled. "I'll take your word for it." She dropped into a chair opposite him.

"I understand Tanya's special," she said.

"Danny tell you that?"

"Not hard to figure out that you and her have a history."

"Not a long one."

"They don't have to be long to be intense."

"I don't even know if it was, Bernie. It happened, that's all." He pulled a deep breath. "When my wife was killed, it ended."

"You don't have to talk about it, Peterson."

He grunted a laugh. "Easy way out?"

"Your choice."

"My wife gets buried under a cement truck with her boyfriend, and I fall apart. I hurt everyone like I was getting even. I left my daughter to run the streets then run west. Abandoned Tanya in a drug rehab centre. Not much to brag about."

Bernie winced. "I knew some of it, but . . ."

"It's okay."

She placed an iPad on the table and swiped to the page she wanted. "Missing Persons first?"

"Sure."

"Nothing until this morning. Vernon Rumley. He owns Coastal Communications. High profile, big spender. Likes to gamble. Goes to Vegas whenever the mood hits. His staff said he often disappears for a few days, long weekend, on the spur of the moment. They saw no reason to report him missing until he was a no-show at a meeting with a major client."

"Sounds like a prime candidate."

Bernie agreed. "I had Gloria build a file on the guy." She swiped to a new page. "His company hit the skids during the recession and hasn't recovered yet." She looked up. "You don't care about numbers, right? Revenues, net profit?"

He shook his head. He trusted her computer savvy and data analyses. He hadn't developed the knack for them and probably never would.

"Chattel loans for most of what the company owns," she continued, swiping from page to page on the iPad. "It's outstanding debt in a line of credit that's pushing half a mil. Rumley borrowed two hundred thousand of that less than six weeks ago. Gloria ran credit checks on him and his wife. It turns out they both hold three bank credit cards, as well as American Express. His are all maxed out."

"What'd he do with the borrowed money?"

She swiped back a page. "It went into the company bank account and was withdrawn two days later."

Peterson's eyes lit up. "What about his wife? Didn't she notice her husband wasn't home?"

"Busy woman. Her name's Lisa Cusack. She owns a

children's clothing store, marginally profitable. It probably gives her something to do."

"I'm glad I didn't say that."

"I thought I'd say it for you."

"What else?"

"She's on the board of the Theatre Foundation and recently stepped down from the board of the symphony."

"Well connected," Peterson said.

"Very."

"That still doesn't excuse her for not reporting him missing."

"She confirmed that her husband often disappeared for days at a time. She thought nothing of it until his office called about him missing the meeting."

"There's an understanding woman."

"I doubt they have much of a relationship."

"What does Danny say about all this?"

"Until there's a body, there's no homicide, and Vernon Rumley is a Missing Persons file. He could turn up any moment, and if he does, Danny wears egg for wasting time and resources on a file that belongs to another department."

"What about you?"

"I'm off the record, and that's between you, me, and Danny." She slid Peterson a Post-it note stuck to a photo of Vernon Rumley. "Lisa Cusack's vitals."

"What about Cassie Colpitts?"

Bernie clicked open another file. "I pulled records on her, Logan Morehouse, and Kenny Paul," she said. "Cassie bounced through foster homes. She's not your love-and-be-loved kind of kid. Troublemaker in every one. No charges until the one for unlawful possession of a firearm, a 9mm

Browning. She was fourteen years old, six-months' house arrest. You know how it works: underage carries for the dealer so he doesn't go down for weapon possession. Lucky for her the nine came without a toe tag."

"Who was the dealer?"

"You're going to love it — Willie Blackwood."

"It gets complicated," Peterson said.

"Doesn't it?"

"The mother is gassed and working the street," Peterson complained, "and do-gooders screaming if the court comes down hard. No discipline, no responsibility." He flicked his head at the teenage girls wasted in the corner. "They become what we make them."

Bernie watched his face shrink into a frown.

"What else?" he asked.

"A sidebar on her in a report from an undercover cop. Fifteen and she had a child. Blackwood's, from what the undercover said. I don't think it went too well. Blackwood kicked her out and put her back on the street. Six months, a year later, she hooks up with Morehouse. She's already on a downhill ride and he's no bargain. I have a couple of pages on him."

"Sum it up."

"Scum bag. Charged as an accessory for break and enter when he was twelve. He was the lookout. There's not supposed to be a juvie record of that." She lifted her eyes to Peterson and smiled. She continued, referring to the iPad. "Simple possession when he was fourteen. Again a year later. The first got him a warning not to do it again. The second got him a much sterner warning. The judge told him he *better* not do it again. He dropped out of high school at sixteen. That was five years ago. He went back the following September. A front for selling illegal smokes and pimping teeny boppers on the side. Then he expanded into other schools. Got caught. Tossed. Never graduated. The last few months, he and Cassie Colpitts have been selling smokes, girls, and coffee sweetener. You still want to find her?"

"I'm a promise keeper. What about Kenny Paul?"

Bernie swiped the iPad. "A long list of assaults, B and Es, drug possession with no arrest, and one count of dealing cigarettes. He uses the Indian reserve as a cover." She slipped Kenny Paul's photo from a brown envelope and passed it to Peterson. "Did six months. Still on parole. Morehouse and Colpitts funnelled his stuff into high schools, probably the universities too. They parted ways a couple of months ago."

"We know why?"

"Ask Kenny."

"I doubt he'd answer my questions without a badge."

"That never stopped you before." She passed him another Post-it note with the name Diddy Parks, street address, and apartment number. "Danny thinks I should go with you on that one. I keep it official."

Peterson made a face. "I thought you were off the record."

"A woman's touch might help, and you know it," Bernie said. "Danny doesn't want faces popping into your head."

"Mother hen."

"Do you blame him?"

Peterson let it go. He leaned forward, elbows on the table. "Congratulations are in order."

Bernie shook it off. "Easy collar," she said. "Two jugheads in a pub arguing over Preparation H. One pulls a knife. The other balls his fists. The knife wins. I had half a dozen willing witnesses. It wasn't hard to put a case together for manslaughter."

"I heard the knife had a big-time lawyer," Peterson said, "and I heard he gave you a hard time in court."

"He tried to stick me with a messy investigation. No glue."

"You taking bets on how much time the knife gets?"

"Most money is on an easy three, out in two."

"Anything else going on?"

"You mean what are you missing downtown now that you're out in the cold?"

Peterson shrugged.

Bernie brought him up to speed on the in-house gossip and behind-closed-doors shenanigans. Policy changes, internal reviews, and what cop had been called on the carpet and disciplined for playing fast and loose with overtime.

"What about you? You doing all right?" she asked.

He shrugged.

"That means not too good." She waited a beat. "You need anything? I'm serious. Don't give me the rock 'n' roll eyes. I've been there. Eight years ago, almost nine."

"Been where?" Peterson challenged.

"Head stuck up your own butt," Bernie said. "Clawing for a way out. I lost my partner, my best friend, and almost lost myself. No time off, so nobody knows."

Peterson saw she wanted to tell it, and he wanted to hear.

"He was military, JTF2, special forces. I'm a cop and never knew what he was doing. He couldn't tell me. Top secret."

She looked past Peterson to where the teenage girls were. They had gotten up and were putting on their coats.

"He'd go away and I'd never know where," she continued. "Then one trip he doesn't come home. A roadside

IED. Southern Iraq. I'm not supposed to know where he was. I'm not supposed to know anything. But I do. I know how to ask questions. I know where to look for answers. What's he doing in southern Iraq? We weren't supposed to have combat soldiers there. Don't ask, they tell me. We were common law, but that didn't matter. The Army circled the wagons. He got military honours but no ceremony. No Highway of Heroes. Nothing!"

He saw the tears well and reached across the table to hold her hand.

"This government shafts vets!" she said. "Cutbacks. No counselling. I wanted to drop out of everything, and the only one I could talk to was my six-year-old son."

She squeezed his hand and let it go.

"I clung to him like you wouldn't believe. Him and the job, that's what kept me together. And a priest. We still talk, but not about religion. We talk about me and my son, about the job. I started talking to him about you."

"Me?"

"That you need help the way I did. Are you getting any?"

"Group session," Peterson said. "Along with paramedics and a couple of veterans. A lot of bullshit."

"Does it help?"

He looked at her as though she was talking gibberish.

She got up. "I got to go," she said. "It's your call on time and day we visit Diddy Parks."

"Let's go early morning," he said. "Better chance of Cassie and Morehouse being there."

CHAPTER
TWELVE

Two hours later, he was on the highway out of town when his phone rang. It was Danny.

"Your friend Leon hit town about three forty-five this afternoon," Danny said.

"No more doubt that he's coming?" Peterson asked.

"Wishful thinking," Danny admitted. "The problem is we can't make a move until he does."

"You can't," Peterson corrected. "I'm not dressed in blue anymore."

"Don't be stupid!"

"Nothing stupid about it. I'm out here with no one watching my back. What would you do?"

There was a long silence before Danny responded. "Where are you?"

"A few clicks from the reserve. Social call."

Peterson passed a snowplow tidying up the shoulders and spilling salt brine over the highway. Then he took the next exit and followed a secondary highway about three kilometres to a snow-packed road that skirted a scar of clear-cut left by a provincially funded pulp and paper company. Peterson had read somewhere it was a disputed tract of land the Mi'kmaq claimed as theirs and the company argued belonged to the Crown.

The snow-packed road soon gave way to cleared pavement where the reserve started. Streetlights were few and far between, and house numbers at the roadside had been buried in plowed snow. But Peterson knew where he was going. He pulled into the driveway of a split-level behind a silver Chevy pickup. A floodlight caught him square, and the front door opened before he reached the steps. Joe Christmas stood haloed in the doorway. He squinted at the visitor then sagged at the shoulders on seeing it was a friend whose friendship had been stretched so thin it was almost see-through.

Peterson stood at the bottom step wearing a penitent's smile.

"She's home if you're checking up," Joe said, his face rigid. He stepped out and closed the front door behind him. "And she's clean, if that makes a difference."

"She's out and she's home," Peterson said. "That's what matters."

"You pulled strings for her and I'm grateful," Joe said, "but that's the extent of it. You don't get off easy, Peterson. Not for putting my daughter away in the first place."

Peterson felt the strain on their friendship.

"I'm not looking for gratitude," he said, his voice flat and even. "And I'm not checking up. Sometimes a favour pays off. I'm just glad I had one owing before they made me a civilian."

Joe's face softened, but not by much. "What do you want?"

"I'm looking for someone."

"No badge, no business here."

"Just a little conversation, Joe."

"With who?"

"Kenny Paul."

Joe snorted. "You're still crawling with low-life."

"The spots don't change in such a short time."

"You think they ever will?"

"I can hope," Peterson said.

"That's a four-letter word for you."

Peterson shrugged, nodded. "Kenny Paul?"

Joe thought about it. "Bad news. He hangs at a shack, up the gravel road past the new fire station. You'll know the one."

Peterson started back for the Jetta, the cold air making his knee throb. Limping. Joe's voice stopped him.

"Him and a friend, they live like they got nothing to lose, Peterson. Your gimpy leg won't cut it."

"I just want to talk," Peterson said, opening the car door.

"Talk?" Joe flashed a lopsided smile. "Not your strong suit." He went inside the house.

Peterson drove past the band office and through a neighbourhood of upscale homes, past the rec centre and arena, and through a stretch of tired, 1960s bungalows, many in need of repair. He rounded a wide curve, and had it not been for the bright yellow truck parked in front, the white walls of the fire hall would have been invisible against the snow-blown field behind it. Across the street there were

91

several empty tree-lined lots and, farther on, a burned-out bungalow that was like a gap in a toothy smile. Another half click and the paved road tracked to the right. Straight ahead was a ploughed path to an open field with a clapboard shack near the back.

Peterson killed the headlights, made a three-point turn, snugged the Jetta to the side of the path, and sat for several minutes watching the shack. Music and bright light spilled across the snow from the two curtainless windows in the front. Fainter light spread from windows on both sides. He figured there were four rooms, one the width of the shack in front and two bedrooms and a bath at the back. No front porch. Between songs he heard a woman's voice. Then a man hollered and another man hollered right back. The front door opened and a man stepped out and walked to the woodpile at the side of the shack, where he loaded his arms. The man's step was unsteady. Drunk? Stoned? He had left the front door open to accommodate his return with an armload of wood, and through it Peterson saw a man and a girl huddled together in a stuffed chair. Another girl crossed the room and stood in the open door, closing it after the man had made a second trip to the woodpile.

Peterson made a face. Women complicated it. Men always played twice as hard and twice as stupid when women were present. Peterson tapped the Ruger in his coat pocket then reached under the driver's seat for the twelve-inch steel cat's paw, a tool he carried whenever he wasn't sure what he was walking into. He ran it up his sleeve and cupped it in place. Then he snapped open the plastic cover on the dome light and loosened the bulb. He didn't want the light alerting those in the shack when he opened the car door.

The driveway angled to the right of the cabin, where a late model Ford Explorer was parked. Peterson walked a rut on that side of the driveway and rounded the SUV. Then he duck-walked beneath the front window, rising just short of the front door. He rubbed the ache and stiffness from his bum knee then peeked through the window to confirm the layout of the shack. It had the undecorated flair of a back-country camp, with pressboard walls and overhead lighting from a sixty-watt bulb in the centre of the room. Before an open fireplace were two unmatched upholstered chairs with the stuffing poking out, a guy and girl snuggled in each, one couple toking, the other splitting a beer. A dozen empties littered the floor around each chair. On the right side of the room there was a utility kitchen with a small table and two straight-back wooden chairs. The sink against the outside wall was stacked with dirty dishes.

Peterson hammered the front door and slipped back to the window to see if the men were reaching for something to arm themselves. The girls were off their laps and standing and looking ready to run. Both in see-through blouses. Tight jeans. One had red streaks through her brown hair; the other had shaved her head on one side. Jailbait, to Peterson's eye.

The men stayed put. Cocky. Not worried about someone at the front door. One of the men, the good-looking one, early twenties with gelled hair and a bullshit smile, the one Peterson recognized as Kenny Paul, chinned the girl nearest the door to open it.

Peterson was back in place when the door swung wide and the shaved-head girl held it for him to step inside.

"Who the fuck are you?" This was Kenny Paul.

"Nobody you'd know," Peterson said, no challenge in his voice. He stepped to one side as the girl closed the door.

Kenny Paul stayed in the chair, inching his hand down the side of the seat cushion. The other guy got to his feet, which put him close to a rack of fireplace tools.

"That right?" the other guy said. Cropped hair, puffy face, eyes lit like he had a line or two stroking his nerves.

The girls backed over to the kitchen, knowing the game their boyfriends liked to play.

"I'm just here to talk," Peterson said, holding up his empty hands.

"About what?" the other guy asked.

"Logan Morehouse," Peterson said, aiming the name at Kenny Paul. "I'm looking for him."

"Why's that?" Paul asked. His hand went deeper between the seat cushion and chair arm.

"He owes a friend of mine," Peterson said.

"He owes a lot of people," puffy face said and faked a laugh.

"Yeah, but he owes my friend more."

"For what?" Paul asked.

"Keeping him in one piece."

"Your friend his bodyguard?" puffy face joked.

Peterson shook his head and lowered his hands. "Just a do-gooder who likes being paid."

"Why bring it to us?" asked Paul, his eyes showing that his hand had found what it had been reaching for.

"You and Morehouse ran smokes together. I heard you were pretty tight."

"Not that tight, and I ain't paying for what he owes."

"I'm not asking you to. I just want Logan Morehouse."

"He ain't here!" The other guy insisted, squaring his shoulders, getting ready. "So fuck off!" He eyed the distance between his hand and the poker.

The move wasn't lost on Peterson. "Who are you, hot shot?"

"I'm your worst fucking nightmare," puffy face said, remeasuring the distance to the poker.

Peterson dropped the cat's paw into his hand. He fixed Kenny Paul with a stare that was all balls. His voice went cold. "If fuckhead goes for the poker or you go for what's in the chair, I open your head first. Otherwise he shuts up and you tell me what I want to know."

Both guys just stared, sizing him up, suddenly worried about playing over their heads.

"You don't talk," Peterson pressed, "and you get three visitors, like Scrooge."

"What the fuck you talking . . ." Kenny Paul said.

"Only, your visitors come all at once. They take noses first. Then fingers. The nose is all cartilage, just takes a blade and a flick of the wrist. Fingers mean hacksaw or pounding the blade through bone. Hurts like hell. So I'll say it one more time — Logan Morehouse."

The two of them looked apprehensive. Then Paul raised the hand that lay in his lap and said, "I'm holding nothing." From the side of the seat cushion his other hand came out empty. He gestured puffy face to sit down, then swung sharply to the two girls and ordered, "In the bedroom and close the door."

The girls scrambled and the door slammed. Paul turned back to Peterson. "We split a while ago," he said. "Logan moved up in the world."

"From cigarettes to ice cream," Peterson said, sounding as if this part of the story was old news. "Left you behind to peddle smokes and hustle teeny boppers."

"Fuck you!" Paul snapped. Their eyes locked. "I make enough."

"Now that you've hooked up your own supply."

Paul and puffy face exchanged nervous looks.

"Not my business," Peterson said. "I want Morehouse, and I heard he was into something else, something with a little bit of muscle." Peterson was making it up on the go, remembering Tessa Morehouse's mention of the two big guys meeting separately with Logan outside The Tower.

Paul said nothing, his tongue working the inside of his left cheek. Then he said, "He came around waving money but never said what he was into."

"That was when?"

"Not long after we split."

"Six months ago?"

"Less than that. Big money, big risk. That's what he said."

"What else did he say?"

"Nothing."

"I don't buy it."

"That's how it was!" Paul's voice climbed half an octave then fell. "He was selling, man. Maybe he had a big score."

"You got a name of this supplier?"

"Fuck knows! It could be anyone juggling fifty rocks at a time. But Morehouse was in and out, you know. Off and on with this and that. Weed. Crack."

Peterson recognized the dodge for what it was.

"Let's talk present tense," Peterson said.

"What?"

"What's Morehouse doing right now?"

Paul shrugged. "I don't keep up with the man's doings. It's not like we're friends."

"That sounds like you're skating around something you don't want to say."

"We're talking people that'd waste my ass."

"Like who?"

"Like I ain't saying, man!"

"Yeah, you're saying," Peterson said. "Because you either talk to me, or you talk to my friends."

"I ain't talking to nobody!"

"Yeah, you're talking. All you got to do is hold out your right hand."

"What?"

"Hold it out!"

Paul held out his right hand.

"Now look at it," Peterson said.

"Look at it?"

"Look at your hand, Kenny."

Paul's head turned toward his outstretched hand. "I'm looking at it."

"Now count your fingers."

Paul's jaw dropped. He turned back to Peterson. "Who are you?"

Peterson pulled a crazy-man face, the one he had often

97

used when he was playing bad cop during an interrogation. "I'm your worst fucking nightmare," he mocked.

Paul kicked his legs out straight and pounded the chair arms with his fists. "I'm fucked! I'm fucked, man!" He continued pounding the chair arms and shouting.

Peterson waited for Paul's tantrum to pass then he stepped closer. Lowered his voice. "Who'll know you talked? Just me and your new friend here. And you can shut him up as soon as I'm out the door."

Paul lifted his eyes to puffy face, who threw open his arms in a gesture of submission.

"You know me," the other guy said. "I'm zipped tight. Nothing, right! Not a fucking word."

Paul shifted his head toward Peterson. "Bad motherfuckers, man."

"Names!"

Paul raised his fists and shook them in front of his face. "Cowley Pike and Tommy the Brick."

Peterson held his surprise down tight. "Doing what?" he asked.

Paul squirmed. "I don't know."

"One more time, what were they into?"

"He wouldn't say. I asked, but he shut right up. But I knew it was big, you know, he had that shit-eating grin."

Peterson heard the rattle in Paul's voice, like a pebble in a drained barrel. He'd got all of what Kenny Paul had to give. "Show me what's in the chair," he ordered.

Paul dug beneath the seat cushion. Swallowing hard.

"Bring it out with two fingers," Peterson said.

He did as he was told, pulling out a .22 Smith & Wesson.

Peterson took the pistol. "You want to play the big time, you'll need something bigger than this. You should stick to selling cigarettes." He pocketed the cat's paw and reached behind himself for the doorknob. "So what do you think? Should I tell Cowley and Tommy the Brick you were asking for them?"

Paul shouted, "No, man," and sank deep into the chair. The other guy chewed his lower lip.

Peterson was outside in one stride. He slammed the door. His adrenalin was high. Heart pounding. Gasping. He tore the car door open and tossed the .22 onto the shotgun seat, figuring it could be a throwdown if he ever needed one. He returned the cat's paw beneath the driver's seat and flopped behind the steering wheel and laced his fingers against the sudden exhaustion that always followed a confrontation. Then he started the car and flicked on the wipers to clear off the new-fallen snow.

The wipers kept time with his thoughts as he drove through the reserve and considered the complications that Cowley Pike and Tommy the Brick brought to his search for Cassie Colpitts. By the time he reached the snow-packed road, Peterson had soft-pedalled through half a dozen scenarios that put Logan Morehouse into the same game as those two thugs. Then he noticed a black SUV with no headlights riding his ass.

He flicked the wipers to high speed and gunned the engine, had the front end pawing air. He sped down the winding road, checking the rearview, throwing up clouds of fresh snow, fishtailing, and skinning the snow banks.

The SUV kept up, using the Jetta's taillights to get

through the curves. Peterson reached for the .22 and set it in his lap. He now had the Jetta at 120. Snow-heavy spruce and birch flying by. He tightened his grip. Nerves firing.

At the first straightaway, the SUV closed the gap. Then its headlights came on high and flashed into Peterson's side and rearview mirrors. The blinding light shining ahead turned the flakes into a blowing white curtain.

Peterson hit the brakes and slowed into a turn. The SUV swung left, caught a loose patch, skidded, straightened out. Then it came side by side within a foot of the Jetta. Peterson glanced in. The driver was slunk low behind the wheel, a passenger riding tall and going eye-to-eye with Peterson. Brush cut, broken smile, and unflinching stare. It was Leon Ferris. Then the driver floored it, and the SUV ripped ahead, kicking up a snow cloud that swirled around its taillights till they were out of sight.

Peterson braked to a stop. He was shaking uncontrollably, and his breathing came short and choppy. He stared at the windshield as though he saw something terrible embedded in the glass. Then he gripped the .22 and extended his arm. Stared at it, threw open the door, and struggled from the car. He slipped and fell to his knees. He yelled and raised the .22 and fired into the blowing snow, emptying the clip.

CHAPTER
THIRTEEN

No sidewalks, no playgrounds, no trees. Just strained nerves crowded together in a jungle of concrete-and-glass apartment and condo buildings built to feed city council's hunger for density. It was the kind of high-rise development that greased palms and blind eyes allowed to get off the ground. The kind that promises minimum wagers an affordable, upscale today, but delivers ghetto-style living tomorrow. And from what Peterson saw at 11:08 p.m. — open trunks and handoffs through car windows — it was a dope peddler's paradise.

He sat at a corner table in a twenty-four seven Tim Hortons on the ground floor of one of these high-rises. Lacing and unlacing his fingers. Watching a kid in baggy pants, his ass hanging out, hustling Triple C and nose candy in the parking lot. Beemers, Audis, Chevs, Fords, and VWs, it made no difference, all hit Timmy's drive-through for cover then drew alongside the kid for a quick exchange.

One girl, thirteen pushing twenty, came inside to use the toilet to pump herself up before going bow-legged in the back seat of another car. Peterson watched her in and out. Skinny and slack jawed from sucking a crack pipe or whatever else she used to cook her brain. Walked crooked back into the parking lot. It stoked his anger at the creeps who hosed these kids with drugs and ravaged their hopes.

He calmed when he saw Patty Creaser pass by the plate glass and enter the coffee shop. She lived upstairs but had to access the coffee shop from the outside.

Peterson more or less smiled and shrugged apologetically as he rose to greet her.

"No need to apologize," Patty said, anticipating his first words. "I probably sleep as little as you." She pointed at his coffee mug. "And if I drank as much of that as you, I'd sleep even less."

"So what can I get you?"

"Herbal tea. Any kind."

Peterson went to the order counter and turned in time to watch Patty remove the sheepskin coat to a pink blouse and matching scarf. When he returned with her tea, she smiled with eyes that she had taken time to highlight.

"I'm glad you called," she said.

"I just sort of found your number in my coat pocket," Peterson said, embarrassed.

Patty shook her head with affection. "You really know how to flatter a girl."

"Not much practice."

"It shows."

"I needed to talk and . . ."

"You just happened to pull my name."

Peterson saw that she was kidding him. He sipped the black coffee and the cup shook in his right hand.

She saw this and the way his eyes were flickering. "Talking helps," she said, just above a whisper. Consoling. Filled with understanding. "It doesn't make the problems go away, but it does make them easier to face."

"Who said I have problems?"

"You did when you called. You said something happened and you needed to talk."

"I said that?"

Her dark eyes looked into him, at the thundercloud inside. She said nothing.

"And that makes you think I have problems?"

"I'm a social worker, Peterson. I know what cops do and what they see. It's not hard to guess what's going on. You're not the first cop or ex-cop I've had coffee with. I also have a friend who's a cop. I asked her about you."

Peterson couldn't speak.

"I came didn't I?" she said. "You're not the only one with a past. I was married once."

He looked at her.

"My fault, not his."

Peterson smiled. "Who am I to judge?"

She slid her fingers across the table to touch his, and he curled his over hers.

"You want to talk about something else?" she asked.

He nodded.

"I grew up on a small farm, thirty acres," she said, with-drawing her hand and wrapping it around her tea. "My

103

parents had greenhouses for flowers and herbs. We sold them at the farmer's market and local grocery stores. I loved it. Country girl in jeans and flannel shirt. No traumatic past. I grew up happy. How about you?"

Peterson shook his head.

"Favourite movie?" she asked, shifting gears.

"I don't watch them. They're nothing like the real thing."

"That's the idea, Peterson, to get lost in the make-believe."

"How do I make believe when I see what's going on in that parking lot? I can't make believe just to ignore what's happening. I don't want make believe."

"I have a stack of files on my desk," Patty said. "Each one a person, and all of them want make-believe. It's the reality of their lives they don't want. They choose big-screen TVs and Xboxes over food. I can't blame them when I know just how miserable they have it. So I'm juggling and they're juggling, and the truth of it is, I can't make it any better for them. They know it. They've known it the whole time. So they turn to make-believe. How else do they live with the way they have to live? Deep down I want them to face up to it and do something. But I also know it won't make a difference, for one or two maybe, but not for the majority of them. It's a dead end."

Peterson knew where she was going with this and admired the way she was getting there.

"They can't do a damn thing about their reality," she continued, "or what they can do won't make much of a difference. But you can. You're facing the reality of what you do; at least you think you are. But I don't think you want more of it. I think you want less. In fact, I think you want none of it because of what it's doing to you. And that's the reality you're not facing. It's the reality my clients won't face."

He grimaced.

"I'm sorry," she said. "I'm not being fair."

He reached across the table and took her hand. Their eyes met and remained that way for a long time. Then he said, "City boy. Some summers in the fishing village my father came from. Country drives with him on Sundays. We used to go to a river and walk the trail alongside it. There was a tree that hung out over the water, and I once went hand over hand on a branch. Then I froze. My father kept yelling for me to let go and drop into the pool underneath, but I couldn't. Of all the things, tough neighbourhood and all that, hanging on to that limb is what I remember most. I dream about it. Wake up sweating. I don't know why. I don't know whether it's because he was yelling at me or because I was so scared."

He looked out the window, uncomfortable with what he had just said.

"There's more to that story, isn't there?" she said.

He shook his head. That was as far as he was going along that road.

"What about a happy memory?" she asked.

"I don't know. What do you want?" Then he smiled. "I was ten, maybe twelve, and we used to slide down this saw-dust hill on pieces of cardboard. They were grocery store boxes that we opened up and flattened out. And the hill was like a mountain of sawdust from a company that made furniture. It was fun. We played like those days would never end, and not wanting them to, not wanting to go home."

Peterson grinned at the memory, and Patty saw the joy

in his eyes. He usually chewed more words than he spoke, yet here he was gabbing away like it came easy. They talked about being kids for another twenty minutes, then they both rose at the same time.

"Thanks for meeting me," Peterson said.

"Thanks for calling." She beamed at him. He smiled back, then he opened the coffee shop door for her and walked her to the entrance of the apartment building.

"Not the best neighbourhood to be living in," he said.

"My clients live here, why shouldn't I?" She opened the lobby door and turned to face him. "How about a real date next time? Movie? Dinner? I don't care. My treat."

Peterson's smile again was genuine and his response was honest. "I'll call."

"Promise?"

• • •

As he drove away from the coffee shop parking lot, his mind was less lathered than when he had driven in. At the traffic light at Dunbrack, he hung a left and checked the rear-view for anything keeping close. After midnight on a weeknight, traffic was almost non-existent, and the traffic light was more like a four-way stop. Nevertheless, he turned left three more times to circle back to the Dunbrack traffic light, this time turning right. He zigzagged the side streets through a district of bungalows and fourplexes, until he emerged on Main Avenue. He drove into a strip mall and parked between two Harleys in front of a bar. Riot gates on its blacked-out windows. Steel door. Above the door was an unlighted sign depicting an overflowing beer mug and the name Plenty More. He turned his cell phone to vibrate only and climbed out of the Jetta.

No cover charge, but the bearded bouncer in full leathers scrutinized him as he went in. Inside, dark wood panelling and deep shadows secured the anonymity of the half dozen strays who were scattered about and pounding back whatever launched them into insensitivity. Raunchy guitar chords from tinny speakers pained the ears more than it did the heart. A whiny female on a tiny stage in a dark corner sang along. She wore jeans and a black leather vest, no shirt, relying on her twelve-string and long brown hair to cover what the vest didn't.

No heads lifted when he entered and made for the bar, but Peterson knew he'd been noticed. As a big man, clean cut, in a brown field coat with a piece outlined in his right pocket, he knew he'd be ID'd immediately in a bar whose clientele wore black leather and denim and rode the bikes parked out front.

A beefy cue-ball tended bar, a weekend rider and part-time hood named Greely. He wore leather and chains. Peterson knew him as the kind of man who showed muscle but was eager to back off when a scrap came close.

"You got some nerve coming in here," Greely said in a deep voice, like he carried his balls in a barrel.

Peterson slowly scanned the place. "I don't see anyone that can show me the way out."

Greely looked past Peterson to the bouncer on the door.

Peterson caught the look and said, "Ten-to-one he's working off a parolee's IOU. My word over his gets him back in a narrow room on the same cellblock as your cousin. I doubt he wants to play."

Greely swallowed it. "So what do you want?"

"I want to do your cousin a favour. I hear he's having a rough time."

"You ain't a cop no more."

"Twenty-three years earned me a lot of favours. I cash one for your cousin, sweeten his stay, and the time he has left goes easy."

"And how does he get that?"

"You tell me about Cowley Pike and Tommy the Brick."

"Why ask me?"

"Because you and the Brick were so far up one another's asses, it was like you had two heads. Then Cowley walks in and you walk out."

"That just makes me close up tighter."

"Maybe this will open you up. Everybody knows your cousin's doing your time. Bar fight breaks out, your cousin and some wannabe biker. The hammer on the wannabe's head was more your style, especially as you clocked him from behind."

"You can't prove that."

"I don't have to. Your cousin knows what he did for you, and now it's your turn."

Greely scowled. Peterson knew the fat man would take a swing if only he had the courage.

"Cowley Pike and Tommy the Brick," he urged. "Tell me where they are, what they're doing, and who they're doing it for."

Greely grumbled what sounded like, "Fuck you."

Peterson pushed back from the bar. "Your cousin asks how come his hard time just got harder, you tell him because you lost your voice. Or maybe I should pass it down." Peterson turned to go.

"You're a son-of-a-bitch, you know that?"

Peterson turned back. "I forgot how to be anything else. You talking now?"

Greely called to the bouncer on the door. "Jerry! Look after the bar a minute."

They went out the back door and sat in Greely's white F-250 pickup. It had a Harley stanchioned in back. Greely turned the engine and left it running. Put the radio up to interfere with any recording of the conversation. The windows began to steam over.

"Pike and Tommy are busting up dope deals, sweeping the streets for whatever they can get," Greely said. "A gun to the head of the seller and one to the buyer. They're making money, but not like they got to open a bank account. One night Tommy comes in and has a few. He says him and Pike were upping their game."

"When was this?"

"I don't know, a couple of weeks ago."

"What were they playing at?"

"Brick didn't say."

"What *did* he say?"

"He said they were on to something."

"Like what?"

"Like something that pays better than shafting street dealers."

"So where's Pike and the Brick now?" Peterson asked.

Greely shrugged.

"That's the answer that eases your cousin's pain."

"Doing their thing. I haven't heard from the Brick since him and Cowley made the connection."

"And kicked you out."

"I run a bar. That's more than enough business for me."

"I meant Tommy's bed."

Greely went deadpan. "Too bad that girl didn't put one in your fucking head."

"Too bad, huh. Logan Morehouse?"

"What about him?"

"You tell me."

"Smokes, coke, small-time, strictly hand to hand."

"Tommy never mentioned him?"

"Not to me."

"What about his girlfriend?"

"What am I, a census taker? If he has one, more power. But I don't know who the hell she is, and I don't care. You done?"

"Not yet. What do they drive?"

"I don't know. Pike likes heavy duty, you know, 1500 Big Horn, something with a cab."

"Sleeping where?"

"C'mon," Greely groaned. "It gets out, I don't have much protecting me."

"You got nothing going for you now."

"I'm in one piece."

"Tell me where, and your cousin gets privileges."

Greely thought for a moment, then said, "Back rooms in that crack house on Maynard. I don't know the address. Next door to that company that demolishes buildings."

Peterson pulled the photo of Vernon Rumley from his shirt pocket and showed it to Greeley. "Know this guy?"

Greeley hit the dome light and took a look. He shook his head and switched the light off. "We done now?"

"Yeah, we're done."

Peterson walked back through the bar, tempted to say something to Jerry the bouncer, but passing it up. Back outside and in his car, he turned on his ringer. He punched in Tanya's number and got a recording from her wireless service that the customer was not available. Her phone was off. Then he hit speed dial for Danny. Similar message. This was new for Danny Boy. When they rode together, their phones were always on, twenty-four seven. Family and love life had never interfered with their duty to the job and to one another. Now Danny was off the clock. He had found what he had long been looking for — someone to go home to.

CHAPTER
FOURTEEN

Peterson drove through the Maynard Street neighbourhood and spotted a black RAM 1500, V8 diesel parked in the driveway of a boarded-up house. He ran the licence number through Jamie Gould on the night shift and got the name he was looking for — Cowley Pike. Then he made one more sweep, this one to check side streets, his eyes on the rear view. He may have been running down Pike and Tommy the Brick to find Cassie Colpitts, but he still had Leon Ferris in the back of his mind.

He parked alongside the chain-link fence at Dominion Recyclers and watched for activity in the vinyl-sided building next door. He knew what usually went on behind its graffiti-scarred walls and red-streaked windows. A cud of memory had him chewing the past. When in uniform he had raided plenty of crack pads, hauling out the wasted and unwashed. Closing a place down, boarding it up, only to see another just like it open a block away. The futility of police work. It was like playing backyard tag.

He reached for the cat's paw under the seat and slid it up his sleeve. He walked over to the house, avoiding the ice chunks thrown to the sidewalk by a plow. He took another over-the-shoulder look before stepping onto a stack of cinder blocks leading up to the door. The stink inside made him gag. Streetlight through the windows papered the stained walls a pale yellow. It was 1:22 in the morning and pipeheads were wall-to-wall inside with their heads on fire.

He high stepped through the trash in the hall and past a kitchen that had been stripped of plumbing. A glance into the bathroom revealed it too had lost its guts. Side rooms had mattresses on the floors, six to a room, each cruddy beneath the teens lolling in six shades of hopelessness. Beside them were cardboard boxes for nightstands, their tops covered with vials, tinfoil, razor blades, crack pipes, and parts of ballpoint pens.

In one room, a girl rose on an elbow and looked at him. She was young and bony, with bloodstained eyes. A current went through him and his revulsion spilled over into a pool that had no bottom. He turned from that room and looked into the one across the hall. One room like another, all with hollow-eyed teens with their youth hacked off.

Leaning against the wall outside a closed door at the end of the hall was a skinny guy wearing a who-gives-a-shit expression. He eyed Peterson and grudged him a nod. There was recognition on both sides.

"Fuck you doing here?" the guy mumbled.

Peterson now knew what was coming down. "I got a girl back there that needs getting out."

The guy lifted his eyes to the ceiling. "And I got an Ontario warrant second floor," he said. "Bad guy with a long list of priors. Don't fuck this up, man."

Peterson tried the closed door. It was locked.

The guy smiled. "Whorehouse on the other side. Alley entrance. Which side your girl cooking on?"

"Give me ten minutes," Peterson asked.

The guy held his smile. "We're not multitasking."

Peterson pivoted and was out the front door in a hurry. He ran around the crack house and down an alley, which he now realized connected to the side street where he had seen the RAM 1500.

There was muscle on the door to this side of the house, an overweight slimeball with chin hairs wishing to be a beard. They each gave the other the once over.

"You lost?" the slimeball asked.

Peterson shook his head.

"Then show me the money."

Peterson pulled his wallet and opened it.

"Credit cards ain't worth shit," slimeball said.

Peterson removed a handful of tens and twenties.

"Pay the one you fuck."

Inside, he paused in a green-painted living room with outdoor furniture and smut for wall hangings, reading the place for what it was. Then all hell broke loose on the crack-house side. Screams and shouts. A gun went off.

The whorehouse erupted. Doors were thrown open and whores and johns, in various stages of undress, ran nine ways at once, desperate for a way out. In the hallway, Peterson pressed against a wall, picking out faces. Not seeing those he was looking for, he sidled along the wall, against the rush. He opened a closed door to a suite of rooms and saw Pike, the Brick, and Morehouse racing from one bedroom into another, gathering clothes and belongings. Then Morehouse dragged a girl out from one of the bedrooms.

"Cassie," Peterson called.

Time slowed, and he could register every detail. Pressboard side tables with bare bulb lamps that drove shadows up the beige-painted walls. Holes punched in a hollow-core door. A blue damask loveseat with worn arms. Empties lying where they had run dry. And there was Cassie staggering and turning toward him with a hopeful look on her face and reaching out her free hand as though pleading for him to help.

He lunged forward and grabbed her hand. Then he chopped Morehouse's arm to break Cassie free. He pushed her behind him, dropped the cat's paw into his hand and brought it up hard into Morehouse's stomach.

Morehouse whooshed air and doubled over.

With his hands on her hips and his head on a swivel, Peterson pushed Cassie into the now-empty hall. She fought him until he told her that her mother had sent him. Then her legs buckled and she leaned into his hands.

"Thank God," he heard her say. Then a solid blow caught him across the back of his neck and sent him colliding with a wall and then the floor. His brain was numb and his arms limp. He felt the cold barrel of a pistol briefly against his cheek and heard a man shout, "Let's go!"

He heard the back door slam. He pulled himself to his

feet and stumbled to the door. His legs were wobbly, and he missed a step, sending himself sprawling and struggling for breath. He crawled to the back wall, pulled himself to his feet and staggered onto the side street where he saw the RAM 1500 backing from the driveway and throwing gears. Heading his way. He stepped into the street and stood his ground in the gun sights of the pickup, waving his arms. The driver hit the headlights and gunned it. Peterson jumped clear of the passing truck. In the glow of streetlight, he saw Cassie looking at him from the rear window.

FIFTEEN

The Office had closed hours ago, but Cotter was still inside, sweeping, adding receipts, taking stock, anything to keep from going upstairs where he lived alone with furniture he didn't like.

Peterson tapped on the window and Cotter let him in.

"You too," Cotter said.

Peterson nodded.

"Some nights are harder than others," Cotter said. "And there are some hours that are the worst of them all."

"Tell me about it," Peterson confirmed.

"I'm having a beer. You want something other than coffee?"

"Something cold."

"How about orange juice?"

Peterson nodded and sat at the bar. "Fill a towel with ice."

"What happened?"

"I promised someone I'd find her daughter and help her out of a jam."

Cotter was wrapping ice in a bar towel. "And someone else didn't like you finding her."

"Something like that."

"The one you promised, that wouldn't be a wired up Tanya Colpitts?"

"She wasn't always strung out like that," Peterson said.

"She's been turning tricks since I opened this joint." Cotter handed Peterson the towel.

"Does that mean I shouldn't help her?" He winced as he pressed the towel to the back of his neck.

"Who am I to say who you should or shouldn't help? But if the daughter's anything like the mother, you have your hands full. Then again, that's how you like it. Sometimes I think you drag the streets looking for those no one else would touch with a ten-foot pole."

"The girl's tied up with three hard-asses."

"And the ice on your neck says you need help."

Peterson sipped his orange juice. "Not yet."

Cotter sipped his beer.

"A guy came looking for you," Cotter said. "A little guy with a chip on his shoulder, you know, little dog, yappy bark. I've seen him around, but never in here. Then he comes in, says your name. Says he has a message and leaves a number."

"The Runt," Peterson said. "He works the street for whatever he can hear. Sells it, usually to the drug squad. Danny and I bought his goods once or twice. Strictly small change, but sometimes he comes across with something solid."

From his side pocket Cotter dug out a slip of paper with the Runt's number and slid it across the bar to Peterson.

"God forbid I should interfere," Cotter said, "but a beer delivery guy saw Leon Ferris up at the Horseshoe Tavern late this afternoon. He was violating his parole and bragging about how he was going to mess with some cop."

Peterson nodded. "I'll add that to my list."

"From the looks of it, that's a long list."

"Getting longer."

"I always figured you were more fucked up than me," Cotter said. "I take pride in saying that. Everybody wants to think they're better than someone else. No matter how screwed up they are, no matter if they're smoking butts from the gutter or panhandling change on a corner. And for what, huh? For ten cents' worth of blow, a forty-minute high, and then they're back down and on the corner, back shovelling shit against the tide. Even these losers want somebody they can piss on. Why else do we put people down for being black, brown, Jew, Indian, you know what I mean? We stub them out because it raises us up. You're shaking your head. You don't agree?"

Peterson smiled, removed the towel, and rolled his head back and forth. "So, I make you feel better about yourself."

"You waltz in, and I think I'm King Tut. Janice said the same thing. She said no matter how bad she feels about herself, when she comes to work and sees you, she feels better. She said seeing you is like driving through a shabby town and seeing whoever sitting on a curb, brown-bagging it. She didn't say it to be mean, Peterson. She thinks the world of you. I shouldn't tell you that, but she does. She just said it because the other day we were talking about customers. I don't know what got us started, but we were adding up what we knew about the regulars and the ones who show up for a quickie so they can go home to face the old lady. You know what she said about McGovern? No, I shouldn't tell you that."

"What'd she say?" He replaced the ice-filled towel on his neck.

Cotter winced as though he didn't want to tell tales out of school but he was going to anyway. "That McGovern pinches her ass whenever she walks by. The guy's, what, eighty-five, pushing ninety, in here every afternoon, and he's pinching her ass like he found gold. Janice told him off a few times, you know, when he started doing it, but then she said, what the hell, if it gives the old guy something to look forward to, why not? Besides, she hasn't had a feel or anything else in years. I told her that makes two of us, but she didn't take the hint. I mean, don't get me wrong, I don't pressure Janice with nothing, but if she offered, I wouldn't throw her out of bed. Right now, this stage in my life, I wouldn't throw nothing out of bed. How about you? You getting any?"

Peterson sipped his orange juice. "What else did the Runt say?"

Cotter snickered. "That's the other thing. You don't give much away. We know you're fucked up, and we know why, but that didn't come from you. That we can see, and from what we hear, none of it comes from you."

Cotter drained his beer and pulled another, then came around the bar and took the stool next to Peterson. "Leon breaks parole, you call it in, and it gets Leon off the street. But you won't do it. I know you won't do it. I'd call it in, but if anyone finds out, it puts me in the middle. I'm going day and night looking over my shoulder. And it's not like he was in here drinking. He was in the Horseshoe, so technically it's none of my business, but really it is because I was a cop and because you're one of my regulars, you got to be the most regular customer I have, and on good days, I mean good days for you, I sometimes think of you as my friend. But not every day. There's many days you're one big pain in the ass."

Peterson finished the orange juice and pushed the glass to the backside of the bar. "The Runt, what'd he say?"

Cotter wiped foam from his upper lip. "He said he had something you were looking for, not like it was a thing, but more like it was information."

"That's all?"

"He said for you to call and wrote down the number I gave you."

Peterson laid the wet towel on the bar and slid off the stool.

"So what do I do, Peterson? Do I call it in or not?"

● ● ●

Peterson was back in the Jetta when he called the Runt. A thin voice answered, "About time."

"You got something for me?"

"Yeah. The subway under the tracks in about an hour."

Peterson knew the place, a dimly lit concrete tunnel under the railway tracks, a few hundred meters from the south-end container terminal. The inside walls were a graffiti gallery. One end opened to a dead-end street and a two-storey red-brick building that housed an advertising firm slumming it as an image thing. The other entrance caught some spill from the terminal's mercury vapour lighting. Peterson drove past this entrance to see if there was anyone in the subway. There wasn't. He drove back and parked beside the Mission to Seamen, a squat grey building not much bigger than a railway shanty.

Three in the morning and the Mission chaplain, a burly man Peterson knew and liked, was still at his desk by the window and on the phone, probably chasing down three hots and a cot for a sailor who'd jumped ship.

Peterson waited in the car and watched two gantry cranes unload shipping containers that were stacked six high on a carrier's deck. He cranked the window and let in the sound of distant voices and the yelp of metal on metal coming from behind the twelve-foot chain-link fence. He checked his watch and it was just an hour since he had called the Runt. He walked over to the subway to have a look.

The Runt was standing under one of half a dozen caged lights that cast the subway in alternating pools of light and shadow. He signalled Peterson to come in. Peterson shook his head and waved for the Runt to come out. The Runt shook his head and Peterson walked back to the Jetta. He was inside and ready to start the engine when the Runt showed outside the subway. Peterson got out and walked back.

"You don't trust me?" the Runt said, brushing his shoulder-length brown hair off his face. He wore a dark overcoat that dragged on the ground.

"It's more a matter of knowing better. For ten bucks you'd set up your mother."

"More like twenty, Peterson."

"What do you got?"

"I got thirty bucks to occupy your time."

"From who?"

"I'm not supposed to tell."

"But you will."

"For ten bucks."

Peterson peeled off a ten spot and passed it over.

"Take a guess," the Runt said.

"Leon the Neon."

"Close but no cigar. Cory Ferris was the big tipper."

"How long am I supposed to stay here?"

"I think getting you here was all Cory had in mind."

The Runt followed Peterson back to the Jetta. "For another ten I'll give you something else."

"You've already been overpaid. I've had a long day, Runt. You got something to tell me, tell me!"

"Leon's wearing a long coat."

"Back to his old ways."

"He's always liked the feel of a pump-action."

• • •

As he turned into the driveway, his headlights swept the blue split-level. The drawn blinds on the living room windows caught his eye. Peterson had kept the house just as his wife had left it three years earlier, and she had never drawn the living room blinds. She had liked the hominess of lamplight spilling from the front windows, fooling neighbours and passers-by into thinking life inside was all tranquility and soft-spoken words. He saw the curtains had been closed up on the second floor as well.

123

He climbed from the car, pulled the Ruger, and held it behind his right leg as he walked to the front door. He used his phone light to inspect the door lock for pick marks. No scratches, but there was the faint indentation from what Peterson figured was a bump key lifting the driver pins and jimmying open the lock.

He killed the light and used his key. Then he crouched, eased the front door open and duck-walked inside, quickly closing the door behind so as not to appear as a silhouette. He let his eyes adjust, catching hints of streetlight slipping between the closed curtain panels in the den.

He closed his eyes, held his breath, and felt through his senses for the presence of someone else in the house. Apprehension urged him to crawl from the house, to back out the way he had come, but he stayed put. He was scared like the time in that domestic dispute in a trailer on the outskirts of the city when the muzzle of an old Lee Enfield .303 was stuck into his chest, the husband bawling that he wanted to die and would take Peterson with him. He had watched the man's jerky finger on the trigger. He had forced himself to look the broken man in the eyes, to speak to him. Calmly talking the husband's anxiety down and his own courage up. Feeling the other man's feelings himself by dragging his mind through his own disillusions and disappointments.

He talked to himself now in his head, talking himself out of being scared, talking to himself to feel through the darkness and to listen. Nothing imposed itself on him, other than what he always felt when he came home — his wife's spirit imbued in the upholstery and dark curtains. He listened for creaks or rustles from the distant rooms. He heard only silence, as though the house too was holding its breath.

Slowly Peterson rose to his full height. He pressed his left hand against the small of his back, angled his body, and advanced with the Ruger pointing the way. He reached the far wall of the living room, and now, with both hands on the Ruger, speed-scanned the dining room then craned his neck toward the kitchen. The microwave and stove clock emitted enough light for him to see that no one was there.

The switch to the overhead in the den was on the living room side of the wall. He pressed his chest against the jamb, raised the Ruger with his right hand. He flicked the switch and sidewinded into the sudden blast of light, scanning the den with the Ruger. No one was there.

He killed the overhead and started up the stairs. Halfway up he saw a thin band of light escaping under the door to the master bedroom. He rolled over and climbed the stairs on his back, shouldering his way up tread by tread. He had a two-hand grip on the Ruger, his right middle finger on the trigger and his index along the barrel so he could point and shoot.

The door to his wife's sewing room was open. So was the one to his daughter's bedroom, doors that had been shut for over three years, rooms he had not entered since long before that.

He reached the second floor landing and backed up the wall to a standing position. Then he sidled along to the sewing room. He carefully placed the car keys at his feet, reached around the jamb, hit the light switch and kicked the keys into the room. He aimed the Ruger into the sewing room, saw nothing, spun around and heel-and-toed across the hall to stand with his back against the wall beside the door to his daughter's room. He lunged into the bedroom and dropped into a crouch, knowing his silhouette against the sewing room light made him an easy target.

No gun blast. Nothing but the sound of an empty room.

He crept toward the light seeping beneath the closed door to the master bedroom. He stood clear of the door, reached to turn the knob, and threw the door open. Quick glance in. Then another and another. Overlapping glances covering the entire room. Then he saw it, and seeing it buckled his knees.

He stumbled forward. The Ruger hung at his side. His mouth stretched wide in a groan.

On the bed was the dressmaker's form from his wife's sewing room. It was dressed in his wife's black knit skirt and black blouse. The arms of the blouse were folded on the chest.

CHAPTER
SIXTEEN

An egg-white morning. Snowy streets. Behind the wheel of her Chevy Cruz, Bernie was negotiating the early bird traffic onto the bridge to the east side of the harbour. Peterson rode shotgun, hands in his lap, eyes glazed in moody thought.

"So don't tell me!" Bernie said. "Leave me guessing if that's what you want to do. I come in and find you asleep at the kitchen table with a loaded .38. That has me worrying. And not for you, for me! This isn't by the book, Peterson. You're a civilian assisting in a police investigation, and you know how Fultz will go for that. He'll have a conniption if you flip out and something goes wrong. Then I wear it. Danny too."

She breezed through the toll with a bridge pass, took the first exit ramp, and hung a left at the light. She glanced at him. His frown was set in concrete.

"We could dust for prints," she said.

Peterson spoke to the road ahead. "This is between him and me."

"That's not how it's done and you know it. None of this macho stuff. You lay a charge, and we haul Ferris in. His prints match those in your house, and he's off the street and doing whatever time he has left and then some."

Peterson didn't answer.

Bernie glanced at him. "I'm getting nowhere, right?"

Peterson looked her way. "If anything goes wrong, I'll cover for you."

Bernie harrumphed. "The way Danny covered for you?"

A smile twitched at the corner of Peterson's mouth. "No mention of the times I covered for him?"

Bernie's eyes lit up and then dimmed as she turned into a maze of three-storey apartment buildings in a neighbourhood that was on the police books for its social problems. She checked addresses.

Peterson looked at his hands in his lap, his fingers curling into fists. Bernie parked outside a building that had started falling apart on day one. He was slow to get out, feeling anxious about entering a building where there was always trouble.

"Are you carrying?" she asked.

"Will you cuff me if I say yes?"

"Just being cautious."

"About my reputation?"

"Leave it in the car."

He opened the passenger door and tucked the Ruger under the seat.

"All it takes is someone getting the wrong idea and this place becomes a shooting gallery," she said.

"I heard about that," he said, his voice giving Bernie a lot of respect. "Third-floor apartment, Mexican stand-off, and you wouldn't back down."

She laughed it off. "Too scared to make a move. Thirty seconds and the guy gave up. I heard you faced it yourself at the container terminal. You and a drug dealer five feet apart, guns pointed at each other's head."

"Danny told you that?"

"He did."

Peterson looked past her to the building. "Different ending," he said. "My guy didn't lower his weapon. It's a good thing yours didn't come to that. It stays with you, Bernie, never goes away."

They entered the building. Vintage 1990s. The foyer looking as though it had been built during a hurricane. They took the stairs, hugging the wall, breathing through their mouths to avoid the smell of body fluids. On the second floor, the hallway was no better with the worn carpet exuding the damp stink of cigarette smoke and burned onions.

They stopped outside apartment 202. Bernie tried the door and gave Peterson the eye that it was unlocked. She opened it. Then he knocked.

A twenty-something sat at the kitchen table nursing a Diet Coke. Six fifty-seven a.m, and she was still on the clock, working through a list of regulars. Black panties, no bra, tats on her arms and legs, a criss-cross pattern of four-inch scars on her back, and skinny enough to count her ribs.

She responded warmly, probably thinking Peterson was an unscheduled walk-in. When she saw Bernie behind him, she stood up and backed away from the table. Her pupils glowed from what she'd been popping.

Peterson gave the apartment the once over. Unswept and unscrubbed. Kitchen table and chairs scrounged from curb-side pickup. Big-screen TV. Sofa with the guts hanging out. He peeked into the bedroom on his way by. Unmade bed. Soiled sheets. A box of condoms on the pressboard dresser. It was like walking into the Skype images that his daughter sent, and when he looked at the girl strung out beside the kitchen table, his heart emptied.

Bernie held up her badge. Her voice was firm and reassuring. "You're not in trouble. We just want to talk. Are you Diddy Parks?"

The badge and Bernie's calmness helped ease the girl's nervousness.

The girl shook her mop of dirty blond hair. "I could be."

"Why don't you put something on and we can talk," Peterson said.

Bernie followed her to the bedroom and waited at the door as the girl pulled on jeans and a blue work shirt. They went back to the kitchen and sat in mismatched chairs at the wooden table that had a wide crack running the length of it. The girl tapped a smoke from a pack of Players and set the pack down beside an ashtray that was gagging on butts.

"So where's Cassie?" Peterson asked, preferring to stand, leaning against the white fridge.

"She's not here." The girl fumbled for a lighter.

"We can see that," he said. "She coming back soon?"

"She hit the road. No big deal, right?"

Bernie jumped in. "Where did she go?"

"On the move."

"You're not being too helpful."

"What do you want? She gets a call and off she goes."

"Morehouse too?" Peterson asked.

Parks lit the cigarette and drew deeply. "Where he goes, she goes."

"Just the two of them?" Peterson asked.

"As far as I know."

"Where does that leave you?" Peterson pushed.

"I get leftovers."

"Does that include the pick-me-up?"

"When they come by, he rocks the cradle and I get high."

"How often is that?"

"Whenever."

"So where are they now?"

She dragged on the smoke. "Like he'd tell me, right? They went. End of story."

"Did she want to go or did he force her?"

Parks became angry. She blew smoke. "Yeah, she likes getting knocked around. We all do. Isn't that why men do it?"

"Not all men."

"Well I haven't met the one who doesn't."

"Did Morehouse hit her?"

She answered with raised eyebrows.

"But she sticks around," he said.

"You know how many times she tried to go?" She spit out the question. "The last time he used a coat hanger on her. Dragged her back." She stabbed a finger toward the hall. "Look in the bedroom. That's her blood on the wall. He wouldn't stop until she told him what he wanted to know."

"What was that?"

She took a long drag and smoke streamed from her nose. Suspicious look. Reluctant to say any more.

"I know we're cops," Bernie said, "but we want to help. That's why we're here. It doesn't go beyond this room. I promise."

Parks weighed it and then responded. "She said a street, Titus Street. That's all I heard. Then he called me into the bedroom and told me to clean her up. He called her a tough bitch. He said the Needle taught her how to take a punch."

"When was this?" Peterson asked.

"Ten days, two weeks."

"And they left together."

"That's what I said."

"With no one else?"

She shook her head.

"What about two guys, one big, the other blond with glasses, they ever come around?"

She shook her head and said, "I got a client any minute. I got to get ready, make the bed, freshen up."

"Thank you," Bernie said, and turned to leave.

Peterson had one more question. "What about you? You ever think of getting out?"

"To do what?"

"Get straight. Get a job. Have something, a life better than this."

"You think I can just walk out the door? You think it's as simple as that?" She looked at him like he had two heads, then she removed a partial set of dentures. "He used a hammer. You know what happens if I try to run away again?"

132

She replaced the dentures and crushed out the cigarette.

Back in the car Bernie said, "That doesn't get you closer to finding her."

Peterson had been staring at the apartment building. He reached for the Ruger under his seat.

CHAPTER
SEVENTEEN

"I'm making scrambled eggs and monkey dicks," Robbie Yorke said. James Robin Yorke, Detective Sergeant, retired. Sixty-nine, overweight, well groomed. He'd put in thirty-two years of police service: six as an MP in the army, two in Winnipeg, the rest of his time here. He'd worked a beat, went undercover, then back in a patrol car, climbing the ladder. He had always been a cop's cop who stood tall in uniform and taller still whenever he flashed his detective's badge.

"Black coffee and toast is good for me," Peterson said.

"You're getting eggs and sausage. You look like hell. Every time you come, you look worse."

"And here I spruced up for the occasion."

Yorke worked the galley kitchen in his three-bedroom bungalow like a short-order cook in a diner. Back and forth between the fridge, counter, and stove. Cracking two eggs at once, six eggs for the two of them, adding milk, grating cheese. "You don't have the job no more," he said, "so what's grinding at you?"

"I'm still working, but not on the payroll," Peterson said and walked into the dining room to see the photograph he liked, Robbie in his dress blues and his wife, Kitty, in an evening gown, at the ceremony where Yorke received a distinguished service medal. "Danny throws me bones and I get to chew."

"You making a meal?"

"Sometimes. I work my sources. Follow leads and ask questions he and Bernie can't. I'm also looking for a teenage girl, a possible witness. I'm doing it for her mother."

"Her mother?"

"Old friend." Peterson saw the shadow marks on the wall above a sideboard where two police citations had hung. "You redecorated."

"What?"

"You took the citations down."

"I took a lot of things down. Tell me about this girl."

"She got mixed up with a low-life. Talked to her mother about a gun and clothes covered in blood. At least that's what the mother said."

Peterson returned to the kitchen.

"The mother's not the most reliable," he said. "But some of what she told me holds up. From what I put together, a well-dressed guy took a taxi to Canal Street to meet someone."

"The girl?"

135

"That's what I'm thinking. Someone used her for a set-up. Only there's no body. But there is a missing person who fits, a businessman named Vernon Rumley."

"What about the low-life?"

"Logan Morehouse. Thick file. Smokes, drugs, running with two guys who are always on the muscle."

"What does Danny say?"

"Danny needs a body to get involved."

Yorke poured the egg mixture into the heated frying pan.

"Eyewitness to a hit, and now missing," Yorke said. "You might as well start looking for her underground. The other one, Morehouse, he's either on the run or sharing the same hole."

"Not yet anyway. I saw them last night, in the back room of a crack house off Maynard. I almost had her out."

"Yeah?"

"One of them nailed me from behind." Peterson leaned against the fridge. "I got something else, someone who wants me to get a backhoe," he said. "A snitch named Turtle. He never delivers the whole story, you know, always holding back to protect himself. Like two years ago he had us digging for a dealer named Jonah off the 107 behind the industrial park. We never knew Jonah was a hit until he told us. I think he was guessing what someone did with the body. Half a dozen holes and we had nothing. Then another source had us looking in the back of a freezer in that Lakeside packing plant. There's Jonah on a hook surrounded by two-hundred-pound hogs."

"So what's this Turtle have you looking for now?"

"That's why I'm here. Turtle says he heard Blackwood talking about a body buried in Laurie Park, says it goes back a long time, thirty years. I did some night work and found that thirty years ago a woman went missing. A housewife, two kids. Her husband came home from work and she's gone. No note. No reason for going."

"I remember that," Yorke said. "Her car was still in the driveway, purse and credit cards in the house."

"At the same time, almost to the day, Carlisle Martin went missing," Peterson said.

Yorke was turning the eggs with a spatula, dropped it and picked it up. "Fucking hands," he said. "Don't get old, Peterson. Nothing works the way you want it to." He held them out. "Look at these knuckles. Sometimes I can't hold my dick to pee straight."

Yorke plated the eggs and sausage and gestured for Peterson to sit at the kitchen table. He sat opposite.

"I was undercover when Martin disappeared," Yorke said. "I can't lie about it, not to you, not now. I didn't do my job, never saw it coming. We had Martin in our sights. He was back and forth to Montreal. Talk had him in line for bigger things, the Niagara region was one possibility, and we wanted to nail him before he made a permanent move. I was the source and I got blindsided. Martin disappeared. Taken out? Who knows?"

"You think he was taken out?"

"It could be. Or maybe he shuffled some money his way and found himself a quiet place to hide."

"And it could be someone put him in the park."

"Like I said, who knows? That guy Turtle tell you where?"

"Campground, but no site number."

"I doubt the department wants to turn the park inside out," Yorke said.

"Not unless Turtle comes up with a number."

"How likely is that?"

Peterson shrugged. "He might hear something else."

"Eat!"

Peterson did as he was told, scoffing down his eggs and sausage, feeling comfortable with the man who had taught him police work, who had showed him how to play the street and get results, the man whose example had taught him that the job was everything, that it was the measure of who you are, and that bad work on or off the job follows you forever.

"That was a long time ago," Yorke said between mouthfuls. "They hustled me in from Winnipeg. I must have told you that, how they gave me a rap sheet and jail time so I looked like a thug. The things I had to do just to stay above water. You've never been undercover, so you don't know. Fuck up once, blow my cover, and I'm a dead man, simple as that. Back then Willie Blackwood was just an up-and-comer. Ruthless. I watched how he got his nickname, the Needle. A kid named Stebbins ratted someone out, not Blackwood, but someone else. Everybody suspected the Stebbins kid but he wouldn't say he did it, not until Blackwood put a flame to that needle he always carried, getting it red hot then sticking it into the kid's eye. Fuck! I never heard someone scream so loud."

Yorke ate another forkful then pushed the dish aside. "That's another thing about getting old," he said. "You can't eat the way you used to, and you don't sleep. Up three or four times a night. Not just to pee. You just wake up and can't go back to sleep. Thinking. Thinking about nothing, and a lot of times thinking about things you want to forget."

"Like what?"

"Like nothing. I can see you don't sleep. Afraid to close your eyes?"

"Maybe."

"Don't kid me, Peterson. I've been there and back. A buck for all the times I fucked up and I could buy a new car."

"You were a good cop."

"Not that good. There's a blind spot in everybody. I wasn't much of a husband. I drank my marriage dry. I think Kitty stayed with me only because she had nowhere else to go."

"C'mon, you're talking like you're tapped out."

"Maybe I am. Maybe I've had enough. I look back and there's a lot of things, a lot of things, I wish I'd never done."

"There's a lot of things we all wish we'd never done," Peterson said.

"Yeah. You live a cop's life, and you come home with more regret than satisfaction. It's when the regret goes cold and you don't feel it no more, that's when you got to worry. That's when you do things prayer won't pay for. You want a drink?"

"I'm good with coffee."

"Yeah, me too."

Yorke picked up the plates and set them in the sink. He ran cold water into the frying pan and set it back on the stove to soak. He drew a deep breath and let it out. Then over his shoulder he said, "Carlisle Martin. I regret that part. Sometimes you just don't look far enough down the road to see what's coming."

CHAPTER
EIGHTEEN

He sat with the six others in the former classroom, them talking and him not listening. Through the high windows, he watched a light snowfall. He felt the cold and the helpless sense of going nowhere and getting there fast. He thought about his daughter and Cassie Colpitts, and about Cassie reaching to him, and about her face in the rear window of the pickup. He thought about his daughter running from the house three years ago and not reaching back to him, shouting "fuck you" over her shoulder, like she didn't need him for anything but still yanking his chain with phone calls and not letting him hear the sound of her voice.

He tuned in to the others in the room telling about things they'd seen and what they felt. Then it was his turn.

"I used to dream I was putting a puzzle together," he said. "A jigsaw puzzle. And I had pieces that didn't fit, a lot of pieces that didn't go with my puzzle, but I kept trying to make them fit, jamming them together, forcing them. I thought I had two different puzzles mixed together. Then I realized the extra pieces meant nothing to me. They belonged to someone else. And that scared me. I wanted to find this person and give them the pieces to their puzzle, because I was hoping they'd have the pieces that would fit mine."

The bearded guy leaned over his knees and looked hard at Peterson.

"Why were you scared?" Dr. Heaney asked.

"Scared? Because I had the pieces for other people's puzzles, but I knew they had none for me. Somehow I knew my whole life would be looking for and never finding my pieces."

The bearded guy was still staring at him.

"I know what you're saying," the guy said. "It's like we're all carrying pieces that don't belong to us, pieces that belong to someone else."

CHAPTER
NINETEEN

He had his spiel worked out before visiting Lisa Cusack at her children's clothing store. He told her he was a retired police detective helping the department with missing persons investigations. Cutbacks and staff shortages had opened the door for retired detectives to volunteer their services. His interview with her was a follow-up to one she had given to two uniformed police officers. He didn't even have to flash his phony badge.

She asked if they could talk away from the shop. She usually went home at three to fix supper for her mom. He followed her to a nearby neighbourhood of modern two-storey houses, each four thousand square feet minimum, with built-in garages, multiple rooflines, and brick driveways cleared of snow. She turned into the driveway of a light grey house with dark grey corner boards. He pulled in beside her black Audi S6 and followed her through a side door into a mudroom and then a kitchen with stainless steel appliances, black granite countertops, and chalk-white cupboards.

She called to her mother, who answered from a distant part of the house, and went to say hello to her. When she returned, she asked if he wanted coffee and tossed her car keys onto the centre island. She removed her coat and draped it over a stool back. She was wearing a cranberry-coloured pantsuit

"Black," he answered, unbuttoning his field coat but leaving it on. He sat at the island and watched her fuss with two Keurig coffee cups.

"Vern and I have lived separate lives since we were married," she was saying. "Convenience really. Passing trains, that sort of thing. We like one another and get along well when we're together, which doesn't happen very often, super busy, which is probably why we still like one another. I can't say that for a lot of couples I know. They separate and divorce. We found a way that works for us. Does that explain the first question you didn't ask?"

"Uh huh," he said, noting how easily she told it, as though she had practised it a hundred times. Getting it out all at once. "What's the answer to the second question I didn't ask?"

"I have no idea where he is," she replied. "We both go away for days, sometimes a week at a time, without the other knowing where. That's why I wasn't worried, not until Burton called." She caught Peterson's questioning look. "Burton Allen is the company's office manager. Vern missed an important meeting with a major client. He's reckless, but not that reckless."

She slid a white mug across the island to him. Manicured nails, pampered hands, show-off sparkler on her ring finger.

"But you're worried now," he said.

"Everything considered, yes." She sat down on a stool across from him.

"Like what?"

"Like money problems. Burton told me more than Vern would want me to know."

"How bad?" Peterson asked.

"To the limit," she said. She raised the mug but didn't drink. She set it back on the island and looked at Peterson. She no longer seemed quietly confident. In an instant, she had gone from early forties to deep middle age. "Vern lost a lot of money in a bad investment. That's all Burton said about it, but by just saying that and nothing more, I know Vern is in way over his head."

She lifted the mug again, and this time she took a sip. Peterson waited for her to figure out how to say what she wanted to say.

After a couple more sips, she began. "We had dinner together over a week ago. Vern was nervous. He said it was the money he'd lost, then waved it off like it was nothing. He's a pleasant man, and when we do get together, it's like a date, a first date, and he's Prince Charming all over again. He wasn't like that last week. Then, he got a call, which he took, which was against the rule we had set years ago about no calls when we're together. He said hello and that was it. The caller did all the talking. Vern looked worried. I asked what that was all about, and he said a deal with a guy named Bates."

"Jackie Bates?"

"I don't know. Vern just said Bates and that he had to settle some money matter with him and get everything back on track."

Peterson watched her reclaim her dignity by forcing a smile and blinking away her distress. Separate lives. He wondered whose idea that had been, because to watch this woman struggle through the worry and fear she now felt, he didn't think it had been hers.

"What do you think was going on?" he asked. "The bad investment, I mean. What do you think that was all about?"

She looked out the window at a copse of white birch, its bark peeling into papery strands and its eye-like markings looking back. "You mean something dirty," she said.

"Not the word I would have used, but real close."

"Illegal then," she said. She nodded. "Especially with Jeff Marshall. They go to Vegas together. Jeff's a dentist. Always looking to 'double up,' as he calls it, make money. He talked Vern into becoming slum landlords together on a small apartment building. It does all right, but it's not the money-maker Jeff believed it would be."

"Where's the apartment building?"

"Across the harbour, near the power plant."

"And the phone call your husband received at dinner, any guesses what that was about?"

She shook her head. Then she drew a deep breath and asked what she had wanted to ask since they had started talking. "He's in serious trouble, isn't he?"

CHAPTER
TWENTY

Peterson parked twenty metres from where a bevy of uniform cops were combing the snow banks along the road that ran from the north-end container terminal and under a highway off-ramp and harbour bridge. The sound of rush-hour bridge traffic spiralled downward. Rain-cold clouds had blown in off the water and darkened down the already darkening day.

The road was half potholes. On one side was the harbour, on the other was a garbage-strewn ditch. Beyond the ditch was the rusted track of a little-used railway siding, and beyond that a thicket of scrub bushes and knotweed. A driveway crossed the ditch and railway track to a dirt parking lot where truckers stored flatbeds with empty containers. A police cruiser blocked access to the parking lot, and at its far end, in the crossbeam of two high-powered lights on stands running off a portable generator, Peterson saw a green Toyota Camry sitting among spindly trees and brown stalks and cordoned off by yellow tape.

Peterson walked past the cruiser to where a uniform cop and Nicky Demers, an overweight vice-squad cop in jeans and a parka, were drinking coffee and shooting the breeze. Nicky saw Peterson and lifted the yellow tape for him to duck under.

"How come you and me always get to see the grunge?" Nicky said. His high voice did not fit his size. They shook hands, then walked together over to the Camry.

"Maybe it's the places we hang out," Peterson said. "Why are you here?"

Nicky opened his arms. "This is whore heaven, and I'm the lucky son of a bitch who gets to drive through here looking for whatever's going on. I spotted the car a couple of hours ago. It's hard to see into those weeds. Danny figures it's been here for a while. That's my excuse. What's yours?"

"Danny thinks I know the victim."

"Must be your lucky day."

"They're all lucky."

"Yeah, sure. Mine too. But at least you can sit back and count your pension."

"You got thirty years, you can call it a day."

Nicky made a face. "I'd miss knowing things." They stopped thirty feet from the abandoned car. "Like cuffing that guy at Walmart, the toe sucker. You hear about that?"

"No."

"A woman's trying on shoes and this guy drops down on the floor and starts sucking her toes. Security had him wrapped up before I got there, but what he said to me, you

147

know, you can't make it up. The guy said he saw her feet and it drove him nuts. Like he wasn't already driving nails without a hammer. I'd miss that stuff."

There was a cluster of people around the green Camry, Danny among them. He saw the two of them approach and walked over. "The victim has an ID, but that's no guarantee."

Bernie nodded to Peterson from where she was standing at the open trunk. Janet Crouse, in a blue forensic suit and booties, was crouched in the passenger side. She was a big woman, and she looked uncomfortable at being squeezed tight. She looked up and smiled at the sight of Peterson. He smiled back, threw open his arms, and pretended to give her a hug. She pretended to get one.

"I never thought I'd miss you," Crouse said, struggling out of the car.

"Give him five minutes," Danny said.

Peterson looked past Danny at the body of a woman slumped behind the steering wheel. Danny stepped aside for him to get a better look.

Peterson's guts tightened when he saw the victim's face. It was Tanya, her eyes wide open and jaw dropped. Her right hand held a Glock 20. It looked like she had swallowed the Glock and blown out the back of her own head.

Peterson turned away. The smell in the car sickened him. He pressed both hands to his mouth to hold back the outrage fighting to get out. Then he lowered his hands and said, "It's her."

They walked back to the yellow tape.

"You all right?" Danny asked.

"I'm fine."

"You don't look fine."

Peterson balked. "It's not the first gunshot to the head I've seen."

"That doesn't make it any easier. It sure as hell doesn't for me."

They walked in silence until they reached the yellow tape, Peterson with his head down, hands shoved into his coat pockets. "There used to be something that made us obey the law. Not because it was the law, but because it was the right thing to do. But now there's nothing keeping people from doing whatever they want. Nobody cares about anyone else but themselves."

"They never did," Danny said. "We've been at this for over twenty years, you and me. Not much has changed, except there's more of it, a lot more of it. Drugs upped the ante. But you measure it out, go long term, and we've been hurting one another since day one."

They ducked under the yellow tape and walked toward Peterson's car. "How deep was she into it?" Danny asked. "It looks like suicide, but I have my doubts and I want to get it right."

Peterson looked up at the headlights streaking the dark sky. "Someone tried to make it look that way."

"What makes you say that?"

"The company her daughter's boyfriend kept."

"Like who?"

"Like Cowley Pike and Tommy the Brick."

Danny's face lengthened.

"A Mi'kmaq kid named Kenny Paul, he and Morehouse hustled smokes together until Morehouse made friends with Pike and the Brick. I talked to Greely at that biker bar. Pike and the Brick were jacking drug deals for petty cash. I think

Morehouse and Cassie were part of it. Greely said Pike and Tommy were into something else, upping their game."

"Like how?"

"Big score. That's what Morehouse told his sister. They were jacking drug deals, not scooping from big-time players, not according to Greely. Then something comes up."

"Like what?"

"Like something that put them on the run."

Danny gestured back at the Camry. "And you think that's because she blabbed about what her daughter saw?"

"So do you."

"Let's say I'm now open to the idea. You have a name for the guy her daughter saw killed?"

"I think it was Vernon Rumley," Peterson said, and he brought Danny up to date on Rumley's file without telling him it came from Bernie and a staffer named Gloria.

Danny heard him out, then he said, "How does he connect with Pike and the Brick?"

"And Morehouse and Colpitts."

"Yeah, them too."

"I'll have a better idea once I talk with Jackie Bates."

"What about?"

"Rumley owed him more than he could afford."

Danny hardly took a beat to work that one through. "You and Bates go back."

"Not as friends," Peterson said.

Danny broke out a smile. "But he owes you."

"I got a charge dropped a few years ago, shaky evidence, and the Crown agreed."

"You planning on using that to do a sit down?"

"I am."

Danny threw back his head and blew out a breath. "If anyone asks, I called you here to get a quick ID on Tanya Colpitts. We didn't talk about anything else."

"Covering your ass," Peterson said.

"If what you're saying doesn't work out, then I'm covering my ass."

Danny went back to the forensics team and the abandoned car. Peterson climbed into the Jetta. He felt exhausted. He wanted nothing more than to lie down and rest his head. He started the engine and drove across the ditch and along the potholed road. As he approached the container terminal, two RCMP cruisers passed on their way to the crime scene. There was a uniform and three plainclothes in each car and, as they passed, each gave Peterson a good look.

CHAPTER
TWENTY-ONE

A half hour later, Peterson turned down the service lane behind Gainer's Pub. He drove past the back doors of shabby two-storey row houses that were only one room wide, snow was piled against their ruined fences. He parked behind a house with long fat icicles dripping off the eaves. The house had grey, paint-peeled clapboard. Lights were on, upstairs and down. His eye went to the red-tuck-taped bedroom window on the second floor. Three years and still not fixed.

He checked up and down the lane. No tail. No Leon Ferris. But he had the feeling that eyes were on his back.

He reached into a duffle bag in the back seat and pulled out a pair of latex gloves, then walked up the shovelled path to the back porch where snowmelt had pooled on the deck boards. A loose board squeaked. Balusters were missing from the railing. Weathered windowsill. A typical rental with an absentee owner. Eight hundred a month, which Tanya paid in cash.

Music played from somewhere in the house, a classical piece. A cello and a bass. Tanya's taste in music had surprised him. He remembered waking up alone in her bed and walking downstairs to find her sharing her morning with CBC Radio 2, humming along, dragging on a cigarette, and stoking her showered and powdered body with strong black coffee.

He tried the door and it was unlocked. As he slipped inside, he glimpsed someone playing neighbourhood watch behind a curtain in a window across the lane.

Streetlight from the service lane was dimmed by streaked windows, making the eat-in kitchen drearier. An empty coffee mug sat on a pine table, with a ladderback chair pushed aside. Cold popped toast was in a toaster on the counter. Beside it was a coffee maker with the warmer still on and burned coffee in the carafe. She'd left in a hurry.

He looked at the chair in which he had sat for six consecutive mornings, drinking Johnnie Walker to flush the guilt and douse the shame. And he looked at where she had sat across from him on those mornings, in a blue housecoat she wore off her shoulders to entice him into staying longer than he intended. She had sat there writing in her pink vinyl journal.

"You do that every day?" he had asked.

"No," she had answered and watched him button his shirt. "I write down good things that happen, and there haven't been many of those. You're in it."

"How's that?" he said, tucking in his shirt.

"The way you're helping me get straight."

"You writing about last night?"

"Uh huh."

He now opened the fridge door, examined the contents, smelled the milk. After closing the door, he stood still and listened to the hum of appliances and the distant voice of a CBC announcer waxing on about the harmonic and structural complexities of Béla Bartók's two violin sonatas.

He read the fridge notes. Hurley's Plumbing Service. Kit Kat Pizza and Donairs. Discount Fuels. Tim Rosen Handyman. There was a computer-made calendar that was five years old, with a photo of a smiling Cassie Colpitts, age ten maybe, arms folded in a pouty pose.

He turned from the fridge and suddenly faced a three-year-old memory that kicked hard. The red flowered apron on the peg beside the stove, the apron she had worn that time when she had heated up a President's Choice meat lasagne, a thank you for cutting corners to get her into rehab. The apron she hadn't been able to take off fast enough.

He followed that memory along the front hall, past the living room, the two of them stumbling on the stairs, shedding what they wore. Then he winced at recollecting the day he'd come back down those stairs in a hurry and answered the call about the Buick on the shore road crushed under an overturned cement truck. He went home to his daughter. He hadn't been there in more than a week; hadn't slept there in nearly a month. She was crying in the kitchen. She had heard the bad news from a neighbour.

He climbed the stairs and stood outside Tanya's bedroom. Reluctant to go in, remembering the two of them doing what he regretted doing, taking advantage of her, talking riddles when she was talking hope.

He opened the door and double clutched at remembering her on the bed, her long brown hair wild over the pillow. Then the memory became her gunshot head in the car, her sightless eyes and colourless face.

From the radio beside the bed came the wistful sound of strings reaching into darkness. At least that's what Peterson thought. His eyes filled and he dropped into a chair beside a dresser.

He sat there staring at nothing for a long time. Then he pulled himself together by being a cop. He searched the bedroom, as a way of pretending the dead woman with the back of her head blown off was a normal part of his job. He opened dresser drawers and combed the closet. He examined the computer desk and computer, searching the files and appointment calendar on the desktop. Nothing in the last two days, but a busy girl the week before. He wrote down the names of her appointments.

He went online and clicked on her website and scrolled through her lightweight promises to horny men. She had left no phone number for them to reach her. Email responses only. There were several photos to turn the johns on. She looked good. She looked younger. She looked like he remembered her, lying in bed as he had gotten dressed, the floral sheet partially covering her.

He returned to the kitchen where he sat at the table and slowly scanned the walls and counter, looking and feeling at the same time, giving his cop sense a shot at working it out.

He went back upstairs and looked at the undecorated walls. His eyes went to the top of the dresser, then to the top of the nightstand. He went back to the computer and looked at her photos. There were sixty-seven pictures in all. None of her daughter. There were no photos of her daughter on top of the dresser, none on the nightstand, none on the walls of the bedroom. Other than the calendar on the fridge, there was nothing to suggest Tanya had a daughter at all. In the time they had been together, Tanya had not spoken of her daughter, not once. Foster homes might account for that, no relationship until the girl became a teen, the girl only reaching out to her mother when she became pregnant and had a child. He thought about what Tanya had told him about texting back and forth, perhaps trying to make amends, trying to catch up for time lost.

Back in the kitchen, he opened the cupboard above the coffee pot and found the pink vinyl-covered notebook inside. He sat with it at the table for a few minutes, thumbing through. He saw his name and read the entry. Frowned. Then he pocketed the journal and leaned back and looked out the window to the back lane. He got up and followed his instincts across the service lane to the brown house where he had seen the curtain move. There was a light on inside. He walked over and knocked on the back door. No response. He knocked again. This time the porch light flicked on, and a pregnant thirty-year-old opened the door. No smile on her pasty face, just a hint of fear in her brown eyes. He smiled to ease her concern and flashed the phony badge, which he knew would be difficult to read in that light.

A toddler screeched from a playpen in a small room off the kitchen. The woman threw up her hands, beckoned Peterson to enter, and went to the bawling child.

"She just woke up," the woman said. She held the child, cooing motherly things that had Peterson shifting in the doorway. It took a few minutes for the child to settle and for the woman to tuck her down in the playpen. Then she came from the room and gestured for Peterson to take a seat. On the table were a cup of tea, a can of Carnation, and supper dishes, a service for one.

"I'm sorry about that," Peterson said, referring to waking the child.

"It's all right. She's back down now." She pulled a deep breath and blew it out. "I don't know what I'm going to do with two."

Peterson put on the friendly face he had used when door knocking for information on a case. The woman responded with a faint smile.

"You saw me enter the house across the lane," he said.

She nodded.

"I'm a retired police detective," he said, covering up for using the phony badge. "My name's Peterson. There's been an accident—"

"I know."

Her response caught him off guard.

"How do you know?"

"Mrs. Huskins called and told me. She heard the whole thing. We're friends. I mean, not real friends but friends like the way I am with Tanya. We talk sometimes."

"You know what Tanya does for a living?"

"I see the men going in. I see the deliveries. It's not like I'm watching her. I don't snoop. I sit at the window with my baby, rocking. You can't help but see what's going on."

"Did you ever see her daughter visit?"

"I didn't know she had a daughter."

"Did you see anyone go in last night?"

157

"No, but Mrs. Huskins did."

"She told you that?"

She nodded.

"What's your name?"

"Marilyn Goss."

"Marilyn, which house does Mrs. Huskins live in?"

"The green one next to Tanya's, the one that has no back porch. You have to go around the front if you want to get in. There's an alley three doors down."

• • •

Mrs. Huskins was at the front door waiting. She must have been watching from a back window, saw him enter Tanya's place, saw him cross the service lane and visit with Marilyn, saw him cross back over to her house and disappear down the narrow alley between the sets of row houses. She was in her mid-sixties, well worn, probably living off old-age security and, like most, barely getting by. She stood her ground in the front hall. Overhead light, twenty-watt bulb, saving money.

"You're here about the woman next door," she said, not waiting for introductions, voice like a pigeon coo.

Peterson didn't bother with the badge. She would have seen him flash it at Marilyn's back door. She was also the type who would have looked it over, carefully. "Marilyn said you saw someone enter the house next door last night."

The old woman nodded. "I also heard the yelling. I think they hit her. It sounded like that. You live in places with paper for walls and you know what wife-beating sounds like."

"You said 'they.'"

"Two of them."

158

"Did you see their faces?"

"You a policeman?" she asked, as though it had just occurred to her to do so.

He smiled. "Retired. I'm doing legwork for the department to cover off cutbacks."

"Legwork?"

"Someone, anonymous call, reported Tanya Colpitts as a missing person," he lied. "I'm checking it out. Did you make the call?"

Mrs. Huskins snorted. "I made a call a few years ago. I learned my lesson."

"What about the two men?"

"One was tall, like you, strong looking."

"Hair colour?"

"They wore toques, black or maybe blue."

"And the other guy?"

"He was shorter."

"Did you see their faces?"

"It was dark."

"You told Marilyn there'd been an accident. How'd you know?"

"They dragged her out and threw her in a car."

"What kind of car?"

"I don't know cars."

"You get a look at the licence plate?"

She answered with a hard stare.

"What about her daughter? She visit her mother much?"

The old woman rolled her eyes. "A girl came by sometimes. I didn't know it was her daughter."

He went back to the Jetta. Bernie was parked behind it. Two squad cars pulled up behind her and left their headlights and flashers on. He opened the door for Bernie to get out. They stood in the bright light.

"Did you go inside?" she said.

He nodded.

"Touch anything?"

"You know better than that."

"It doesn't come off good for us if you—"

Peterson's glare cut her off. "The woman next door saw two men enter Tanya's place last night. You might get more out of her than I did."

She watched him walk to his car and stand beside it. "Are you all right?" she asked.

He looked at her in the hard light, gathering herself after having seen Tanya in the car, holding down her feelings the way he had done, or was trying to.

"I'm fine," he answered. "I'm just fine."

CHAPTER
TWENTY-TWO

Peterson drove the shore road to the sharp curve near a beach where he had sometimes taken his wife and daughter. He pulled into the beach parking lot. It had been ploughed, but was slick with freezing spray. He lowered the windows and listened to the waves for a long time, then he got out of the car and walked back along the road to the sharp bend. There he said something out loud then turned around and walked back to his car. He leaned against the front end and listened to the waves some more.

When he felt the cold he got back in the car and sat with the windows down. After a while he took Tanya's journal from his coat pocket. He turned on the dome light and opened the journal to the page he had read when sitting in her kitchen. A poem.

The sudden loss of you has left me hopeless.
The sudden loss of you has left me in fear.
The sudden loss of you has left me heartless.
The sudden loss of you I cannot bear.

He popped the glove box and pulled out the sealed pint of Johnnie Walker. He rubbed his face and cracked the seal and had one sip, then toyed with the bottle, tempting himself to have another, and maybe another after that. He put the pint back in the glove box and drove home.

Many of his neighbours had already put the trash out for curbside pick-up, and a few had left their window curtains open, letting the lamplight out. Peterson had no trash, just a dark house he hardly lived in.

He looked over the outside of the house but saw nothing to suggest the intruders had returned. He let himself in and inhaled the cool damp smell of emptiness. He flicked a switch and the overhead lighting accentuated the brittle feel of the living room that he seldom sat in, a room he had trashed a few times after his wife's death at that sharp curve on the south shore road, and again when his daughter ran away after telling him she knew what he was.

As much as he hated the living room, he had not changed a thing, not the rose-coloured drapes and walls the colour of cinnamon, and not a stick of the blue damask French Provincial furniture. For him, the room was a bad memory, now merely a passage to the wood-panelled den that was his office and his bedroom.

In the den, between the brass-studded leather love seat and leather recliner, was a computer desk and an iMac that Billy Bagnall, the tech nerd at the police station, had revved up for him. There was a bar fridge on the far side of the recliner, and on the wall behind it were seven paintings of men's faces, all set against dark backgrounds. Peterson draped his coat over the back of the recliner, turned on a table lamp, and sat at the far end of the loveseat outside the yolk of lamplight. He set the Ruger and Tanya's journal on the seat beside him.

For several minutes, he sat there thinking. Then he made his way upstairs, flicking lights on and off as he went.

In the master bedroom, he stood heartbroken at the foot of the bed. Then he removed his wife's skirt and blouse from the dressmaker's form and carried the form to the sewing room. He returned to the bedroom and stared at her clothes on the bed.

He entered the walk-in closet and hung the skirt and blouse on her side. Then he stripped naked, crossed through the bedroom to the bath, and punished himself with a cold shower.

He shut off the shower and pulled back the curtain. His reflection in the mirror over the vanity was nothing to admire. The gunshot scar on his chest had darkened down. Raised and rough. The surgeon just getting it done and not fussing over what it would look like.

With a shaky hand, he lathered and shaved, watching the blade so as not to look into his own eyes. He dressed in whatever came to hand, a blue-checked sports shirt, tan chinos. Then he returned to the den, sat at the computer, and clicked on his daughter's latest email.

He had once tried not answering her phone calls, but that had lasted all of two days. Now she called him using phones with unfamiliar numbers, phones she had boosted off drunks or johns, making it impossible for him to call her. She never spoke. There was only ever an image sent to hurt him. Using her life to get even. This one was a photo of a used condom on a soiled mattress in a fleabag room.

After staring at the photo for a while, he put the computer to sleep, swivelled from the desk, and reached for the Ruger on the loveseat. He clicked the safety off and stared at the gun. Then he clicked it back on. Then off again. He started to cry.

His cell phone rang and he let it go to voice mail. When he stopped crying, he checked the caller ID and saw it was Patty Creaser. He clicked on the safety and set the Ruger back on the loveseat and hit dial.

"I just called you," she said.

"I was in a bubble bath."

Patty laughed. "It must've been nice."

"It was."

"I know it's short notice, but I just got two tickets to the hockey game tonight. I was wondering if—"

"Yes."

"That was easy. We'll miss the first period, but let's meet in thirty minutes outside—"

"What about right now?"

"Right now?"

"Right now."

"I still have to—"

"Take your time. I'll be downstairs in the coffee shop."

"Is something wrong?"

"Nothing's wrong. I'll be in the coffee shop."

• • •

They sat three rows back from the penalty box and saw plenty of action during the second period as the Seadogs and Mooseheads fought more than skated, piling up minutes in the box as though the team with the most infractions would win. Twice Patty hugged Peterson's arm when the home team scored, and twice he hooted like a long-time fan.

They held hands as they negotiated their way up the stairs to the concourse. He was scanning the crowd the way he'd been doing the entire game, as he'd been trained to do. Midway to an exit, Peterson saw Ferris turn as he passed through the double doors. Leon caught Peterson's eye and smiled.

● ● ●

They were in the car when Patty brought it up. She had said nothing about it on the way to the game, but now, with the question coming out of the blue, Peterson figured the bullet hole in the car roof had been on her mind from the moment she had climbed into the car.

"It happened," he said.

"But I don't understand how something like that just happens."

Peterson drove for a couple of blocks, then said, "Let's not ruin a good night."

Patty offered him her hand and he held it tight. "Then how about this?" she said. "What does T. J. stand for?"

"Tom Jones," he said and looked out the side window, grinning.

Patty laughed. "Not really, does it?"

Peterson shook his head.

"C'mon, what does it stand for?"

Peterson smiled and let go of her hand to turn up the radio. An oldies station was playing a rock 'n' roll song with a sax ripping at the eardrums. He was straightening up when a vehicle blew through a red light and slammed into the rear passenger side of the Jetta. The airbags exploded. The car spun. Patty screamed louder than the wailing sax and the shriek of crushing metal. Tires screeched at being driven sideways across the pavement. Another scream. A bright flash. Then a sudden squeal that ricocheted throughout the car and shattered into coloured streaks of light and a horn blast. There was a second crash, with less impact. This one on the driver's side. The radio went dead. Then a sudden stop, then a slow settling of sound, and then silence.

Peterson opened his eyes to a folded windshield, deflated airbags, mangled metal, and a blanket of crumbled glass. He saw a streetlight through the buckled roof and watched the traffic light change from red to green. He tasted blood and his body felt wet from the waist down. He flexed his fingers and wiggled his toes. His arms were pinned to his sides, and the steering wheel was in his face. Patty was slumped in her seatbelt and leaning toward him, her eyes closed and her face bloody. He said her name but she didn't stir. Then he smelled gasoline, and that scared him into squirming his arms free and trying to pull himself out from under the steering wheel. He was crammed into a tight pocket between the centre console and the caved-in driver's side door. He shouldered the door but it didn't budge. Then he reached and touched her face, and then her neck to feel for a pulse. He said her name again, and again she did not stir. "I can hear the sirens," he said. "We'll be all right. Hang in and we'll be all right."

Then he did hear the sirens, and he said out loud, as though saying a prayer, "Not like this. Don't let it happen like this."

CHAPTER
TWENTY-THREE

In a four-bed ward divided by beige curtains, he slouched in an armchair, holding the blue johnny shirt from opening and exposing his hurt body. There were dark purple bruises on his left side from thigh to shoulder, and fifteen stitches in his forehead. The sore head had earned him a bed for overnight observation. Every hour on the hour a nurse had entered his curtained cubicle with an LED flashlight, looked in his eyes and asked him the same questions: how many fingers did he see, what city did he live in, and what day of the week was it?

He had only one question for her: how was Patty Creaser? She didn't know. It was not until the nurse's 5 a.m. rounds that she had an answer. "She's on the fifth floor, room 519, and she's doing fine."

The nurse couldn't be more specific than that, so Peterson decided to take a look for himself. He walked past the nurses' station without being noticed and rode the elevator down to the fifth floor. Patty was in bed 519b. An inflamed zipper of stitches extended from her jaw to above her blackened right eye. A temporary cast held her right arm in place. There was a bar-like contraption on her right leg. As he watched her sleep, his brain flashed with images that had him groping the bed sheet and gathering it into a ball at his chest. He could not hold back the overwhelming feeling of shame.

In a neighbouring cubicle, a nurse was taking a patient's vitals. Another patient groaned. The nurse pulled the curtain and saw Peterson. "You shouldn't be here," she said.

"We were in the car together."

The nurse smiled. "She's doing well. She'll be with us a few days after surgery. So, why don't you go back to your room and get some rest?"

Peterson went back to his room. Though he lay on the bed, he did not sleep. A few hours later, Danny poked his unshaved mug around the curtain and tossed onto the bed the change of clothes and winter jacket he had brought for Peterson.

"They must've scraped you out of it," Danny said. "And your girlfriend's even luckier. Had the pickup hit a couple of feet the wrong way, she'd be in a box. How long you here for?"

"A head test sometime today and I'm out."

Danny looked the ward over. Two guys were snoring, the other one was talking through the drugs he had been given. Outside, a nurse walked the hall pushing a cart with a squeaky wheel.

"Not soon enough," Danny said. "C'mon, get changed and we'll go downstairs for coffee."

Peterson crawled from the bed, unwrapped the gown, and let it fall.

"From this side, you look like a grape," Danny said.

Peterson winced at pulling the T-shirt over his head, and again when he lifted his legs into the boxers and then his chinos.

"Stolen car," Danny said, as they made their way to the cafeteria, along hallways that were Sunday-morning quiet. "The driver ran, and I'm betting there's not a single print inside."

"I don't need forensics to know who was driving."

"It wasn't Leon."

"It was Leon. He was at the hockey game. I saw him."

"He was there with his parole officer and five other ex-cons under supervision. He's playing it like a model citizen. They all went for coffee and donuts after."

"Then it was Cory."

"Cory doesn't have the balls. Anyway, he was in the Horseshoe, and one of the waiters, I know the guy, said Cory was there late, watching some martial arts shit. So that tells me you didn't see the driver of the pickup."

"I didn't even see it coming. The hockey game I remember, and driving home. Then, I don't know, I remember being in the car and not being able to move, but I can't remember getting out."

"If it wasn't for seat belts and airbags," Danny said.

They joined the morning shift of hospital workers gassing up with coffee for another day of working short staffed. Danny got the coffees and joined Peterson at a table by the back wall where they could talk unheard.

"Loaves and fishes," he said as he swung a chair around so they both could sit with their backs to the wall and watch the morning traffic in the cafeteria.

"What are you talking about?" Peterson shrank into his shoulders.

"I'm talking about working here," Danny said. "Staff do that miracle every day. Shortages. Talk to the nurses, they'll tell you. Not enough staff, not enough beds, and way too many patients. But there's an easy out. Set an upper age limit for eighty, and you cut the number of patients in half. Who's the woman?"

"A friend," Peterson said.

"Hard to believe."

"Isn't it?"

Danny drank from his coffee. "It wasn't Leon, but it was no accident. We found a second stolen pickup abandoned on the opposite side of the intersection. I think the plan was to make you into a sandwich and one of the drivers chickened out."

Peterson watched two doctors in surgical scrubs make for a nearby table. He recognized one of them from a few years back when a murder suspect with a gunshot wound had been in emergency. Peterson had pestered the doc to give him five minutes alone with the man, but the doc wouldn't give him five seconds. He turned back to Danny. "A guy gets muscled into a car, taken for a ride, blown away. Cassie tells Tanya and Tanya tells me." There was a hitch in his voice. "You believing me now?"

Danny didn't answer. Angry pride.

"Maybe I'm making someone nervous," Peterson said.

"Maybe you should stop poking your nose in."

"Maybe I should crawl away and hide."

"Maybe you should do just that."

Danny rubbed his jaw. "Your friend, how's she doing?"

Peterson stirred his coffee. "Broken body," he said. "The army calls it collateral damage."

Danny spotted Bernie at the entrance to the cafeteria and caught her eye. She grabbed herself a coffee and then negotiated through a shift change of RNs and LPNs. She drew up a chair and sat facing the two men.

"I saw the car," she said to Peterson, but he was staring at nothing, distracted by thoughts.

"Anything more on the pickup?" Danny asked her.

"They're dusting for prints." She turned back to Peterson. "I'm sorry."

Peterson made no response for a few moments until he returned from wherever his mind had gone. "You know how many?" he said, his voice rising. "And I can't bring them back. She's up there in that window, and I can't bring none of them back. She wants me to, but I can't."

He shot up from his chair and bolted for the exit. Stumbled against a table and crashed over a chair.

Bernie and Danny caught him on his way down.

A nurse was the first to respond, then another nurse and two surgeons. The first nurse examined Peterson's hospital bracelet.

"Car crash," Danny told her.

• • •

The neurologist ordered a battery of head tests and another night in hospital. Bernie brought him the cell phone and spiral notebook from the smashed car. He could get the cat's paw after he was discharged. As for the Ruger, she had turned that over to a volunteer gun-forfeiture program. The pint of Johnnie Walker, safe in its plastic bottle, she had kept for herself, telling him he didn't need it while doctors were peeking into his brain. "That's a medical report I'd like to read."

Patty went into surgery that afternoon and was still heavily drugged when Peterson visited her that night. Her broken arm was now in a hard cast and sling. Surgery on the open fracture in her leg had to wait until she was stable from her other injuries.

After he was discharged the next day, Bernie drove him home and brought him up to date. There were no prints in either of the trucks. Both of them stolen off a used-car lot. Security cameras turned off. "Someone made it convenient," she said.

They ate Subway sandwiches at his kitchen table. Small talk, like she was holding something back. Then she said it. "They try once, they'll try again. Next time they might not screw up."

He knew what she was asking, and knew that she knew he would never back off.

After she left, he popped a few Tylenol 3s and slept where he always slept, in the recliner. He woke up late the following morning without a headache and drove to the hospital. Went to the gift shop, then to the fifth floor where he stood for a few minutes outside her room watching the traffic in the hallway, feeling uncomfortable with what he was about to say but knowing he had to say it.

Patty's nurse had her sitting up in bed. Her hair was washed and combed, and her drug-dopey eyes brightened when he came through the door carrying roses. As he sat beside her, she reached for his hand and held it tight.

There were two other occupied beds in the room. Both patients had their curtains pulled shut, and one had her television cranked for an interview about sports bras and running pants. Sun blasted through east-facing windows, and he repositioned the visitor's chair to keep the sun from his eyes and so he could face Patty.

They did the How are yous? and How are you feelings? then Patty said, "I'll need plastic surgery after the cut heals."

"They say how long that'll be?"

"A couple of months. I put in my order for a prettier face."

"I like what's there," Peterson said.

She pointed to the stitches.

"It's not as bad as you think," he said.

Patty tried to smile. "You don't make a good liar."

"You don't know me that well."

"Getting to know each other is part of the process."

"After the other night, I'm not safe to be with."

"The other night was an accident."

"No it wasn't."

Patty frowned as she fought through the painkillers to comprehend what he meant.

"Someone ran into us on purpose."

Patty tightened her grip.

"I've been turning stones someone doesn't want turned," he said. "They'll probably try again, and I don't want you getting hurt."

174

Her face flushed. "I already have been. So what are you saying?"

"That I can't stop turning those stones."

"Can't?" The line of sutures and black eye accentuated the hard look she gave him.

Peterson held her gaze.

"But you're retired," she said.

"A friend asked me to find her daughter. The girl's involved with some pretty bad people who may have killed someone. Now my friend is dead."

Patty closed her eyes as though that would shield her from his life rubbing off on her.

"My friend's daughter is out there. She's in trouble."

Patty let go of his hand and turned her face to the sunlight.

"There's no conscience in the drug business," he said. "People get hurt, people get killed, and the dealers and users don't care who."

Patty looked over the rooftop of the emergency room to a snowy field that was a community garden in the summer. She looked at the closed curtains around the other patients' beds. She looked at him. "So we're ending something that just got started."

"It's better this way."

"For which one of us?"

Her words stung him the way Tanya's had stung when she had said much the same thing.

"It's not safe, and anyway I don't have much to give," he said.

"You're a detective, and you haven't figured it out. I'm not asking for much."

CHAPTER
TWENTY-FOUR

He woke in his den, curled on the floor beside the loveseat. There was dried blood on the split knuckles of his right hand. He hauled himself to standing, and his knee hurt from walking the streets all night, the way he had once walked them in search of his daughter. Only last night he had been searching for Cassie Colpitts, showing her photo to anyone who would stop and look.

Just before sunrise, he had poked his nose into an abandoned warehouse on the waterfront where homeless teens jungled up for body heat and self-defence. Same place he'd looked for his daughter. That's what had driven him to punch a wall.

He made coffee and drank it. Then he hauled a steamer trunk from the basement up to his bedroom and into the walk-in closet. He gathered all his wife's clothes from the rack, stuffed them into the trunk, and pushed it under the rack where her clothes had hung. Then he ducked under his own rack of clothes and pulled out a shoebox, which he carried downstairs to the den. He set it on the loveseat beside him and opened it. Inside was a police department registered SIG Sauer, a gun he had wrestled from a dirty cop named Andy Miles. He'd kept it as a souvenir to remind himself how bad it could get. There was a full clip inside the box. He pocketed the SIG and clip in a tan duffle coat his wife had given him for Christmas one year, but he had never worn.

He locked the house, opened the driver's door of the Jeep Cherokee he'd rented, and got in.

Just then Danny pulled his Malibu into the driveway. He got out and climbed into the Cherokee.

"Anything?" Peterson said.

"Not with the pickup trucks."

"What with?"

"We're getting pressure to call it a suicide."

"Because she's a whore?"

"That too," Danny said. "Her prints and only her prints are on the gun. Drugs in the car. Her blood tested positive. Headline reads: Whore needles up and kills herself."

"You believe that?"

Danny pursed his lips. "I think someone worked hard to make it look that way."

"What about the two guys at Tanya's?"

"The old woman told Bernie exactly what she told you."

Peterson said nothing.

Danny opened the glove box. It was empty.

"I heard you were working the downtown last night," he said. "You're supposed to rest. But not you, no, you're out there shaking trees."

"I was looking for Cassie Colpitts."

"You don't have a good record with lost souls. You know that, don't you?"

Peterson made a face.

"There's no telling you anything, but I'll tell you anyhow. You want to look for the girl, look for her. But for everything else, back off."

Peterson still didn't answer. Thinking.

"Did you hear what I said?" Danny asked.

"I heard."

"But you won't take advice, will you? You never do. Someone says don't stick your nose in there, what's the first thing you do?"

"When something smells bad, I like to know what's rotten," Peterson said.

"What smells this time?"

"I still have to talk to Jackie Bates."

"When's that?"

"Later tonight, after I sit down with Lewis and Bigger."

"You and Lewis don't get along," Danny said.

"We're on speaking terms."

"Yeah, sure. The conversation ever run to how you slapped him around for hitting on your wife at a police barbecue?"

"That was a long time ago."

"And you're an elephant."

"Maybe this elephant has a good reason to forget."

"When's the meeting?"

"Tonight, up the hill in the parking lot where the gays hang out."

"Lewis sending you a message?"

"It's good cover for three guys sitting in a car."

Danny snickered. "Keep me informed. I can't back you up if I don't know what you're doing."

• • •

Fog horns at the harbour mouth and on the inner islands growled safe passage to the tugs and container ships, and they answered back with low grumbles of their own. They were like a small chorus of Innu throat singers taking turns going solo to complain about the thick fog on the water. Fog also hung in the trees of the large park at the southern edge of the city. The smell of evergreens filled the heavy air.

Dr. Beatrice Heaney extended both arms, her palms up and filled with birdseed, enticing chickadees to land on her fingertips and eat. When they did, her face lit up. So did Peterson's. She shook off the excess seed, pulled on her red thrummed mittens, and unhooked the cane from her left arm. They walked along the snow-packed Bridle Path, at her pace.

"And she was waving to you from the window," Dr. Heaney said, picking up where they had left off.

Peterson walked with his head down and didn't respond.

"Do you recognize her?" Dr. Heaney asked.

Peterson nodded. "Them. It's not just her. It's like she's changing faces, and I see one at a time. But then it's like they're all together in this one face, or I see them all in this one face."

"But you recognize the faces."

179

He nodded again.

Two dogs and their walkers passed by, then a pair of joggers. He and Heaney continued walking in silence. They descended a small hill.

"I'm standing there looking up at the window. It's high up in a building. High. And I'm a kid and I'm looking up. My father's pointing and I'm looking up. She's all in white and . . . I don't know if it's the sun or what, but everything's bright. So bright it stings my eyes."

He looked at Dr. Heaney as though to confirm the psychiatrist was there. "I'm talking crazy, right?"

"No you're not."

"Yes I am, because it makes no sense. All the blood, heads blown apart, and I'm seeing their faces on a woman dressed in white."

• • •

He walked alone back to the park's parking lot and saw Bernie in her Chevy, the driver's seat pushed back, laptop open on the steering wheel. A bag of take-out was on the dash. The radio was tuned to a country station and it was blasting. Her head and shoulders were bopping to a twangy driving song. She was so absorbed she didn't see him approach. When he tapped on the passenger's side window, her head snapped up. She killed the radio, closed the laptop, and got out of the car.

"Where's Danny?" he asked.

"Putting out a fire on a file that went sideways. Remember the sniper shooting from eighteen months ago?

We now have a witness who's lost her voice. Danny isn't happy. You want a burger? I brought you one."

Peterson shook his head. "I don't eat lunch. Never did."

"Danny eats all day," she said. "Western sandwich here, BLT there. Timbits in the afternoon. How'd you last together for so long?"

"Maybe we didn't worry about what the other was doing."

"That a hint?"

"Not from me."

They leaned against the car and watched a young woman trying to corral her golden retriever between two cars in order to leash it. "That dog gets loose in the park and she'll never get it back," Peterson said.

"You ever have a dog?"

"My father didn't like dogs."

"What about your mother?"

"Never had the chance to ask her anything."

Bernie finished off the burger and tossed the wrapper and napkin into a nearby trash barrel. "We're getting pressure to close the Colpitts file."

"Danny said."

"He's pushing back, but it's coming down hard."

"What do you think?"

"I don't like wrapping a file too fast."

"When I find the girl, you can put the file to bed."

"Only if she saw something and will tell us what she saw," Bernie said. "As it stands, we don't have a body. Rumley's still a missing person."

"I'll find the girl."

"You better, because if she saw something, she's in

trouble. And if she didn't, and she's hanging with Pike and Tommy the Brick, she's still in trouble."

They watched the young woman head down the path into the woods, her dog on the leash.

"I have the background check on Dr. Jeffrey Marshall," she said. "Successful dentist. Real-estate investor through a holding company. Slum landlord. He owns a strip mall and six twelve-unit apartment buildings."

"And Rumley's a partner in one of them. A silent one, if you didn't pick that up."

"You're ahead of me."

"Not by much. Now tell me why you're here. You could've called me with the details on Marshall."

She turned to face him. "I'm worried about you."

He faked a smile.

"So is Patty Creaser," she said and noticed how his cheeks flushed, either from anger or embarrassment. "I was curious about her, so I paid a visit. C'mon, lose the look. Asking questions is what I do for a living. She likes you Peterson. I mean she really likes you. Don't ask me why, but she does. She's not happy with you calling it quits. You can say what you want, but you're not walking away to protect her, and you know it. Nine years and I'm still wearing body armour against meeting another man. So don't think I don't know."

Without a word, he pushed himself off her car and crossed the parking lot to the red Cherokee.

● ● ●

Peterson caught up with Jeffrey Marshall outside his dental office and followed him through the mall and into the parking garage. From about twenty feet away, Marshall beeped open the locks on his silver BMW Cabriolet. He was opening the driver's door when Peterson slid along the passenger's side and leaned over the hood.

"What the hell!" Marshall said.

"My name's Peterson, ex-cop, ex-detective."

Marshall quickly scanned the parking garage.

"It's not a stick-up," Peterson said. "I just want to talk."

"About what?" Nervous eyes still looking for help.

"Vernon Rumley."

"No idea," Marshall said, and got into the car.

"You walked him blind into a bad investment."

Marshall glared at him, got back out. "I did no such thing."

"That's how his wife sees it. And now he's missing."

Marshall again dropped into the car and slammed the door.

Peterson swung around to the driver's side as Marshall started the engine. He leaned to the window. Took a chance. "What did Vernon do that got him killed?" he shouted.

Marshall said nothing, but the panicked look on his face did. He backed out of his parking spot and spun the wheel for the exit.

Peterson watched him go. He didn't have what he was after, but he had something.

● ● ●

He followed a hunch and visited each of Marshall's six apartment buildings. All were cheaply built and not well maintained. Three were clustered on the same block in Fairview, and on their own had turned the blue-collar neighbourhood into a slum. Outside, one of them was where Sammy O, a big time drug dealer and Willie Blackwood's delivery boy, had ducked a bullet.

He button-holed tenants, said he was thinking of renting here, and asked how much they were paying, saying he didn't want to be fleeced by a landlord he didn't think was on the up and up. He pretty much received the same answer from everyone: low rent and no amenities. Two buildings had bedbug issues, which the landlord had cleared up, but took his time doing it. There were drug dealers in four of the six, and one entire floor of another building had a lot of in-and-out traffic, all men.

There were a few empty apartments in all of the buildings, which, according to several tenants, had never been rented for as long as they had lived there. Another thing stood out: five of the six buildings had a third-party ATM in the front foyer.

CHAPTER
TWENTY-FIVE

Midnight. Peterson waited in the Jeep in the parking lot outside an eighteenth-century hilltop fortification in the centre of the city. A forty-foot-deep ditch encircled the stone fort. He quickly lost interest in the car hopping and partner exchange in the parking lot and watched the steady flow of car and pedestrian traffic on the street below. He picked out the unmarked units and the cops in civvies who patrolled the street and the two bars within one short block. Weekend or weekday nights made no difference. There were always plenty of hammerheads and college boys drinking courage then going one-on-one over what was said, what was done, or over which girl smiled and what guy smiled back.

Ten minutes later Lewis and Bigger pulled in, and Peterson climbed from his vehicle and into the Honda CR-V. They left the car running for heat. Lewis sat in the driver's seat, running a hand through his wavy brown hair. He wore his usual snarl, and Eddie Bigger, his hair close-cropped and framing his big ears, flashed his little-man's look of defiance. Both turned when Peterson settled in the back.

Lewis pointed at the stitches in Peterson's forehead. "One of your many friends?" he asked.

"Car accident."

"Hit and run, wasn't it?" Bigger said. "Another customer doesn't like what you're selling."

"If that's what you heard."

"Hot off the press," Lewis said. "Now what's on your mind?"

"The Mounties bust a big shipment offshore and the supply to the city goes dry," Peterson said, settling back into the shadows. "I want to know how that stirred the pot."

"What's it to you?"

"Some street dealers never ran short. One of them was a kid named Logan Morehouse."

"Low level and not worth our attention," Lewis said, but the way he shifted in his seat confirmed for Peterson that Lewis knew more about Logan Morehouse than he was saying.

"What's this Morehouse to you?" Bigger asked.

"He has a girlfriend," Peterson said, "Cassie Colpitts. I'm looking for her."

"Why's that?"

"Her mother asked me to."

"Didn't you once have a crush on the mother?" Bigger said. He enjoyed saying it.

Peterson kept his cool. "Neither one of us would piss on

the other's good side," he said to Lewis. "So let's talk and get it over with."

"Nothing to talk about," Lewis said. "You're not a cop, so why should we tell you anything?"

"Because I have something that might interest you. With the right police work, it's something that would make Willie Blackwood uncomfortable."

"You got something on the Needle?"

"I got something that points in his direction."

"That's not as good as pointing right at him."

"If you don't want what I have, we'll call it a night." Peterson reached for the door handle but Lewis gave him the stop sign.

"If it's good, we'll listen."

"A buried body, a thirty-year-old cold case that someone just put a match to," Peterson teased.

"A cold case takes too much time to put together," Lewis said.

"Not if you know where to dig."

"Do you know where to dig?"

"General vicinity."

"Convince us," Lewis insisted.

"I have two names, solid. They could fill in the details."

Lewis and Bigger exchanged looks. "It better be good," Lewis said.

Peterson grinned and leaned forward to make sure they saw.

Lewis and Bigger exchanged another look, then Bigger nodded and turned the radio on. Lewis rubbed the back of his hand across his nose. He twisted around to face Peterson.

"Product usually comes in over land. Truck, car, it varies. Then the Mounties got wind of a shipment coming by water. They made the bust, three watertight bales over the side of a mother ship. GPS transponders. They collared those on the mother ship and the two in a Cape Islander following the GPS signals. Low levels on both sides, all scared shitless to talk."

"The Mounties choked the supply," Bigger added. "Temporary, but it has its immediate results."

"No product, no sales," Lewis said. "Turf wars start. More threats than take-downs, you know, drive-bys at houses, accidental victims, an eighteen-year-old girl ends up a quadriplegic. All this time Blackwood has a stash he feeds out in goody bags. Corner-store dealers were standing in line. Sammy O was his delivery boy. We think someone used all the hit and miss as cover and followed Sammy to where Blackwood keeps a stash and a hoard of money. Or maybe they knew where it was and waited for Sammy to open the door. Nothing neat about it. Sammy ducks a couple of shots, and the street's not talking about who did it."

"You'd think God struck every street juggler in the city deaf and dumb," Bigger said. "Only thing leaking out is they took cash and only some drugs. Private use, that's what we figure."

Peterson remained straight-faced, not giving anything away.

"We heard Blackwood knows who they are," Lewis said. "Has them on a string."

"You have names?"

"Nothing definite," Lewis said.

"What about Cowley Pike and Tommy the Brick?" Peterson suggested.

"They slam doors on back alley dealers. This was out of their league."

"Anything on a businessman named Rumley?"

Bigger turned to Lewis, who shook his head.

"That's not up for trade," Lewis said. "Your turn."

Peterson didn't let it show that Lewis had confirmed what he had suspected. Now he had to play his side, thinking they could ride it awhile and get nowhere. Without saying his name, Peterson told them about Turtle overhearing Willie Blackwood talking about a body that's been buried for thirty years in the campground in Laurie Park. He also made the connection to the sudden disappearance of Carlisle Martin around the time the body was buried. Neither Lewis nor Bigger had been cops back then, so Peterson filled them in on the nature of the drug business in the city in the days of Robbie Yorke and Cotter. Peterson also gave them the name of another old-timer, Jimmy Stiles, who worked undercover back then. He was gambling these drug-squad cops, especially Lewis whose ambition exceeded his ability to drag himself higher up the food chain, would gobble up the chunks he served without checking if they were any good.

"How solid is this information?" Lewis said.

"The man's a snitch," Peterson said. "Take it or leave it, whatever you want."

"And he overheard this conversation?"

"That's what he said."

"This guy, he delivered solid stuff before?"

"He led Danny to Jonah's body in the meat locker."

Both cops nodded at the same time. "And the campground's all you got?" Bigger said.

Peterson knew that Bigger was asking this to make sure

Peterson didn't have his own hand on the rabbit in the hat. "The snitch can't narrow the search any tighter than the campground," he said.

"That's a big place to search for a body," Bigger said. "And thirty years is a long time ago. Possible sources may all be dead."

"It's good information," Peterson said. His hand was already on the door handle. "All you need is someone who can draw smaller circles."

CHAPTER
TWENTY-SIX

Peterson knew Jackie Bates from way back, as a busy man who ran three payday loan operations and loan sharked out their back doors, playing it tight with the local politicians and keeping the cops off his back. Jackie squeezed juice from the underemployed, the minimum wagers willing to give five percent per day and secure the debt with whatever they owned. Vehicle owners got a half a point discount by putting up the title to their vehicle, along with an extra set of keys. Miss a payment and Jackie's repo men paid a visit.

What never got said, but Peterson knew, was that Bates's real money was in the jewellery and twenty-per-cent-a-day vig from the casino rats and coke blowers who were *personae non gratae* with the banks and credit unions. These were the over-extended nouveau riche with images to maintain. They were blackjack flatliners and high rollers who threw craps on both sides of the table.

Men were always the big losers and big borrowers, but women were Jackie's most reliable customers. They were sitting on their collateral. And Jackie had the connections to sell it. He also ran a high-stakes game from the upstairs of a pizza joint on a main drag that ran from downtown to out of the city. Three tables. Cash only. No IOUs except for the ones Jackie covered for a straight twenty percent per day. That's where Peterson went.

He parked and walked two blocks to read the street, passing a couple of stick-to-the-ribs ethnic restaurants, a burger joint, a fried-chicken shack, and a handful of quick-stop retailers for commuters on their way out of town. At that late hour, the street was bored with nothing to do.

A ragged old woman sat in a narrow alley between a sports shop and a tattoo joint, holding her own against the cold night in a torn overcoat and laceless shoes. She was a has-been hooker with nowhere to go.

"Yeah, I know," Peterson responded to her hustle. "Pimps don't provide pension plans." He reached for a five-dollar bill, changed his mind, and made it a ten.

There was muscle on the back door to the pizza joint, two bouncers who knew Peterson from days gone by. They had words, but after a call to upstairs they opened the door and ushered him to the low-lighted stairway to the second floor.

Upstairs, fifteen guys, all ages and colours and ethnic heritages, a regular multicultural night, sat five to a table. Most of them were in shirtsleeves, and one still had on a blazer and tie. There was more muscle in the room, and one of them pointed at the door to Jackie's office.

It was a low-overhead operation. Bates's office had just a desk and three chairs. The cushy, high-back swivel was for him; the metal folders were for the losers looking for a loan. Nothing on the walls, no landline, and no stocked bar. The street pegged Bates as living like a monk, but Peterson knew better. Jackie had a wife and three kids tucked away in a vast ocean-view two-storey on the South Shore. He had a one-bedroom condo in town so he didn't have to drive home tired. Peterson nodded and Jackie nodded back. Peterson didn't sit.

Jackie sat up straight with his hands folded on the desk, the cuffs of his blue Oxford button-down rolled up once. His full head of brown hair was untouched by that Grecian stuff, but sprayed in place for a night's work. His sharp brown eyes and tight smile gave nothing away.

"I don't usually talk to middlemen," Jackie said in a soft voice that underscored the neutrality of his expression, "but you've always been an exception."

"What you owe me doesn't need paying back," Peterson said.

"I know. I also know you ain't looking for a loan."

"Vernon Rumley," Peterson said, adding a big smile as though he and Jackie were bosom buddies.

"He hasn't been around lately. I thought maybe he skipped off to Vegas to win what he owes me. What's Rumley have on you?"

"Friendship," Peterson said.

"You don't have friends, Peterson," Bates said.

"Long time ago."

"Worst kind, always coming back to haunt you. What does he want?"

"More time."

"We're not talking cab fare."

"He owns a business. He's good for the money."

"Not that good. He's missed two payments already, or didn't he tell you that?"

Peterson held back his surprise. "So you take a few extra points for late payment."

"I take them anyway," Jackie said. "It's not like I haven't seen it before. The shitters come to me because they have no credit. Never did. Some have assets I can touch. Others have pretty wives. The rich and famous, the south-end snobs, they only come after the banks cut them off. They need cash and have assets they won't sell. The image thing, you know. Big boat, big cottage, big house, big fucking debt. I show them the dotted line for a few hundred grand, and if they miss a payment, the boat belongs to me. You know how many boats I own? Fill a goddamn marina. So I rent them back for the sake of appearances."

Jackie sipped his coffee and wiped his mouth with the back of his hand.

"Rumley has nothing," he continued. "He's way over-extended. No free asset I can touch. I doubt he could scrape together enough for a cup of coffee. But that's my fault. I made the loan thinking he could pay. Due diligence I didn't do, not until he welshed. Then I found out he gambled on a bad investment. He listened to the sweet nothings of money."

"What bad investment was that?"

"I thought he was your friend."

"Old friend. Worst kind, remember."

"The kind that walks you off a cliff. But you don't have the money to cover what he owes. So, who does?"

Peterson shrugged.

"C'mon," Jackie said. "You come here looking for time. Time for what? Rumley could have all the time there is and he still couldn't pay. It's not Rumley who needs time, it's someone else."

Peterson stared him down.

Jackie's expression never changed. "His wife? Not a chance. She comes from money, but so what? Old money learned long ago how to keep what they have. Deep pockets with fishhooks sewed inside so they can't reach the change. Not his wife, so who bails him?"

"He promised he'd pay, that was enough for me."

"Song and dance, Peterson. Rumley promised what needed promising to get you, or whoever, to do what he needed doing. There's a poem. You didn't know I read poems."

"Never would have guessed."

"More my wife than me. But there's one by this poet named Rilke. It's about a guy who's getting married, and at the reception, Death comes to take the guy. I can't remember his name. Some Greek name. Anyway, the guy panics. He tries to bargain with Death. One more year, he begs. Then a month, a week, a few days, one day, this night, his wedding night. Death refuses the deal. Then the guy pushes his mother and father forward and offers them as his replacement. See what I mean? The guy'd do anything, say anything, to get out of a bad situation. That's Vernon Rumley getting you or somebody else to cover for him. He wants time, like two or three weeks would make a difference. Anyway, Death is still standing in the doorway. As for the guy's parents, Death didn't want them. Too old, he'll soon get them anyway. Death says, 'No deal.' Tell Rumley that. And tell it to whoever wants to cover off Rumley's debt. I want cash now, or Rumley gets hurt."

Peterson pursed his mouth and nodded. He tried again. "What was the bad investment?"

Jackie tented his fingers under his chin. "You don't want to hear the end of the poem?"

Peterson shrugged. Jackie smiled.

"Then the bride comes forward," Jackie said, "and offers herself to Death. She's beautiful and has the whole of her life in front of her. Yet she ransoms herself for her husband. And Death takes the deal."

"What are you asking, Jackie?"

"Who wants to cover off Rumley's debt?"

"You need to know?"

"Professional pride."

"What was the bad investment?"

Jackie leaned back in the chair, arms crossed behind his head. "He had a sure thing. That's what they all say. Rumley puts down a couple to get back four in thirty days. The guy hocked his business to raise the cash. Only the sure thing wasn't as sure as Rumley thought. Never is."

"What's the investment?"

"Two for four in thirty days, you tell me what turns money that fast."

Peterson made a face halfway between wonder and scepticism. "How does a small-time businessman start playing with black money?"

"Lawyers and accountants, Peterson, they make the world go round."

Peterson shrugged. "Then Rumley loses and comes to you to keep his business going."

"A business that's not doing too good. That's my mistake. So who wants to pull Vernon Rumley out of the pisser?"

"Same Grim Reaper who came for the bridegroom," Peterson said. "He paid Rumley a visit. No negotiation."

"The fuck you talking about?"

"Someone took Rumley for a hike," Peterson said, pressing his luck that the panic he'd seen on Marshall's face was confirmation that Rumley was dead. "Your name came up. Pound of flesh?"

Jackie held a poker face. He stroked his jaw as he thought about it. "There's no percentage in smoking a guy who owes me money."

"You just said he couldn't pay no matter how much time he had."

"You have nothing on me."

"I don't need anything. I just need to whisper something to the right pair of ears. A homicide investigation shuts you down, you lose ten times what you loaned Vernon Rumley."

"This sounds like you're making me an offer."

"You wipe Rumley's loan, nothing goes back on his wife."

Jackie thought about it for a New York second. He agreed.

Then Peterson leaned over the desk, going face to face. "Who did Rumley invest in?"

Jackie took his time, weighing his options. Then he said, "Everybody's playing gangsters, you know what I mean, underworld shit. Big fucking laugh, because the under-world doesn't go very deep. Names? I don't ask for too many names. What I don't know won't get me hurt. I know my place, Peterson. So if you want to shut me down on a trumped-up homicide investigation, you go ahead. I'd lose money, but that's all I'd lose."

CHAPTER
TWENTY-SEVEN

Reggie's Place. Elbow room now that the early bird crowd was fed and gone. Peterson headed for his usual corner table, with Angie the waitress not far behind, carrying his burnt toast and an empty mug in one hand. He sat and she pointed the coffee pot with the other.

"You expecting company?"

Peterson looked where she was pointing. Jonathan Hillier was standing in the doorway and looking around. Peterson caught his eye, and Hillier walked over. His drawn face offered what passed for a smile. He removed his tweed cap and stuffed it into a pocket. "Other than the stitches, you look much better than the last time I saw you," he said.

Peterson acknowledged the compliment.

Hillier pointed at the burnt toast. "But you're still eating like a drunk. Of course, I'm eating off the same menu." He extended his hand. "Always a pleasure, Peterson."

"You working?" Peterson said.

"Off the record now and again. Consulting work. Legal research for those without a conscience. Plugging holes in cross-examination rehearsals."

"You had a good go at me a few times in court."

"The last time, I shredded your testimony, if I remember right."

"Your client still went to jail."

"Back on the street, from what I hear," Hillier said. "We can't lock them up forever. And we don't hang criminals anymore."

"It wouldn't do much good if we did." Peterson lifted the mug but waited to drink. "Too many others with a sweet tooth and plenty of them with no conscience for the lives they ruin."

Hillier grimaced. "We both have daughters," he said. "We both know how they buy what they use. And we both know who's shitting in our streets. Let's not talk about what hurts." He sipped the coffee. "I wrote a stage play about a disbarred lawyer."

"You know the material," Peterson said through a mouthful of toast.

"I do, don't I? Only, my hero makes a comeback. That's not going to happen with me. I don't even know if I want it to. Besides, consulting on the side pays the bills, keeps me busy, and I'm not sitting in the pressure cooker." He tried his coffee. "You got something you want to talk about?"

"Lawyers working the shadows."

"Open the Yellow Pages," Hillier said, then waved his words away. "That sounds like sour grapes."

Peterson shrugged. "You helped a client influence a witness. You went down, and he didn't."

"Willie Blackwood doesn't do time. I knew that when I agreed to represent him." Hillier's voice snagged on something in his throat. He swallowed. "I stood up for the guy who'd been supplying my daughter with drugs, maybe not directly, but I knew he owned the supply line. I did nothing to stop him. I defended him, for Christ's sake, and I defended others just like him, maybe not as ruthless, but just like him. So what does that say about me?"

Peterson knew the regret and helplessness Hillier was feeling. He had felt it for years, a feeling that had driven him to the bottle. Nerves crackling, fists clenching and unclenching at thoughts he could never shake, mental images of young girls flagging down cars and choking on the buzz dealers sold them off the street. And when he felt it, he could barely hold down the urge to snap a round into a high-powered rifle and just shoot someone.

"Tell me about the lawyer you're looking for," Hillier said.

"Could be a lawyer, maybe an accountant. I heard someone was lining up investors to bankroll the drug business."

"You heard that from a good source?"

Peterson nodded. "A man with his fingers in a lot of pies."

Hillier gave it some thought. "Where's the percentage in dragging clean money through the mud?"

"Double the investment inside of a month."

"Tempting, but now you have dirty money you can't spend."

"Creative accounting," said Peterson.

"How much money we talking?"

"Hundreds of thousands, maybe a lot more."

"Way too much for the accountants I know who run a laundry service. They're into phone cards, phony invoicing, cash businesses that are money losers. The small businesses would tank without cash infusions from their neighbourhood dealers. But these are small-time dealers turning a couple of thou a week. For large amounts you need something big enough to handle it."

"How about six low-rent apartment buildings and a strip mall?" Peterson asked. "Top up the rents with drug money, declare it as rental income, and pay the tax?"

"Now you have large cash deposits that go on record, and personal cheques. It leaves too much of a paper trail. I'd look for something else. As for lawyers, sour grapes aside, there're plenty of them not afraid to earn what they know how to clean. You want me to ask around?"

Peterson nodded and ate the last bit of toast.

"It'll be risky for me," Hillier said.

"You justifying a big fee?"

"I am doing that. What's this all about?"

"A mother asked me to find her daughter. One thing led to another."

"It sounds more complicated than that."

"It is."

"Who's the girl?"

"Cassie Colpitts. She's hanging with a low-life named Logan Morehouse."

"Morehouse I know, the name anyway," Hillier said. "A bit player who alibied for Sammy O about a year ago. The kid only had a couple of minors so the Crown figured his testimony would stand and dropped the charge against Sammy. Only Sammy never came across with his side of the deal, and Morehouse was one pissed-off dude. How does your girl tangle up with him?"

"A user. Morehouse was the icing on the cake."

"Claim to fame?"

"She saw something she shouldn't have seen," Peterson said. "Maybe played a role."

"And you're the catcher in the rye."

Peterson folded his napkin and set it aside. He gave Hillier his hand.

CHAPTER
TWENTY-EIGHT

He was listening to a nurse review the surgical procedure. A metal rod would be inserted into Patty's leg and screwed to the bone. A few hours under the knife, he was thinking. An hour or more in recovery. Then rehab. "How long depends on her," the nurse said, shifting the burden of responsibility to the patient.

He held Patty's hand and waited. Knotted with worry, wanting forgiveness, and Patty offering it with her eyes, at least that's how he saw it, a submission on his part for failing to protect her.

Then her scheduled surgery was delayed an hour. A new technique, the nurse explained, as she gave Patty the OxyContin the anaesthesiologist had ordered. A pre-op painkiller that supposedly lessened the pain after surgery. Patty relaxed, her smile lopsided.

They avoided talking about his trying to end what they had just started. Passing time with chit-chat.

He held her hand as staff wheeled her bed to the elevator. He kissed her forehead and gave her a big smile, which he lost after the doors had closed.

● ● ●

Peterson sidestepped a few icy patches as he crossed the hospital parking lot to his car. Parked beside the Cherokee was a black SUV. Different make and model from the one Cory Ferris had been driving, but that didn't stop him from instinctively reaching to his jacket pocket. It was empty, and he regretted his last-minute decision not to carry the SIG Sauer for a hospital visit.

He had turned off his cell as well. Another last-minute decision when he had entered the hospital lobby. He wanted no phone calls to disturb the visit, as though he wished to seal off from Patty the man he was and, for a while, be the man he wanted to be.

Now he reached under the seat for the SIG Sauer and pulled the phone from his pocket and turned it on. Two calls, two messages. The first call had a Vancouver area code. His daughter's message was fifteen seconds of dead air. The second message was from Robbie Yorke. A message that was short and anything but sweet. "Get the fuck over here!"

CHAPTER
TWENTY-NINE

Peterson entered the dimly lit bungalow and Yorke was all over him. "What the hell you doing to me?"

Yorke sat bare-chested in his boxers at the kitchen table with four fingers of Dewar's in a water glass. The half empty bottle was on the table beside it. A small lamp spread yellow light over the table, accentuating the swollen knuckles on his old man's hands. Hard liquor fired up his face and puckered his baggy eyes. Peterson sat down opposite him and saw the waxy colour to Yorke's skin.

"I'm doing nothing," Peterson said. "What're you talking about?"

"We were friends for Christ's sake, and all of a sudden you send cops hammering my door. Asking questions."

"What questions?"

"Digging up the past about Carlisle Martin." Yorke's

hands trembled and he needed them both to raise the glass for a drink.

"Lewis and Bigger?" Peterson said. "I only told them what the snitch told me."

"And dragged me in."

Peterson bristled at the drunken accusation in Yorke's voice. "I told them if they needed background, you were the man to talk to, or Jimmy Stiles."

Yorke drained the glass and poured another, this one to the brim. He left the glass on the table and leaned forward to slurp a mouthful.

"So what did they ask?"

Yorke swallowed. "They asked if I knew what happened to Carlisle Martin. Only they asked it like I was downtown and they were expecting me to sweat. They said they had a good source."

"A source for what?"

"You know what I'm talking about."

"I don't know what you're talking about. Tell me."

Yorke waved Peterson off. "Who's the source?"

"I don't know what source they have."

"The source who said I picked up Martin at the airport."

"Meaning what?"

"Meaning he disappeared after that."

"So, what are the cops saying?" Peterson asked.

"You know what they're saying."

"I don't know what they're saying."

"They said they know where to dig." Yorke sipped the Dewar's. "They said Martin had three kids. Easy to find. DNA, the whole fucking shooting match. That's what they said. You know what I said? I said, you got something else to tell me, put it in a warrant. Just like that. Cocky, you know. But I'm shitting bricks, because they're saying I had something to do with Carlisle Martin."

"Like what?"

"Like him going AWOL for thirty years."

Yorke went at the Dewars, two hands. His face went maudlin. His voice slowed. "I had the job. Kitty had nothing. Cop's wife. No kids. Alone most of her life. You know how many times she threw that in my face? You know how many times she walked out?" He held up both hands and spread his fingers. "But you tell them nothing. You can't. The job. You love it and hate it, right? The fuckin' job."

Peterson nodded. "Did you pick him up at the airport?"

"What?" Yorke looked at the glass in his hands. "I was undercover, you understand? He was outside arrivals waiting on the curb. Habs sweater. Always wearing it when he came back from Montreal. Showboating because Tony Bones had given it him. Like it was a fucking badge. Tony fucking Bones. Nothing happened down here without Tony's say so."

"After the airport, then what?" Peterson asked.

Yorke continued to look at his hands.

"Do I have to hear it from Lewis and Bigger?" Peterson pressed.

"You've never been undercover. You got no idea when you're in deep." Yorke looked at Peterson. He sipped the drink. "I don't want it coming out. After I'm dead, I don't care. But it comes out now, you and a lot of other people get hurt."

Peterson wanted a shot of Dewars. He needed a shot just to go on listening. He reached for the bottle and tilted

208

it to his lips. One drink, he thought, one drink to dull the edge. But one drink meant two, and two would have him climbing all over himself and drawing blood. He set down the bottle. "Let me hear it from you, Robbie. Whatever it is, let it come from you."

"Then what? Cuff me?"

"I'm not a cop anymore, you know that."

Peterson got himself a glass from a cupboard and filled it with tap water. He moved his chair closer to Yorke and sat, playing it like two pals at the kitchen table shooting the shit. "It's just you and me," he said. "The way it used to be, you talking, me listening."

"That was talk you wanted to hear. Rookie cop, hero worship."

"Now I want to hear more. I want to hear what happened after you picked up Martin at the airport."

Yorke looked at him. "You want to hear it like it happened?"

"Just like it happened."

Yorke looked away to a corner of the kitchen where the light fell off. "I was driving. Zar Tombs was riding in back. Martin got in. Zar was talking, always talking, dopey sounding voice and talking about an M-14. Modified. Sniper's rifle. Some fucker's head big in the scope. Martin asked what's he talking about. Zar said his first kill. Vietnam. He went south and joined for the action, a Canadian fighting in another country's war. He was a crack shot, that's what he said, and he's in Nam sitting in a blind. Authorized kill. Zar's talking and Carlisle's eating it up, asking questions. Zar's telling him four, five hundred yards not a problem. Squeeze it off. Head explodes."

Yorke went silent. Peterson waited him out. Yorke took a sip and continued. "I'm undercover and I can't help thinking the guy was hot shit. It does that to you. What's up, what's down? You lose track. You start making friends with people that shouldn't be your friends."

"Like Zar Tombs?"

"Blackwood, Martin, everybody let him talk. Colourful. What he said, how he said it, hands going a mile a minute."

Yorke took a drink. His glassy eyes were fixed on the corner. Peterson wondered how many times Yorke had played back that night in his head. Peterson sipped water to fill the silence.

"Zar's still talking about Vietnam. How he takes a breath, lets it out. Empty lungs. I'm counting the hairs on his fucking head, Zar was saying. Big shot NVA, and Charlie has no idea it's coming. And that's how you want it to be. That's how my old man checked out, Zar said. A fucking aneurism straight to the brain. Bingo! He's on the floor and lights out. Then Zar leaned in front and said he had to piss. I hesitated. I'm scared. But what can I do. I'm undercover. I back out of it and it'd be me too. Zar yelled, pull in here. I caught his eyes in the rearview, and I swung the car onto a dirt road."

A dumb expression spread across Yorke's face, as though he suddenly realized Peterson was in the room and hearing him relive what he must have relived a hundred times. "What am I talking about?" Yorke asked. "Jesus Christ, what the fuck am I talking about?"

CHAPTER
THIRTY

Cotter knew better than to get too close when Peterson was in this mood. Janice also kept her distance. Others in The Office did the same. They let him stew on his own at a table in an alcove that was seldom occupied. He had grabbed himself a coffee from the urn beside the bar and now sat with his hands wrapped around the mug. His face was rigid, but his mind was rattled and his insides were mush.

There were red, blue, and yellow pot lights above his head, leftovers from when Cotter had booked a blues band on Saturday nights, a money-losing endeavour to hear Cotter tell it. Wrong crowd who came more for the music than the beer. Cotter had tried country after that. Wrong crowd again, heavy-duty drinkers who liked to fight. Damage costs offset bar receipts. He soon gave up on the entertainment and had settled on the tried and true: good pub food and neighbourhood drunks.

The pot lights draped Peterson in a fiendish glow that accentuated the creases in his face and intensified his bloodshot eyes. Eyes that were wide open and fixed on the front door. They narrowed when Lewis and Bigger entered, a quick response to the call he had made less than an hour ago.

The drug-squad cops helloed Cotter behind the bar and negotiated the chairs and tables to where Peterson sat. Lewis pulled up a chair to Peterson's left; Bigger rested his ass on the edge of a neighbouring table. Both had fawning smiles.

Peterson didn't move a muscle. "You badgered an old man."

"We followed up on the name you gave," Lewis said. He laid it on thick. "We asked questions the first time around, cop to cop, getting background on the past."

"Then you went back."

"Yeah," Bigger said, "after we had more to talk about."

"He said you went at him like you had him downtown in the box," Peterson said.

"The man's a suspect," Bigger said.

Peterson glared at him.

"C'mon," Lewis said, "none of us would be here if Yorke hadn't told you something that had curled your curlies. I have an idea he mentioned the skeleton in his closet."

"Or the one in the ground," Bigger added, and grinned.

"You don't have a body," Peterson said.

"Not yet," Lewis answered. "But we have a source with a campsite number. He said a few guys with shovels should find a body with bullet holes."

Lewis caught the surprise in Peterson's eyes. So did

Bigger. He came off the table he was resting his ass on and leaned over the one Peterson was sitting at. "My money's on a professional hit," he said. "Hollow points, two rounds to the head, different calibres. We dig up the body, odds are the flattened slugs are inside the skull."

"You're guessing, and you know it," Peterson said.

"No we're not," Lewis shot back. "You got a hot tip about a thirty-year-old body buried in Laurie Park. You guessed it was Carlisle Martin and parlayed that with us for the inside on the drug game, you thinking it would go nowhere fast. So we asked around. Something nobody's done in thirty years. One source comes out of the woodwork. An old-timer who worked maintenance in the park and slept in the equipment shed when his old lady threw him out. Gunshots woke him up. He saw two guys drag a body into the woods and bury it. He can't ID the two guys, but he said he could put an X on the grave."

"And he's suddenly talking?" Peterson pushed.

"Too scared to talk back then."

Lewis leaned into Peterson's face. "We also have a source who saw Yorke pick up Martin at the airport. We know Martin landed at the airport and was never seen again. I'm betting Yorke said something to you that put him at the murder scene."

Peterson didn't flinch. "Who's the source?"

"Nice try," Lewis said.

"All right, then why's your source talking now?"

"Because we asked around," Bigger said. "He ID'd Yorke as the man behind the wheel that picked up Carlisle Martin."

"He was undercover," Peterson said.

"I've been there," Lewis said. "You protect yourself and

213

your cover, but there's a line. You can walk it, balancing act. I've done that. But you don't ever step onto the other side."

"Sooner or later everybody steps onto the other side," Peterson said.

Lewis sat back and folded his hands at his chest. "We're not after him because you're an asshole. We gave him the benefit. The guy's written up as a hero. I respect that. Eddie does too. We didn't pressure Yorke until we asked around, a few old-timers, retired. Four out of four had the same story. Not a bad word among them. It was like the guy walked on water."

"You don't know him."

"Yeah sure, but how many cops you know wear halos? You said it yourself, sooner or later everybody crosses the line. For most of us, it's a toe, maybe an entire foot. You think they were better in the bad old days? I don't. I think it was the same then as it is now. So Yorke comes up smelling roses four out of four. But number five makes him stink. This cop was working at the airport that night, patrolling arrivals with a sniffer dog. He saw Carlisle Martin grab a bag off the carousel. He made sure the dog sniffed it. Then he watched Martin walk to the street. A car pulls up and Robbie Yorke's behind the wheel."

Peterson stared at Lewis, unsure what to say.

"You want more?" Lewis said. "I'll give you more. I read his file. Clean as a whistle. That's fine. I like to think mine is too. But one thing stood out — the shootout with the gun for hire, Zar Tombs. It went down six months after Yorke comes out from undercover. There's only one report in the file. Sure, there was an investigation, but investigating what? Yorke said Tombs came at him because of him having been undercover. Tombs shot at Yorke and Yorke shot Tombs. There was only one witness to the shootout that capped off Zar Tombs. Jimmy Stiles — the partner of the man who shot Tombs."

Lewis spread his hands on the table, palms up, conciliatory. "That means nothing on its own, but the source we have, the one at the airport, he said the night Yorke picked up Martin, the guy in the back seat was Zar Tombs."

"That still adds up to nothing," Peterson said.

Lewis and Bigger exchanged looks, then Lewis said, "No one wants to hear bad things about a good friend. So you should hear it straight from Yorke. We got it from a good source that Zar Tombs carried a .45 Magnum. Robbie Yorke carried a Smith & Wesson .38. Ask Yorke who has his .38 and Zar Tombs's .45. Ask him whose prints are on those guns. And ask him this: When we dig up the body in Laurie Park, what calibre slugs are we going to find inside the skull?"

● ● ●

Cotter made the rounds of shutting lights, locking cupboards, and bolting the front door. Then he made his way to where Peterson was still sitting under the coloured lights and pulled up a chair.

"You want to talk?" he asked.

Peterson looked up. "Have you ever wished your life would go away?"

Cotter nodded. "There are a lot of nights when I sit at the bar after closing and have a beer by myself. I think about it, my life I mean. No one to share it with. Friends, sure, but that's not the same. I wonder what I did, but that doesn't go too far, because I know what I did. So I stop wondering and have another beer. I'm sixty-seven, and it's all been one big stack of disappointments, most of them my own doing. So yeah, I wish my life would go away. But I fucked it up myself, no one to blame." He leaned forward. "Lewis and Bigger have something to say?"

Peterson looked past Cotter to the bar. "Usual stuff," he said.

Both men shrugged at the same time.

THIRTY-ONE

Peterson pulled open the door to a downtown Irish pub, a Joe Cool hangout for lawyers and businessmen aching to be seen. Most in suits, but some in V-necks and cardigans, open collars. It was lunch hour and busy, with waiters and waitresses shuffling orders of fish and chips and steak and kidney pies, along with sixteen-ounce drafts of dark and light.

Peterson spotted him sitting alone at a table near the crescent-shaped oak bar, sipping froth off a Guinness. Sitting there, in a dark blue three-piece, out in front, disbarred and seemingly unashamed, head up and grinning, Peterson knew Hillier wasn't just making a statement about who the hell he once was. He was rubbing their noses in it.

He nabbed a waiter and ordered a coffee.

"You eating or drinking?" Peterson asked as he lowered himself across from the disbarred lawyer.

"A bit of both," Hillier said.

"Big day?"

"I'm in demand."

They small talked about the snow that had fallen overnight and jammed the commuter lanes with half-assed drivers in vehicles still without snow tires three months into winter. The waiter delivered Peterson's coffee, and as soon as his back was turned their heads went together.

"I have three lawyers that fit the bill," Hillier said. "They operate on their own small offices. All play with dirty money, but one of them plays with a lot of it."

"How'd you get this?"

"You don't want to ask me that. What you want to ask me about is her client list."

"Her?"

"Yeah," Hillier said. "How come we always think it's only men doing these things? Her name is Angelina Samson."

"Don't know her."

"You wouldn't. She keeps her head down, especially after her name came up during that Asian immigrant investment scandal back in '03. No shit stuck to her shoes. A research lawyer, who will remain nameless, passed me her name. Samson represents two holding companies with William Blackwood's name buried in the paperwork."

Peterson grinned. Hillier grinned right back.

"I slum it with the low-life," Hillier said, "while Angelina flies in sushi from Tokyo and calls it take-out."

Peterson raised his coffee by way of a toast. Hillier did likewise with the Guinness.

"I sent you an email with her client list," Hillier said.

"You'll recognize a few. Three or four used to be my clients. Only I got them when they were wearing prison issue. Now they're sporting pinstripes in her office, lining up investors who can shelve their conscience for a month or two."

"You're loving this," Peterson said, sitting back.

Hillier's eyes brightened. "Every fucking moment. You'll need solid evidence to get the legal eagles in the Barristers' Society to investigate. Samson skated on that immigration scam because of friends in high places. Took a little heat. Maybe took it for someone else, a big shot who doesn't like publicity. Favours owed, who knows? That was my big mistake. I piggybacked the losers and gutter snipe. If you want to chat her up, she does a working dinner most days at a chi-chi place around the corner from her office. And if you're talking to her, ask her about ATMs." Seeing Peterson's puzzled look, he added, "It's in the email."

Hillier drained the Guinness and pushed the glass aside.

"You want another?" Peterson asked.

"Client meeting in ten," Hillier said. "I dug some dirt on the Colpitts girl, if you're interested."

Peterson leaned in again.

"Before Morehouse, she bunked with Blackwood and served a one-year probation for carrying his gun. You probably knew that already."

Peterson nodded, and Hillier continued. "But here's what you may not know. Blackwood got her pregnant and she had the baby while she was on probation. You know the rules: no association with known criminals. She chanced it and took the kid to Blackwood. My guy said he beat the shit out of her and tossed her and the kid."

"I knew she had a baby," Peterson said. "She went to her mother but that didn't work out. Gave the baby up. After that she winds up with Morehouse."

"No bargain there. Small-timer living off the kibbles and bits that fall his way, until one day the light goes on. My source thinks the girl brought him something about Blackwood or said something that got Morehouse thinking." Hillier dug a breath mint from his breast pocket and popped it. "I'm giving odds she knew more about Blackwood's operation than was healthy. I'm guessing the whereabouts of the stash house."

"Like an apartment building on Sammy O's turf," Peterson said.

Hillier flashed a big grin. "Owned by a holding company and probably controlled by at least one of the names on her client list. So, what do you think? We sell movie rights, or what?"

Peterson waved him off and said, "What do I owe?"

Hillier shook his head. "It cost me nothing to get, and I'm happy my connections are still paying off. Besides, right now I'm doing an Angelina Samson. I'm collecting favours."

"What are you looking for?"

"I'll know after this client meeting." Hillier smiled. "Remember Brando in *The Godfather*?" Then he frowned and gravelled his voice. "One day, Peterson, and that day may never come . . ."

• • •

Peterson checked the client list on his iPhone as he walked along the busy, slushy sidewalk of a main drag downtown, dodging a stream of pedestrians on their way back to work. Piling up at a crosswalk. Some dressed up to flaunt who they were, others dressed down with what they had. Leathers and down-filled coats. High boots and low cuts. All standing on the corner, rosy-faced from the bitter wind off the harbour, hard-eyed like the surrounding empty office buildings and boarded storefronts, destined for downtown development.

Two names jumped off the list, and he suddenly stopped, jamming the sidewalk flow. He backed up to a store window and thought it through. Not so much the details, but the broad strokes. Angelina Samson lining up investors for under-the-table drug deals. That was easy money. Hand over fist. Lay down two and get back four. A sure thing that wasn't so sure, according to Jackie Bates. But who would've expected it to go south? Like what are the chances a ship-ment gets nailed and the Mounties score a drug bust? The odds go twenty-to-one in your favour. That's what Rumley must've thought, and Dr. Jeffrey Marshall and the other den-tist on Angelina Samson's client list. A trio of conscienceless bastards looking to score big without any thought about the lives they'd be ravaging.

He turned to the store's display of Celtic crosses and small stone altars, of Reiki healers, ankh-decorated mojo bags, and chakra sticks. He wondered at the assortment of snake oil cures and faith healing books for the modern era. Wondered at the misappropriated spirituality that had replaced the brimstone and *hoc est corpus* of the old faith. Wondered if it was all just comfort food for the mind, an old stew stirred up by ordained priests and New Age gurus who promised salvation through amulets, meditations, and magic potions. Jackie Bates was right. Their backs against the wall, too many will believe anything and do anything to save themselves, for now, for eternity.

And that had him thinking about Rumley coming up snake eyes on his first throw of the investment dice. Losing it all and hocking himself to a future that just wasn't there. Now he was missing, probably dead, snatched off Canal Street by Logan Morehouse and company. And that had Peterson thinking about Cassie Colpitts, up to her ears in punks — Morehouse and the two heavy hitters, Pike and the Brick. With what Hillier had given him, and from what Lewis and Bigger had said, Peterson thought he had part of the story. Cassie names the place, and the three roll on it, taking money and some drugs, and shooting at Sammy O in the process. But why did they snatch Rumley? How does his losing on a bad investment connect him to them?

A teenage girl came up and leaned against the same window. She was wearing a long black coat cinched at the waist by a chain, black toque pulled over her ears. It was the girl from the basement on Canal Street, the one who'd overheard Rumley's abduction. They looked at each other. She still had the frown, but her eyes were brighter. He let himself think she was pleased to see him.

"You following me?" he asked.

"I saw you standing here."

"And stopped by to say hello."

She shrugged.

"Did you eat the two twenties?" he asked.

She offered a straight-lipped smile, as much as she was prepared to give. "Yeah," she said. "Soup and sandwich. Side salad."

He chuckled. "Sir Galahad still keeping you warm?"

She stared out at the passing traffic. "He doesn't get messed up as much as a lot of the others. He's pretty good."

Peterson took a moment and said, "Sometimes you lose out if you ask for more."

"Yeah, I know, but sometimes he pisses me off, like, now he wants to move."

"And you don't."

"Like, it's a good crash," she said. "Better when it gets warm, but right now, like, it's pretty nice. Not too cold. Jet just thinks . . ."

"Jet?"

"That's what we call him."

"What do they call you?"

"Worm."

"Worm?"

"I wanted to be a biologist."

"You like cutting them up?"

She made a face.

"Still want to be one?"

She held up her hands, surrendering.

"Why does Jet want to move?"

"Too much action outside the house. Like, he scares easy, you know. I said, four months and we only had, like, two things happen, but he doesn't care. He wants to move to this side. He thinks it's safer."

"It's the same no matter where you go," Peterson said. "And I'm an ex-cop telling you that. So what are you going to do?"

She shrugged, then flashed him a limelight smile. "He is pretty good."

"That's important." He fished for his wallet. "So is eating."

She shook off the contribution and jammed her gloved hands into her coat pockets. "Around," she said and shoved off.

"Around," he said, and watched her until she turned the corner. He went back to reading Hillier's email, about the ATMs. Confused at first. Then surprised at how simple it was.

• • •

Cotter rinsed a glass he'd just washed and set it on a white towel to dry.

It was mid-afternoon and The Office was nearly empty. Peterson sat at the bar. Two regulars played the VLTs at the back, and old man McGovern nursed a beer at a centre table, long face, probably disappointed Janice was working the evening shift.

"You got nothing that'll stick," Cotter said. "You need a paper trail, which you don't have. I doubt the lawyer has left one, not if she's working the deal with Willie Blackwood. The dentists are your best bet."

He reached for another glass to wash. "Did you ask around about this lawyer?"

"She took heat in the immigration scam," Peterson said. "Hillier thinks she covered for another lawyer, big shot in a big firm."

"Figures. One weasel watching another watch the chicken coop. Whatever you got on this lawyer, it'll go nowhere fast. It's like they all bathe in the same tub, wash each other's backs. The same goes for Blackwood. I don't know how many times I stamped warrants for him that ended up on the floor. Friends in high places." Cotter held up the glass to a light, made a face, and washed it again. "So, what are you going to do?"

"Pull a tooth," Peterson said.

"You were always good at that. What about the girl?"

"Still looking."

"Worried?"

"She's with two goons and a creep, doing what the creep says. She wants out."

"Sure of that?"

"He beats her up. And the way she reached for me at the crack house, yeah, I'm sure."

"If you need anything, I know how to get it," Cotter offered.

"Those are things we shouldn't talk about."

"There're a lot of things we shouldn't talk about. But, one thing I want to know. How come Harold Bly owes you? I mean the Mink doesn't give freebees."

"Everyone has something in the closet," Peterson said.

"Don't I know it. Anyway, Janice wants to kiss you. Her nephew may not walk, but the Mink said the kid won't do time. Community service. A stay-in-school order."

Peterson's phone rang. It was Danny.

"Turtle came across something you might be interested in," Danny said. "He won't tell me, only you."

"Where?" Peterson said.

"You won't like this."

CHAPTER
THIRTY-TWO

Peterson knew the place pretty well. He went there often, whenever his mind was a mess or when his feelings ran thick and he needed to weep. He arrived early and drove through the black iron gates and along snowplowed lanes among the headstones. He parked the Cherokee beside his wife's grave. Blown snow covered some of the inscription. He stared out the side window, stared at the headstone, his mind snagged on a memory.

In the rearview, he glimpsed a young couple shortcutting through the cemetery from the high school nearby. When they exited his frame of view, he turned to see them out the side window, but a tall granite headstone, more a monument than a grave marker, blocked his view. He turned back to his wife's grave. He may have been staring at her marker, but he was really looking at himself. He muffled his voice in his sleeve, thinking a thought that was an open wound, thinking that he was spending more time with her headstone than he had ever spent with her.

He looked in the rearview and saw Turtle clearing snow off a wooden bench. He climbed from the car and they sat together.

"What goes round, comes round," Turtle said, rotating a gloved hand around his head.

"If you say so."

"One big circle," Turtle said. "Maybe not a circle, because a circle you'd know you were going round and round, but most of the time we got no idea. So maybe it's like a road, a highway we get on and get off and get back on. Like them cloverleafs on those big highways, New York, L.A. You seen them, right? Making figure eights. Only here the off and on are the same thing. And you're just going round and round, but you can't see you're doing that. You think you're going someplace."

Peterson looked at him, dressed in blue coveralls with a heavy brown sweater peeking from the collar. Shoulders rolled forward. Dark stubble. Sleepy eyes. "Where do you think you're going, Turtle?" he asked.

"Going nowhere, foot on the gas and no goddamn brakes."

"Same ride as the rest of us," Peterson said, not trying to figure this guy out, waving his hand to shoo away what Turtle had been saying. "Danny said you have something to tell me."

"Yeah, I have something. Danny put the screws on about my old lady, so I got something to give, but not to him. He says things, always saying things, and I can't walk away 'cause I put my own balls in a vice. Not much I can do about it. Not now. I got nowhere to go because there's nowhere I can go. There's a big fucking rock holding me down. Same kind of rock you carry around. You're in here how many times? I see you."

"How's that?"

"I got a kid buried on the other side." Turtle turned and pointed across the cemetery. "Seven years old. Bone cancer."

He faced Peterson.

"My wife couldn't take it," he said. "Three kids and one she can't do nothing for. I wasn't much help. I mean, who wasn't telling me to jump? And if I don't jump, my take home is zero. So I'm no help, and she has to do it all on her own. She got worn down, that's what happened. You bury a son and it takes a toll."

He closed his eyes. When he opened them he said, "She didn't abandon the other kids, Peterson. She just needed to get away."

Turtle leaned on his knees and dangled his hands between his legs.

"I don't pray when I come here," he said. "I come every day, sometimes at night if I can't get free. There's a space in the fence over there." He pointed. "I sit on someone's headstone and look at my son's grave. I have lots to say, but I don't say it."

Peterson nodded as though he understood the sentiment. They sat for a while. Turtle fussed his gloved hands in his lap. Peterson stared across the cemetery to the street, and watched a silver F Sport Lexus squeezing into a metered parking space. The driver and passenger did not get out.

Without taking his eyes off the Lexus, Peterson asked, "What you got, Turtle?"

Turtle looked up from his hands. "That day I heard what Blackwood said, when I was fixing his snowmobile, I saw the guy in the truck."

"You said you didn't."

"I did but I didn't. I mean it didn't click, not until I saw him again. I'm in Gainers. I go there, have one beer after I come here. Sit at the back. Like, who sees me anyhow? Two guys were talking. One I recognize as the guy in the truck. Cowley Pike. The other's the fag he hangs with, what's his name, Tommy something."

"The Brick," Peterson said, his eyes still on the SUV.

"Yeah, him. They're talking and I'm listening. Pike, he's two sheets, and the other guy, the fag, he's got eyes, you know." Turtle cocked a finger to the side of his nose in a coke-snorting gesture. "They're bitching about a girl and some guy called Morehouse."

Peterson looked at him. "Saying what?"

"About the two of them being a pain in the ass. Never saying whose stash they were hitting and having to give back the money to Blackwood. Splitting the blow, yeah, but the two of them getting more, like, because they had the plan. The fag said that, and Pike, he started pounding the table because they had it all, blow, cash, and then that Morehouse and the girl fucking up, and Blackwood finding out who's who and what's what. And now they're living in some dump and getting nothing but promises for blowing off that guy I told you about, the one Blackwood said they should bury where he can't be found."

"They talked about wasting someone?"

"They weren't hiding it. A half hour and them going on, and me, like I'm not there. I can't hear it all but I got a lot of it. Like Blackwood having them on a string, payback for them moving on his stash. Playing them to kill someone."

"They say a name, the guy they capped?"

Turtle shrugged and shook his head.

"Was it Rumley?"

"They never said. But they bitched about Morehouse doing nothing, like he can't help lift the dead guy from the car, and all he could carry was a shovel. And the fag saying he never thought a thin bastard could be so heavy. How they'd take out Morehouse if they got a chance. The girl too, from what I heard, so fucked up or scared she couldn't hold the light straight."

"Where'd they bury it?"

"They didn't. They tried but hit a stone floor. The place dark as hell, with the flashlight swinging all over. Pike said it was like being up someone's ass. They were laughing about it, you know, leaving it in there, back against the stone wall, sitting, big fucking grave was what Pike said. What'd they call them tombs, mauser or something?"

"Mausoleum," Peterson said.

"Yeah, that's it."

"Where?"

"They didn't draw a map, for Christ's sake."

Peterson looked back at the Lexus. "And you didn't tell Danny this?"

"Because Danny's on my case, ragging my ass one hundred percent. And you said you still work together, so I figured I'd tell you. It gets to Danny one way or another."

"Then you played me the sob story so I'd get him to go light on you and your wife."

"No story, Peterson. You want to see my son's grave? Is that what you want?"

"I want to know where they left this guy."

"I told you."

"No, you didn't. You're holding back. I get off this bench, and all Danny hears from me is that you held back."

Turtle straightened and made faces as he thought it out. Then he slumped back over his knees and spoke to the ground.

"Maybe they knew I was listening," he said. "I say too much, and it's my ass."

"Just tell me."

"A fort."

"What fort?"

"An old fort. I don't know the name. Out by the mouth of the harbour."

"Where in the fort?"

"A stone building, that's all I know."

Peterson got up and watched the Lexus pull out of the parking space and drive off.

"You going to tell Danny?" Turtle asked.

Peterson looked down at him. "What do you want me to tell him?"

"I want you to go to bat for me, a good word."

"Because you have a son buried in the same cemetery as my wife."

Turtle struggled to say something, faltered, then got it out. "You're asking around about Pike and his fag friend, and about that Morehouse, and showing a picture of a girl the way you did with your daughter. I thought maybe . . ."

"You thought what?"

"It don't matter what I thought."

Peterson said nothing. Sitting there in the cold, with city sounds punching against the quiet that surrounded them.

Turtle balled himself over his knees. He made a low mewling sound. He straightened. "I thought you'd understand. I thought you'd go easy on me."

Peterson saw that the Lexus had circled the cemetery and was now passing by the front gate. It kept going. He turned back to Turtle, who was scrunched into his shoulders. He sat down and thought about Turtle's circular cloverleaf going nowhere, thinking that sooner or later we all just run out of gas. Maybe even welcome it.

"If things work out," Peterson said.

Turtle lifted his head.

"If I find what I'm looking for, I'll pressure Danny for a good word."

• • •

He parked the Cherokee at a meter overlooking the Commons and watched the entrance to the underground parking at the condo complex where Jeff Marshall lived. He had already put together a list of phone numbers from the lobby register. He knew a lot of people used the last four digits of their phone numbers as pass codes to the entrances of their condo or apartment building. For the benefit of the security camera, Peterson had carried two bags of groceries into the lobby and fumbled with these as he ran through the list of phone numbers, punching them into the keypad near the door. The fourth had been a winner, Myrna Cody. He'd entered the lobby, canned the groceries behind an ornamental lemon tree, and waited about five minutes before returning to his car.

By 7:20 p.m., he had gone through a Thermos of coffee and relieved himself twice in an extra cup. His caffeine-soaked nerves were in overdrive, his brain randomly clicking through what Turtle said Pike and the Brick would do to Cassie if they got the chance, thoughts that shrank his stomach, made it hungry for something he refused to eat.

He reached for the crossword puzzle on the shotgun seat to think about something else. He spent ten minutes playing cat and mouse with a clue he couldn't figure: Don't look back. _ _ p h _ _ s. Then he tossed the crossword into the back seat and looked out over the Commons, watching the skaters on the speed-skate oval, daydreaming of being alone on a frozen river, skating nowhere as fast he could pump his legs, his old man watching him from the river-bank. A silhouette against a darkened sky.

A half hour later, Marshall pulled up in the BMW Cabriolet. The garage door opened and Marshall drove inside.

Peterson gave him time to park and ride up to the tenth floor. Then he made for the lobby, punched in the four-digit code from Myrna Cody's telephone number, and entered.

The elevator doors opened to a large brass-framed mirror in a brown-carpeted hallway. His cop knock had Marshall opening the door in a hurry. He wore a blue blazer, tan slacks, and a light blue shirt with the collar open. His face was heavy with worry, and his automatic smile showed his television teeth. Then he recognized the solid-looking man filling the doorway.

Peterson stepped forward. "Remember me?"

Marshall tried to close the door and found that Peterson's angled body prevented him from doing so.

"Rumley's dead, and his wife is pointing at you," Peterson said.

Marshall buckled.

"You want to talk out here or inside? Your call."

Marshall started to say something but couldn't get the words out. Peterson helped Marshall make up his mind by backing him into the condo and closing the door.

Marshall found his voice. "I'll call the police."

"You do that," Peterson said. "Ask for Detective Little or Detective Bernard. They have the Rumley file. They'll be interested in what you have to say."

That scared Marshall. "I have nothing to say."

"We can talk about that."

He led Marshall, now on wobbly legs and heavy feet, through the huge open-concept living space. Pop art and mind-fucker paintings hung on the walls. The furniture was mostly dull coloured and straight edged, the kind that wrote off comfort as a design flaw. Two huge windows looked out to the Commons. He sat Marshall in a armless grey stuffed chair. He remained standing.

"I know about Angelina Samson," Peterson said.

Marshall's face looked like it could cry on sunny days.

"And I know about her funnelling drug money."

Marshall shook his head. "I don't know what you're talking—"

"Yes, you do. You're on her mailing list, along with

234

Vernon Rumley, another dentist named Connors, and Willie Blackwood. A couple of layers of holding companies, but you're there. I looked at your apartment buildings, talked to your tenants. Slum housing at best. Their low rent covers off the mortgage and maintenance, what little of it you've done. Where you make your money, or better yet, where you clean it, is in the third-party ATMs in the apartment buildings and in the strip malls. One or more of your holding companies own them. You refill the ATMs with drug money, and we're talking large amounts. There's no government regulation on where the refill money comes from. Then you transfer money, always under ten thousand, into who knows how many bank accounts held by who knows how many shell companies. One company sends dummy invoices to another, more electronic transfers, until even the cyber trail is nothing but vapour. Then, lo and behold, the money returns to still other holding companies owned by you and Willie Blackwood, all clean as a whistle, and taxable. How am I doing?"

Peterson saw the signs often shown by a suspect undergoing a round of questioning in the box. The brain running a two-minute mile and the eye blinks trying to keep up. Uncomfortable sitting still. Fingers lacing and unlacing. Dry lips. Clammy skin.

"You want a drink?" Peterson asked.

Marshall nodded. "Water."

"Give me your phone."

Marshall pulled his phone from his jacket pocket and handed it to Peterson, who carried it with him to the kitchen. He took a glass from the draining board and filled it from the tap. He returned, set Marshall's phone on a side table, and passed him the glass of water.

Marshall took a big sip. Peterson leaned against the window and folded his arms. He watched Marshall's discomfort, the way the dentist rolled the glass between his hands and stared straight ahead.

"You're no better than Blackwood and his kind," Peterson said. "If I had my way, I'd break your hands so bad you'd never pull another tooth the rest of your life."

Marshall's eyes could not have opened any wider. "Why are you doing this?"

"Because you have a dental degree and no morals. Just tell me about Vernon Rumley."

Marshall stiffened. "There's nothing to say."

"There's a lot to say. You're just afraid to say it. Afraid you'll get what Rumley got." He sat in the boxy grey chair across from Marshall. "The Mounties made a drug bust, and Rumley lost more than just his shirt. He couldn't double up on the next go-round because he's in hock to the bank and to the juicer above the pizza joint. His business is on the skids and, unlike you, Rumley couldn't cover a loss by upselling a dozen or so smiles."

"I don't need to hear any more of this." Marshall started to get up, but Peterson beat him to it and sat him back down.

"It's not just young professionals snorting so they can work more hours or party all night," he said. "It's teenage girls gassed and fucking whoever to stay high. Living in shitholes, with kids of their own they don't want and can't keep. You know how young."

Marshall wouldn't look at him.

"Thirteen, fourteen," Peterson said. "By sixteen they got arms like dartboards." He turned and gestured to the condo. "And look at you — hot-shot dentist, and all you're doing is strangling hope."

"What do you want?" Marshall said.

"What I want has nothing to do with it," Peterson said. "This is about you and what you know."

He pulled out his phone and showed Marshall the photo of Cassie Colpitts. "You know this girl, seen her around?"

Marshall said no, but his face said yes.

"I'll ask one more time, then I go to work on your hands."

Marshall started to shake. "Christ! Don't! Please don't!"

Peterson leaned forward, showed him the photo again.

Marshall looked at it and nodded. "She came to me."

"Here?"

"The dental office. She told me to arrange a meeting with Rumley. He wanted his money back, threatened if he didn't get it, said he'd talk to the cops. She told me to say I'd pay what he lost."

"Why Canal Street?"

"He knew I was buying the abandoned building there. He had wanted in on the development."

"He was broke," Peterson said.

"He had been counting on us making a bundle on the deal."

"The drug deal."

Marshall nodded and craned to look out the window at the cold grey sky.

"Sweet deal goes sour," Peterson said, "and you kissed him goodbye when Blackwood decided to have him killed."

Marshall looked at him. "I didn't have a choice."

Peterson stood. "You do now. Tomorrow the Mounties will pay your office a visit. They'll have a warrant to audit your books, search your office. Following breadcrumbs, they like to say. It may not be a paper trail, but it will take them where you don't want them to go. They'll find it. They may not nail you for under-the-table investments in illegal drugs, but they'll nab you on tax evasion. You'll get short time and a heavy fine for that. But it's the money laundering that'll go down hard. That scores high on the chart. If I can prove it after three questions to your tenants and a good look at the ATMs in low-rent buildings and strip malls, the Red Serge will come away with double the evidence. And here's the kicker: they're going to wonder whose money you've been washing. And they'll work hard to connect the dots. You'll go under the microscope. The box, where they interview you, it'll break you in half." He wrote a couple of phone numbers on a pad on one of the side tables. "You want my advice? Call the Mounties before they call you. Make a trade. Offer what you know about Angelina Samson and the next shipment of drugs for a shorter sentence."

Marshall's hands shook uncontrollably.

"You put yourself on the hook," Peterson said. "I could help if I wanted to, but I don't."

THIRTY-THREE

Peterson entered the restaurant and spotted Angelina Samson sitting with two male associates at a corner table with a harbour view. White tablecloth. Lots of glasses and too many forks.

One of the men had a beard and squinty eyes. The other had a rubber face that moved with every word being said. The woman herself had a forty-year-old face locked against wishful thinking and a body tightened by daily workouts. The severity of her manner was lightened by her girlish way of combing her hand through her shoulder-length brown hair and flipping it.

They had finished dinner and were now talking shop over the last of the wine.

Peterson grabbed the empty seat across from Samson. All three were startled by his intrusion.

"This is hardly appropriate," rubber face said.

Peterson stared him down then shifted his eyes to Samson. "My name's Peterson. I'm an ex-cop."

"How does that interest us?" Samson's tone was dismissive despite her smile.

"I need something cleared up, a case I'm working on."

"You said ex-cop," the beard said, popping the P.

Peterson ignored him. "Give me two minutes of your time. That's all I want." He thumbed toward her associates. "They can stay."

"But I'm not a criminal lawyer," she said.

"Not on paper."

"What does that mean?"

"It means a criminal is a criminal is a criminal."

Samson lost her smile. "I think Josh was right. I think your presence at this table is most inappropriate."

"Does that mean you want me to leave?"

"It does."

"You don't want to help me clear something up?"

"I do not."

"And why's that?" He turned to each of the men in turn. "I had a money question, that's all. What do I know about how big money changes hands?" He fixed his eyes on Samson. "Not like bank transactions. It's more like under-the-table financing."

"If he's not going to leave," she said to the two men, "perhaps we should."

Peterson dangled a carrot. "It's something I'm still in the dark about. A thirty-day investment for a two hundred per-cent return."

Rubber face oohed. "Sweet deal."

240

Peterson kept his eyes on Samson, who ran her hand through her hair and fiddled with a strand. "That's what Vernon Rumley thought," he said.

The eye stutter was what he was after, an ever-so-slight refocusing. A reflex that was hard to control without practice. It was almost imperceptible unless you were looking for it.

"He's on your client list, along with Doc Marshall. You want me to name a few more?"

Samson glared at him with primeval bitterness. "I think it's time you left, or I will call for a real policeman."

"They'll be coming anyway," he said. "Not today, not this moment, but they'll catch up, and you won't like what they have to say."

CHAPTER
THIRTY-FOUR

Later that night, Peterson drove a short section of the 102, going up the on-ramp then down the off, then crossing under the road and going up the on in the opposite direction. He wasn't doing it to ride Turtle's infinite figure eight. He was trying to shake the silver Lexus that had been following him all day. He swung into the parking lot of a Holiday Inn Express, pointed the nose of the Cherokee in the direction he had come, and watched the exit ramp for the Siamese cat eye–shaped headlights. No headlights, no Lexus.

When he was certain he didn't have a tail, he drove to the south end of town and into the hospital parking lot. He counted five floors up and sat looking at Patty's lit window. He knew the glove box was empty but wished it wasn't; it would be easier on his conscience to sneak a sip in the car than to shame himself by stopping at a bar where no one cared if he drank himself blind.

He lowered all the windows to feel the night cold. It was a penance or a scourge of some kind, a way of feeling something to keep from feeling other things. The way he once, as a kid, had pressed his hand down on the spike of a memo holder, feeling it pierce his skin, drawing blood, until he could no longer stand the pain.

He raised the windows and started the Cherokee. He thought about what Cotter had said about some nights being harder than others and that the hours after midnight were the worst. He shifted into gear and thought about the couple of hours he still had to get through.

• • •

Danny was waiting for him in the parking lot, his Malibu parked among the night-shift cars near the back entrance. They walked into the station and past the coffee room, where half a dozen cops were replaying the Habs and Bruins game that had ended in a shootout. Not a word was said as they continued along the deserted hallway and into the Investigation Unit to the back-to-back desks where they had sat and worked together for years.

Danny nodded to three detectives huddled near a cork-board hung with half a dozen photos of people of interest for a stick-up at a downtown TD Bank. Then he sat at his desk and finally spoke. "Did he have much to say?"

"Enough," Peterson said, lowering himself onto Bernie's chair, noticing the tidy desk top, which had always been a cluttered mess when it had been his.

"Did you hurt him?" Danny asked.

Peterson shook his head.

"But you threatened him."

"No more than usual."

"That could be a gun to the head with you."

"Don't get carried away."

There was still tension between them. Danny had eyes on the brass ring, and Peterson's life was long off the rails.

"You left him how?" Danny asked.

"Sitting in a chair, thinking about three to five behind bars."

"You threatened him with that?"

"Not in so many words."

Danny slid over a pad of yellow notepaper to write on. "Tell me how it went down."

"I was never working up a file, Dan." Peterson opened the pencil drawer on Bernie's side, took out a ballpoint and clicked it a couple of times.

Peterson looked around the Investigation Unit, at the room crowded with back-to-backs, like the ones they were sitting at, and at the deputy chief's glassed-in office. "Yeah, I miss it," he said. "But I know my situation. I'm not working up a file to get back in. I was keeping a promise I made to a woman I once took advantage of. Making amends? Call it whatever the hell you want."

He put back the pen and folded his hands on the desk.

"It starts with Pike and the Brick tightening the shank on hand-to-hand deals," he said. "They would interrupt a transaction just before it was about to go down, and they'd walk with cash and drugs. There wasn't a lot of business, but they weren't complaining. A few bucks in their pockets

244

and enough blow to stay high. Then Morehouse shows up with a better idea. He enlists Pike and Tommy as muscle for scoring off one of Willie Blackwood's stash houses."

"C'mon," Danny said, "the drug squad doesn't even know where they are."

"Cassie Colpitts did. A source—"

"What source?"

Peterson let the question hang between them a few beats, then said in a nonchalant voice, "Right now, I'm keeping the public out."

Danny stood up, leaned over the desk, heat in his low voice. "Police business and you know it."

Peterson didn't budge. "Joint task-force, right?" There was nothing smug about his tone, just straight-up daredevil. "They still plumbing empty pipes? How many, ten, fifteen to a team?"

Danny ignored the question.

"You want the rest or not?"

Danny hesitated, then he settled back into his chair.

"Blackwood got Cassie Colpitts pregnant and showed her the door," Peterson said. "She gives up the baby, gets lost on the street, and winds up with Morehouse. He uses and abuses her. She walks out, but he won't let her go. He beats her black and blue, until she offers something to make him stop. One of Blackwood's stash houses. She knew the way, Dorothy down the yellow brick road. Oz was an apartment building on Sammy O's turf. The Tin Man, Lion, and Scarecrow break the door. A gun goes off and blows out a window in Sammy's car. Accidentally on purpose, maybe, to get even for something that went down a few years ago when Morehouse went to bat for Sammy on a possession charge, maybe getting

245

forced into it, maybe never getting paid. Maybe that's why he bit so hard on Cassie's story. All that, I'm not sure about. Somehow Blackwood finds out who did the deed."

"He would've put them in a hole," Danny said.

"But he didn't," Peterson said. "He needed a job done, a job he didn't want any of his crew to get their hands dirty with. He wanted nothing blowing back on him. He needed someone to put someone else in a hole."

"Rumley," Danny said.

Peterson nodded. "Rumley. He and Jeffrey Marshall, and one other dentist I know about were fronting Blackwood's import business. It all ran through a lawyer named Angelina Samson. It was their money invested in the shipment the Mounties busted. The others took their losses, the cost of doing business. Rumley couldn't afford to. He threatened to squeal."

"And Morehouse, Pike, and the Brick paid their debt to Blackwood by capping Rumley," Danny said.

Peterson smiled.

"You can prove all this?"

Peterson shook his head. "That's your job. Mine is to find Cassie Colpitts and get her out."

Danny scowled.

"Go and talk to Marshall," Peterson said. "He lives in the Renaissance Condos. Turn one screw and he's a chatter box."

"Yeah, but Pike and the Brick won't be easy to break," Danny said.

Peterson agreed. "They've been inside too many times. My money's on Morehouse coughing up what you want to know."

Danny squirmed, uncomfortable with asking. "You got a whereabouts on these characters?"

Peterson stood to go. Sly smile. "Not yet.

Danny returned the look. "You find out, you let me know before doing something crazy."

"I'll think about it," Peterson said. "Now I've got to see a man about thirty years of bad news."

CHAPTER
THIRTY-FIVE

The rooming house near the flour mill was everything Peterson remembered. Six boarders, all men, all alone, all unwashed, drunk, and pissing wherever and whenever. The heat cranked high had him mouth-breathing. He called for Jimmy Stiles and received no response. Then he banged open doors and saw what men become when there's nothing and no one in their lives.

Who knew what, and who remembered anything more than the last moment, or maybe the one before that? But they knew their names well enough to sign for the welfare and pension cheques that paid top dollar to a slumlord for a twelve-by-twelve room, caked in filth, and this side of a hole in the wall.

Jimmy Stiles, all 120 pounds of his shit-faced self, once a

bruiser at 210, sat out back in the cold on a broken wooden chair. He cradled a litre jug of Listerine in his lap.

"You got a coat?" Peterson asked him.

"Fuck for?"

"For nothing, Jimmy, not if this is how you're thinking of kicking out. Drink yourself blind then fall asleep. Peaceful. I thought of it myself, only I don't like the cold. I'd end up sitting in ten-below weather with a couple of sweaters on."

Stiles waved Peterson's words away.

"C'mon, wake up! It's Peterson, the guy who used to kick your ass at cribbage, you and Robbie Yorke. Remember?"

Stiles lifted his heavy head and looked at Peterson. His breath smelled like a barbershop. "I'm fucked up," he said, and grunted a laugh.

"You must be on the ass end of your pension cheque to be drinking this shit." Peterson reached for the jug and took it. Raised it to see less than the neck was gone.

"What the—?"

"You'll get it back after we talk."

"What?"

"Remember us playing cribbage?"

Stiles offered a big smile, but his eyes were on the jug. "You never kicked my ass."

It was Peterson's turn to laugh. "Just checking. The truth was I never measured up to you and Robbie Yorke, not at anything."

"You're a good cop. I keep tabs."

Peterson shook his head. "Not like you. You and Robbie had the job by the balls. A two-man wrecking crew. Bad guys didn't have a chance."

Stiles kept his eyes on the jug.

"Undercover, on the street, no one else came close," Peterson said.

"Not how I remember it."

"What do you remember?"

"You know the job. You end up drinking three meals a day." Stiles closed his eyes. "Sideshow. The main stage is nothing but a sideshow."

"How's that work out?"

Stiles grunted a laugh. "If I tell you everything I know, you'll know just as much as me."

"So what do you know?"

"I know if you live the job, you go home and there's nothing there. I know that as a fact."

"What else? Do you know what happened to Carlisle Martin?"

Stiles looked at Peterson. "What do you want?"

"The truth about the night he went missing."

Stiles looked over at the chalky storage towers of the flour mill and beyond that to the lights at the south-end container terminal. "I don't remember nothing," he said.

"Yes, you do. You remember everything Robbie told you. You rode together, how many years?"

Stiles didn't answer.

"Best friends. You know what best friends do? They talk. Sometimes they say things they shouldn't say. Sometimes they say things they need to say. Before you were partners, you were undercover."

Stiles shook his head.

"You know what it was like to go deep on the inside. After you came out from undercover, you and Robbie

250

talked about it. Who else could you share it with? Who would understand?"

Stiles wiped his nose with his sleeve.

"Robbie told me things," Peterson continued, "but not the kind of things he told you. And now you're going to tell me what he said, because right now Robbie Yorke has his ass in a sling. Two drug-squad cops are running him down. I need you to remember."

Jimmy's green eyes were glistening, but they were clear. And his expression was straight up, like he had it together, at least well enough to understand what Peterson was saying.

"I'll talk you through what I know," Peterson said. "You fill in the blanks."

He followed Stiles's eyes past the flour mill and thought he saw someone silhouetted in the lights from the container terminal, someone leaning on the knuckle of a railway hopper that was waiting to fill up with flour in the morning. He kept his eyes on that someone as he spoke to Stiles. "Airport pick-up," he said. "Zar Tombs in back, Robbie's behind the wheel. Carlisle Martin climbs in. Tombs goes motormouth about Vietnam. They exit the highway then turn into the campground. Then what?"

Stiles wiped his stewed face with a dirty hand. He looked at Peterson.

"I don't care if we're here all night and freeze to death," Peterson said.

Stiles reached for the jug, but Peterson pulled it away. "Not until you talk," Peterson said.

Stiles took his time. Chewing his lips to make sense of what he remembered. "A lot of things you don't know until a situation plays out," he mumbled.

"A lot of things, like what?"

"Like what Robbie said. There was a contract."

"Montreal?" Peterson pressed.

Stiles nodded. "Tony Bones. He wanted Martin out. What for? Who the fuck knows."

"And Zar Tombs held the contract," Peterson said.

Stiles nodded. "Maniac. Cap his own mother."

"So they drove to the campground and then what?"

Stiles raised his right hand like he was holding a pistol. "Bang, bang."

"Just like that."

"That's what Robbie said."

"And what did Robbie do?"

Stiles stared at Peterson. "He keeps his cover. Martin's dead already. What's one more in the head, right? It ties a knot. You're in deep like Robbie was, the knots are what keep you alive."

Peterson spat, unsure if the bad taste was from what he'd smelled or what he'd heard. He looked back at the hopper and saw the person still leaning on the knuckle.

"What about the guns they used to kill Martin?"

Stiles choked on a laugh. He coughed it out then muttered something about the guns. He hung his head then lifted it. "It turns a few times."

"What turns?"

"The way you play it. You play it one way, it turns, and you play it another."

"What about the guns?"

"Robbie said it was like Blackwood always knew. And when it played out, Blackwood had him. Back pocket. We're a dozen deep in that pub on Hollis. Robbie more than me, a snootful. He's talking. He says, 'He has me, owns me.' Blackwood could lock him away if he doesn't jump. You try to keep your cover, and it turns. Sometimes it turns and it all goes down the shitter."

Stiles reached again for the Listerine, but Peterson moved it away. "That's why nothing stuck to Blackwood," Peterson said. He lowered his eyes to the ground at his feet. His mouth was too dry to swallow.

"Zar Tombs," he said.

Stiles saw Peterson's face stretched tight. "Robbie shot a dead man," Stiles said. "But that was enough. He couldn't pull the trigger on someone ever again, not for nothing."

Peterson stared at the ground.

"Tombs made a deal with Blackwood to get his gun back, an out-of-town hit of some kind," Stiles said, his voice firm. "There was no deal for Robbie Yorke. None. Then Robbie and me are out from under, and we're on the street together, partners now, and Tombs shows up and demands Robbie protect him the way Robbie does Blackwood. He backs Robbie against the wall and makes his threats. Someone had to shut him up."

Peterson had tears in his eyes. He handed Stiles the jug of Listerine and walked away toward the flour mill. He walked past it and stood in the centre of half a dozen railway tracks. He stood there with his hands at his sides. He heard a yard switcher chugging as it shunted a railcar at the container terminal. He heard metal screaming the cry that was silent in his throat. Then he heard a voice call his name. He looked up and saw someone step away from the hopper. The person wore a long dark coat and a black toque pulled low over his ears and forehead. Peterson knew who it was.

He looked to where Stiles was sitting on the broken chair, sipping Listerine. Tears were still in his eyes at what Stiles had said. He looked back at Leon Ferris. He knew what Leon had under the long coat. He remembered the snow-covered road near the Mi'kmaq Reserve and the dressmaker's form in his wife's clothes lying on the bed. He remembered telling Danny that Leon never goes straight up, that he always works the shadows. And he remembered Danny saying that "Leon likes to play jack-in-the-box." And that brought the tune into his head, and he started humming. With hands at his sides and without reaching for the SIG Sauer in his coat pocket, he walked straight at Leon.

The two men stared at one another as Peterson kept walking forward, humming the tune. Then Leon opened his long coat and raised the sawed-off waist high. Peterson kept walking, his eyes on Leon, his hands still empty at his sides.

He dialled in distant voices, the uncoupling of a railcar, Stiles gagging on a mouthful and spitting.

"Open you up, man," Leon shouted, his voice trembling, his boast lacking conviction.

Peterson kept walking. Humming. He was now well within range of the shotgun. But he kept his face placid and his eyes fixed on Leon.

"Are you crazy?" Ferris shouted.

They were less than ten feet apart, and Peterson saw the sweat leaking from under the black toque and running down Leon's face. Three more steps. Three feet apart, and Peterson grabbed the barrel and yanked the sawed-off out of Leon's hands. He cocked his upper body and smashed the butt into Leon's mouth.

Leon went down hard.

Peterson cracked the shotgun and emptied it. Then he grabbed a fistful of Leon's collar and hauled Leon to where Stiles was still sitting. He shoved the barrel up the back of Leon's pant leg, so he would have a hard time standing up when he came to. Then he dialled 911 and told them what they needed to know. He hung up and speed-dialled Danny. Listened to the recorded message. Left one of his own. Then he sank to the ground, completely drained. Ignored his ringing phone, then shut it off. His back and chest were drenched in sweat, and his hands were smeared with Leon's blood. He sat there with his eyes closed. When he opened them, Stiles was standing over him, a stupefied look on his face.

CHAPTER
THIRTY-SIX

He was parked in the shadow of St. Jude's church, hanging out the door of the Cherokee. Dry heaves. Shedding tears. His heart and soul clicking through a rosary of promises at not knowing if Leon's finger freezing on the trigger had been a blessing or a curse.

He shut the door and killed the car heater. Wreathed his arms around the steering wheel. A wind-stilled hush. Cold creeping in. Blurred swimmings in his brain about that single moment when he believed he was about to die. He'd almost welcomed it.

He straightened up and started the engine. Drove two blocks and pulled over. Closed his eyes. Tried to clear his head. Couldn't. Opened his eyes. He held out his hands and watched them shake.

Twenty minutes later, he turned on his phone and

checked his messages. There were three from Danny, all with much the same message, "Is Marshall calling you? Because he's calling me. I think we have a problem."

Then he listened to Marshall's message. His voice weakened as he spoke.

"Dental degree and no morals. I've been thinking about that. You were right. It was just about money, a business deal. We never talked about it as anything else. We were moving the decimal point, that's what we were doing, that's how we saw it. But it's never as simple as that, is it? When you realize that, it's too late. You can't play it back. Life doesn't have a rewind button."

Peterson sat in the Cherokee in a sort of neutered consciousness, the phone in his lap. He played the message again and listened to every word, motionless, as though moving would change what he had heard. Then he did move and started the car and switched on the headlights. At the corner he gunned it through a yellow light and held that speed across town until he saw the flashers of police cars blocking the road and a fire truck and ambulance parked alongside the curb.

He parked half a block away and walked through flashing coloured lights to where a uniform cop stood sentry behind yellow police tape.

"The wife still letting you out at night?" Peterson asked, going into cop mode, giving the uniform cop a big smile and offering his hand.

"Hey, Peterson, how's it going?" the cop said, shaking hands.

Peterson hunched his shoulders and tightened into the role he was playing. "Who listens, right? How about you?"

"Bitching and complaining. Nothing changes."

"Never does," Peterson said. "So what's with the tape and road crew?"

"Some guy thought he could fly."

"ID him yet?"

"A dentist, I heard. Danny's up there now."

"Can I go up?"

"You know I can't lift the tape."

"I think I know the guy."

"You think?"

"I think. And I have something that might help Danny nail it down."

"Like what?"

"Like a phone message. His last words, I think."

The cop nodded. "Give me a minute. If Danny says yes, I'll lift the tape."

The cop walked over to a parked police car and spoke to another uniform cop who then made a phone call. Less than a minute later, the first cop was back and lifting the tape for Peterson. He hollered to the uniform on the door to the building, "Let him in!"

Peterson had started for the building when the first cop stopped him. "So, let me ask," he said, "you worked the job a long time, a detective for how many?"

"Almost sixteen."

"And you think you know this guy?"

"I think so."

"So, he clears the railing and hits midair. Swan dive, you know what I mean. You think he changes his mind?"

"What difference?"

"I'm just wondering. Eight floors to the bottom, the guy has time to think about it, like maybe a couple of seconds.

258

Seeing the street and no going back. Maybe wishing he had a Superman suit."

Neither of them smiled. Their faces washed with red light. Then the cop shrugged.

"I've seen my share, Peterson, just like you. We used to laugh, right? Dull the edge, you know what I'm saying? Then you get so you stop laughing."

● ● ●

Peterson hit the eighth floor. The uniform cop on the door gave him a frosty reception. A forty-five-year-old hardass, stuck in uniform and blaming it on a glass ceiling.

"What do you want?" she asked, making no bones about her likes and dislikes. "I didn't like you when you were a cop. Even less now."

Peterson nodded. "Some doors swing both ways."

Bernie was standing just inside the condo and overheard the exchange. When Peterson entered, they traded looks.

"You know the feeling," Bernie said. "Sometimes it's hard to trust someone not wearing a badge. And don't scowl at me, I'm not the enemy."

"It's been a hard night," Peterson said.

"I heard about it."

She passed him latex gloves and blue booties. "Danny's on the balcony."

Danny entered through the sliding door and signalled to Peterson to take a seat at the dining room table. He said something to Bernie then joined Peterson.

Peterson slid his cell phone across the table. "Play the message," he said.

Danny played it. He took an attitude. "You came here, threatened the guy to get him to talk, then pressured him about going to jail. Then you play me his message as though that explains it all. You're on the hook for pushing this guy to the edge, and I don't know why you don't feel like shit knowing he took a nosedive because of what you did."

Peterson stiffened, but he didn't respond. He wouldn't give an inch to let on to what he was feeling.

"I don't know how you live with yourself," Danny said.

"You used to live this way too."

"Not anymore."

"Lucky you."

"Yeah, lucky me."

Peterson pointed at the blue paisley tie Danny was wearing. "I remember when you'd show up without brushing your teeth."

"I did a lot of things back then. We both did. But that was a long time ago."

"Not that long."

"Yes, it was."

Peterson got up to leave.

"He didn't jump," Danny said. "I got three calls from him. He was scared. The last message he left, he screamed something about two guys being outside the door. They took his hard drive, daytimer, and whatever else Marshall coughed up before they tossed him. Does that make you feel better?"

They stared at each other. Whatever they had once shared as partners, as friends, it was gone.

CHAPTER
THIRTY-SEVEN

He went home, grabbed the quart of Johnnie Walker from under the kitchen sink, and set it on the floor in the centre of the den. He switched on a table lamp and sat in the leather recliner and stared at the bottle. He felt the urge to do a Jimmy Stiles, by blurring the past and numbing his feelings, even though it would mean waking up with a stomach full of need to do it again, and again.

He reached for the bottle and broke the seal. Sniffed the cap then cradled the bottle between his legs. He removed the SIG from his coat pocket and laid it on the side table on top of Tanya's journal. His eyes went back and forth between the SIG on the table and the bottle between his legs.

He spent the next hour waddling inside his own head, thinking about things he shouldn't be thinking about. Then his phone rang with a Skype call. He answered to an image of a long dimly lit hallway with a closed door at the far end. Above the door was a red exit sign. Then the screen went white.

He set the phone aside and lifted the bottle. He took a mouthful and swallowed. Then he recapped it and hung his head in shame.

● ● ●

He woke cramped on the brown leather loveseat. Tanya's journal was open on the floor. Beside him, the quart was capped with one swallow missing and the SIG was still on the end table. He picked up Tanya's journal. Usually he opened the journal just anywhere and read a single entry, not so much for content as for the intimacy of the scrawl of words. This time he read it from the beginning, skipping over the half dozen pages about himself.

When he got to the poem about Tanya feeling hopeless at the sudden loss of him, he shut the journal.

CHAPTER
THIRTY-EIGHT

By the time he arrived at Laurie Park that morning, one of the campsites had already been backhoed and scraped down about two feet. Men with shovels had dug the rest. The forensics team had erected a tent over the hole. Police tape wrapped around surrounding birch and maple trees defined a perimeter fifty feet out from the campsite. The forensics van was parked near the maintenance shed, and there were half a dozen cops walking around it, looking engaged. An ENG cameraman and female reporter scooted around the perimeter, angling for a shot.

Lewis stood outside the tent, smoking. He saw Peterson get out of the Cherokee and walked to the police tape to meet him. He grunted something by way of greeting, and Peterson grunted back.

The news team closed on them, but Lewis motioned for them to stay away.

"The warrant to excavate didn't take long," Peterson said.

"Knowing where to dig helped," Lewis said. He tried for a smile, and it wasn't the smug one Peterson was expecting. "The Chief always wondered what happened to Carlisle Martin."

"You any closer to knowing?"

"We have a body, or what's left of one. A male, possible mid-thirties. We'll know more after the white coats fuck with the bones. But the front of the skull's blown away, if that tells you anything. Two bullet holes in back."

"A pro hit," Peterson said.

"Or an undercover cop who knew how to get it done." Lewis glanced at the news team. "I know you talked to Jimmy Stiles. And I figure he told you more about what happened here than he told Eddie and me."

"He's a drunk speaking in tongues," Peterson said. "Jimmy's chasing ghosts in a jug of Listerine."

"Coming from you that makes him poster boy for AA," Lewis said.

The tent flap was pushed aside, and Eddie Bigger emerged wearing blue booties and latex gloves. He saw Peterson, drew snot and spat. He walked over to them.

"Good to see you too, Eddie," Peterson said.

"I'm surprised you're still with us," Bigger said, removing the gloves and booties. "I heard the Needle was kissing you goodbye."

"We're still lip locked. Maybe Blackwood can't get enough of me."

Bigger laughed with his mouth open. "Willie Blackwood's not Leon Ferris. Yeah, we heard. Tough guy going head-to-head with a sawed-off. Big deal, right. Only Blackwood doesn't freeze up."

"Willie doesn't do the dirty work," Peterson said.

"Yeah, we heard that too," Lewis said. "Sammy itching to hit back, and your name getting thrown in the mix."

"Is that what keeps you from doing something about it?" Peterson said.

"What's there to do?" Bigger said. "Both sides want to clean house, let 'em. Saves the city a top-up on next year's police budget. You get in the middle, more power to them."

"That's you, Eddie, always working the motto, to serve and protect."

That got Bigger's back up. "Taxpayers, Peterson, not drug dealers and washed-up cops. The time that girl drilled you with a .22, I think half the department wished it'd been an AK-47. You've got friends, but I'll bet there aren't enough to count on one hand."

Peterson smirked. "Check out my Facebook page. I have thousands. And double that on Twitter, all following my every word."

Bigger leaned into him. "Fuck you!"

"That's my next tweet."

"And fuck you again!"

Peterson looked at Lewis. "He's a talker. You must have long conversations together." He turned to go. Turned back. "I take it you didn't find what you were looking for."

Lewis wouldn't bite.

Peterson said, "You dug up a skull like the one on your shoulders — empty."

"You should do stand-up," Lewis said.

Peterson started for the Cherokee.

"Your friend got lucky," Lewis called.

Peterson kept walking.

"We both know what he did here," Lewis urged.

Peterson opened the driver's door.

Lewis shouted, "No halo, Peterson. Yorke never wore a halo."

CHAPTER
THIRTY-NINE

Peterson still had a key to Yorke's bungalow, a holdover from his days on the force when he couldn't or wouldn't go home. Showing up at the door lit like a stumble drunk. There were never any questions on Yorke's part, and no explanations on his.

He opened the back door to a dark kitchen with the shades down. The place stank to high heaven with the same stench he had smelled in the rooming house of the pissy-pants gang. He switched on an overhead light. A whirlwind had blown through the place. Chairs toppled. Pots and pans and broken dishes were everywhere. Two quart empties on the table, one on the floor. The fridge door stood open, food pulled out and scattered. A charred frying pan on the stove.

He followed the stink into the living room. It had fared no better than the kitchen. The TV had been smashed. Holes punched in the walls. The glass-top coffee table shattered by a quart that now lay empty among the glass shards. He turned down the narrow hall to the bedrooms and found Yorke on the floor in the bathroom, curled around the toilet. Shitty pants. Dried vomit down the front of his shirt. More vomit on the floor where he had turned his head to barf.

Peterson stood in the doorway, his hands pressed against both jambs. He gagged but held down the sickening hopelessness that had erupted into his throat. Then he checked Yorke's pulse. Dead drunk. A waxy-faced father-figure sprawled on a bathroom floor, a bull of a man now melted to a puddle of revulsion.

Peterson turned and walked out of the house into a light snow. He reached the Cherokee, spread his hands along the driver's side, and pressed his forehead to the window.

No tears. Just a moan that came from somewhere deep, from a hollow inside that emptied the sound of its high tones, the way a canyon does a voice, and left it barrelling with anguish.

Then he turned and went back into the bungalow. He raised the shades and opened the windows. In the master bedroom, he stripped the bed, found clean linens, and remade it.

Then he hunted down garbage bags, cleaning supplies, and rubber gloves under the kitchen sink. He pulled Yorke from around the toilet and stripped him naked. He stuffed the clothes into a garbage bag. He ran a hot bath and lifted the grumbling, still dead-to-the-world Robbie Yorke into it. He dripped water over Yorke's head and washed his hair. Then he washed the old man's face and under his arms. He rinsed the cloth and lathered it again. He washed the old man's flaccid, stained body. He washed between his legs and cheeks. He washed him as gently as a man with big hands could. He washed him the way someone might wash a corpse, washing away grief, washing away sins that he was trying to forgive.

He drained the water and dried the old man inside the tub. Then he carried him to the bedroom and put him to bed.

After that, he scrubbed the bathroom and bleached the floor. He swept up the broken glass in the living room and the smashed china in the kitchen. He tidied the rooms as best he could. Then he wrote the old man a note about the dig in Laurie Park and how no bullets had been found. "Whether he has the gun or not, there's nothing Blackwood can hold over your head," he wrote. "And from now on, you're on your own."

He placed the note under a salt shaker on the kitchen table and left.

• • •

Peterson parked on the street outside the School of Dentistry, leaving the engine running, the heat cranked, rear-window defrost on, and the windshield wipers flapping on a dry window. In the side mirror, he saw the silver Lexus park half a block away. He checked his watch then looked to the main doors of the red-brick building. A man holding the lapels of his sports jacket closed came out and scanned the street. Then the man saw the red Cherokee and walked over.

No handshakes. None offered. Peterson's early morning phone call had made it clear this was no friendly get-together. The man was Dr. Charles Connors, and, as Peterson had put it on the phone, Connors was his own gravedigger.

Connors climbed into the passenger seat and stared straight ahead. Peterson checked the rearview and saw that the driver of the Lexus was now standing outside the car smoking. Peterson turned up the heat and left the wipers on. Every second swipe, the wipers squealed.

"You know about Vernon Rumley?" Peterson asked. He played his large hands over the steering wheel.

Connors, a Harris Tweed without the accent, shook his head. The cat had his tongue.

"He's nowhere to be found, presumed dead," Peterson said. He reached in back for the morning paper and handed it to Connors.

Connors put it on his lap without looking. "It was on the radio," he said.

"The news left something out. Two guys helped Marshall swan dive off the balcony. Your friend was a big hit."

Connors watched dental students enter the red-brick building. The car was sickeningly hot.

"You want to know why?" Peterson asked.

Connors looked at him.

"Someone saw Marshall and me talking," Peterson said. "They weren't taking chances with what we were talking about."

Connors mumbled something and lowered his eyes to the newspaper on his lap.

"You're a dentist," Peterson said. "You're educated. You teach kids to become dentists. But I'll tell you something. I've busted street-shitters smarter than you."

Connors raised his head.

"A lawyer walks in with a get-rich-quick idea," Peterson said. "And you bite. Did she go to you first or Marshall?"

"Me. My accountant set it up."

"Some accountant. Some lawyer. They're usually paid to keep you out of jail."

"It was an investment," Connors said in the wheedling tone of a panhandler grubbing for change.

"Two hundred thou down, four comes back," Peterson said. "You never asked what turns money that fast?"

Connors didn't answer.

"But you knew," Peterson said. "Of course you knew. Smart guys like you and Marshall, you know how Willie Blackwood makes his living. And you knew what it meant to be bankrolling his business deals. An investment? Is that what Angelina Samson called it? What else did she say it was? A sure thing?"

Connors squirmed.

"There are only two sure things in life," Peterson said. "The last you can sometimes avoid. The first you can't do nothing about. Sometimes it sneaks up, hammers the front door sooner than you expected. And sometimes someone else has more say about your last day than you do. Rumley found that out. So did Marshall." Peterson snapped his fingers. "Now it's your turn."

Connors jerked his eyes to Peterson. "What do you mean?"

Peterson checked the rearview.

"There's a silver Lexus parked half a block away," he said. "It's been following me for a couple of days. The guys inside are the ones who saw me talking to Marshall. Now they're seeing me talking to you."

Connors turned in his seat to look out the blurry back window. He looked at Peterson, his eyes full of fear.

"I checked where you live," Peterson said. "Downtown high-rise, executive suite. Ninth floor. Do you skydive?"

"Oh Jesus," Connors said.

"Neither did Marshall."

"Christ!" Connors began to shake from head to toe. His breathing kept time with the wipers, and the squeal they made sounded as though it came from him.

"You got yourself into this," Peterson said. "Now it's time to get yourself out. The clock's ticking."

Connors stared at the students coming and going from the dental building. He was sweating. His face was pale, and he looked as though he was about to cry.

"This won't be over until they get to me," Peterson said. "I stuck my nose in too far. I know too much. But you, you've got a chance."

Connors swung his head.

"All you need is a paper trail to the lawyer and accountant," Peterson said. "Marshall kept notes, but the two guys took whatever Marshall had. I'm betting you kept records too. Show the cops and they'll connect the dots to Samson and eventually to Blackwood."

He waited for Connors to work through the possibilities. Then Peterson said, "Moral behaviour, they don't teach that stuff in dental school, do they?" He reached for his phone and gave it to Connors. "I got a cop's number on speed dial."

• • •

The two apple dolls were at their posts in wingback chairs in the foyer. Again, one responded to his nod and the other eyed him suspiciously. The lobby had the same sea of grizzled, wrinkled faces, the same constant slow motion of walkers, the same wheelchairs mashed against the bank of elevators.

Peterson entered the breezeway against a herd of shuffling grey-hairs bulked in winter coats and crabbing about the shuttle bus being late. Off the breezeway was the recreation area, and Dinky Toi was in there with three old women squinting over a jigsaw puzzle of tabby cats playing with different coloured balls of yarn. He ignored Peterson's high sign at first, then stepped away from the threesome to join Peterson at a picture window looking out on a snow-covered courtyard. His wide body cut down the grey light coming into the room.

"I got a lot going for me right now," Dink said. "Second chance, you hear what I'm saying? It's not like I don't appreciate what you did, you and Danny. I do, man."

"It sounds like you're ending a relationship," Peterson said.

"I have to be careful."

"About what?"

Dink looked back at the three old women. "They go weeks working on the same puzzle," he said. "Taking turns with a piece, matching colours, shapes. I got others who go all day and stare at nothing. You ever look down the road and see what's coming our way?"

Peterson gave him a dry smile.

"They wear diapers," Dink said. "Some can't wipe themselves when they need cleaning." He looked at Peterson. "I heard you got a virus that could make me sick."

Peterson suspected where this was going. "What kind is that?"

273

"The kind that has more than just Leon Ferris after your ass."

"Leon broke parole," Peterson said. "He paid me a visit and now he's going back to jail. Who else wants me dead?"

With the back of his hand, Dink wiped spit from the corner of his mouth. "Jacking hand-to-hand deals gets overlooked by those upstairs. But storming a stash house and shooting at Sammy O, that was stupid. Sammy's boys are loading up to get even. And Blackwood's okay with Sammy O hitting back. It solves a problem."

Peterson nodded and said, "The problem being Morehouse and friends. They murdered a guy named Rumley on Willie's say-so. That could bite Willie in the ass."

"Yeah, well I don't want to know more than what you just said." Dink held out his hands as though he had something to give. "That girl you been looking for. The word is Blackwood has something against her. Something personal. I'm telling you what I'm telling you because Blackwood wants you to go down with the others. You playing detective pissed him off. They don't know I know. I'm giving you the heads-up."

"It's not hard to figure out. I've had a silver Lexus on my ass the last couple of days. I think I know who."

"That's Blackwood's car. His boys ride it for show."

"They are doing that. Who's your pipe?"

Dink shook his head. "Let's just say Sammy likes to talk. Someone I know likes to listen."

"Did this someone say when and where this will happen?"

Dink looked at him. Smiled. "We been back-scratching how long?"

"A few years."

Dink nodded. "I give, you give."

"That's how it works."

"You pulled my brother's wife from a jam, that false claim as a refugee. You went years and you never said nothing. You helped keep the government from being her travel agent."

"If it worked out, it worked out."

"You did my family good, Peterson. So why can't you just hear what I'm saying? Go somewhere, man. Come back in two, maybe three years when this goes away."

A soft wind eddied in the courtyard and swirled up snow. Dink looked out the window then back at Peterson. "Maybe I should go back to the old ladies before I catch what you got."

"Where and when?"

Dink threw back his head in exasperation. "Where Pike and his friends are hiding."

"Where's that?" Peterson asked.

"They know Sammy's boys are looking for them. If you go where they are, you die with them."

Peterson shrugged. "Tell me where."

Dink shook him off.

He stared Dink into submission.

"They're squatting an abandoned house at Ferguson's Cove. No address, but it's next door to a church. My guy said Sammy made some crack about going to mass after they do it."

"When?"

"Night, early morning," Dink said. "I don't know. Do like the cops and catch them sleeping."

Peterson turned to the window then turned away. He started to leave.

"Don't go there, man," Dink said. "Not alone."

● ● ●

Peterson parked in the alley alongside The Office. Cotter came out the side door carrying a hockey bag. He opened the back door of the Cherokee and set the bag on the back seat.

Peterson lowered the passenger-side window. Cotter leaned in.

"You're not the first cop or ex-cop that's been climbing a short rope," Cotter said.

"I'm just evening the odds," Peterson said.

"It's a death wish, and you know it."

"Is that what you think?"

"I heard about Leon Ferris. I could say something about that, but I won't." He nodded into the back seat. "I used up a few favours to get you this. And I threw in a Kevlar vest. No time for heroes, Peterson. Wear it."

CHAPTER
FORTY

There was freezing rain and fog banked along the coast. The shore road was skimmed with ice. Yet he gunned it, counting on the Cherokee to hold the turns. In the rearview there was only the empty road. He was confident he had ditched the silver Lexus among the side streets downtown.

He was brooding as he drove, his eyes pinched, hands tight on the steering wheel. His head brewed with shame for feelings thick with disappointment. For friendships scoured down to loneliness.

The shore road was flanked by scrub spruce bent like shipwrecked sailors trudging the coast. Spray off the water coated the Cherokee, its wipers losing time to the freeze-up on the windscreen. He almost missed the beige church with dark brown corner boards. Beside it was a two-bedroom bungalow in need of repair. A RE/MAX "For

Sale" sign had been hammered to a roadside tree. The bungalow sat back from the road in a grove of spruce on a four-acre snow-covered lot. The place was a hold-out to all the ocean-view development that was going on around it.

The rundown look and curtainless windows said it was empty. But the black RAM 1500 parked toward the back said that Cowley Pike, and probably also Tommy the Brick, Logan Morehouse, and Cassie Colpitts, were home.

Peterson drove by, checking it out. Then he stopped in the bay of a postal kiosk.

He reached into the back seat and into the hockey bag. He removed the Kevlar vest and a green poncho and set them on the seat. He loaded up the pump action twelve-gauge. He snapped a clip into the SIG Sauer and tucked two more clips into his coat pocket. The SIG he shoved into his waistband. He pulled the poncho over his head and made sure he could easily reach the 9mm.

Cotter had also thrown in an unregistered scoped Springfield 840 30-30. Peterson thought about it for a moment, then zipped the bag and shut the door.

He slipped around the Cherokee, holding the shotgun under the poncho and down along his right leg. He walked back down the road for a hundred metres. The road looped back on itself, and here he cut through a mixed stand of fir and white birch and came up on the bungalow from an angle. Using the tree line for cover, he took position ten metres from the front door on a knoll studded with stumpy spruce.

The high angle provided him a clear view through a picture window. There was a brown couch and a couple of wooden chairs in the front room. He could also see the first few feet of a hallway to the back bedrooms. Through an archway to the kitchen, he made out a table, a chair, and part of an overhead cupboard. What he didn't see was movement.

He watched for another ten minutes, and still the house was quiet. Too quiet, he thought. They either had a bead on him and were waiting on his move, or they were in the back catching Z's for an all-night vigil, expecting Sammy O to hit after dark like Dink had said.

He cocked the shotgun, checked the safety was on, and sprinted for the stairs of the front porch. He crept the stairs to the porch and pressed his back to the side of the door. He clicked the safety off and peeked through the picture window. There was no one in the front room. He tried the door and was surprised to find it unlocked.

He raised the sawed-off to his cheek and entered. His head was on a swivel as he covered off his field of fire, clearing the front room. Then going wide-eyed to see down the hallway and through the archway into the kitchen. He hugged the outside wall, sidestepping with the gun against his cheek. Then he blew into the kitchen and saw Cowley Pike sprawled in a patch of dried blood and spilled bowels. Pike had been shot in the back, his chest and stomach opened up from high-calibre firing hollow points.

Then Peterson sidled along the hallway to the back rooms, past the bathroom with blood smeared on the ochre-coloured tile floor. In the first bedroom, he found Tommy the Brick curled into a ball in a corner. His blank eyes were open, jaw slung, and body shot all to hell.

Dink had gotten it a day late, he thought. And the two bodies in the house had him panicky for Cassie Colpitts.

Peterson checked the second bedroom. No one was there. Between the two bedrooms was an ajar back door. He made for it, came out onto an ice-crusted deck, and saw a lot of feet had beaten a path across the snow-blown field. He followed the path through a wooded area and up a rocky bluff to a walking trail. The trail led to a closed pole gate. The beaten path continued beyond the gate and onto the grounds of the old fort. Peterson squeezed through.

The fort had been a forward gun battery for protecting the harbour. Now it was a historic site, with a stone stockade, ruined buildings, gun emplacements, and walking trails. It was closed for the season.

The footing was unsteady, slushy in some sections, ice-crusted in others. Fir branches sagged under the icy weight. Some creaked at the strain.

He broke from the trees and walked over to the complex of mortared brick-and-ironstone buildings. Swivel cannon aimed at the harbour mouth lined the perimeter. He reached a snowy expanse that served as a parking lot. Stopped. Feeling exposed and vulnerable to those he was tracking. He crouched and weighed his options. Then, like a cat, he hugged the perimeter wall, skirting the parking lot and picking up the trail on the other side.

The trail entered another wooded area and twisted among scrub spruce and birch saplings dripping with ice. It led to the powder magazine, an earth-covered construction designed to withstand a bomb blast.

A narrow brick entranceway led to a closed wooden door two inches thick. Footprints led to and away from the powder magazine. There were fewer of them going away than pointing in. Nearby was a three-foot length of four-by-four. After springing the wooden door, he used the four-by-four to prop it open. Daylight reached into the magazine only so far, then it shredded into dark shadow.

He got out his phone but held off turning on the light. Deciding to wait until he was inside and sure it would not make him a target.

He raised the shotgun and entered. Inside it was even colder than out, and it smelled of earth. There was a small room immediately to his right and enough bounce light to see it was empty. He crept forward into the dark, his back to the brick wall. Listening. Neck hairs up. Pupils wide.

After a few more paces, he held the phone at arm's length and turned on the light. He kept his back to the wall and followed it, feeling his way over the stone floor. Deeper inside. Ten feet. Then twenty. He looked back at the light streaming through the open door, his lifeline from the darkness.

He took two more steps and saw something in the faint glow. A body slumped against the wall, its head hanging to one side, tongue lolling out. He stooped over it and saw it was Vernon Rumley. There was a bullet hole in his forehead. Then he sensed something else not far away. He played the light and saw a hand with its fingers splayed. He moved towards it. The light revealed another body, prostrate, arms outstretched, head turned his way with its eyes open. It was Logan Morehouse. Shot in the back.

He cross-beamed the floor, following it to the far wall, steadying himself, expecting to see Cassie's body. It wasn't there. He returned to stand over Morehouse. Thinking. Turtle had said they had left Rumley's body after discovering the floor was solid stone. Morehouse must have run here to hide from Sammy O. But what about Cassie? Where was she?

He heard shuffling at the open door. He killed the light, flipped aside the phone, spun, and raised the sawed-off just as someone outside opened fire.

Peterson dropped and flattened behind Morehouse's body as bullets pinged off the brick walls, ricocheting ten different ways. The blasts swelled into the roar of a high-speed train in a tunnel. The pain in his ears had him nuzzling his head into the dead man's body.

He chewed the urge to cry out. Then rose high enough to clear the sawed-off over Morehouse and fire at the light in the open door. The shot blasted off the brick walls and screamed back at him, driving him face first into Morehouse's body. The pain in his ears and head was unmerciful. Yet, he pumped in another round and rose and fired.

The door slammed shut, and then there was nothing but the choke of cordite, the fading ricochet of sound, and darkness on top of darkness. It was a darkness darker than the dark behind closed eyes.

He lifted himself off Morehouse's body and sat on the stone floor, still hearing distant cannon blasting inside his head. There was a loud ringing as well, and a crawl of images in his mind. He whispered something to himself, but could not hear the sound of his own voice.

He rolled to his knees. With the shotgun in one hand, he felt the floor for the phone. Creeping forward. Dragging the shotgun at his side. His fingers touched the cold dead face of Logan Morehouse. He felt the fallen jaw. He searched the crevice between the body and the floor. Then he rotated so his feet pressed against Morehouse's body. Using that as a still point, he searched the floor in widening arcs, flattening himself on the floor to reach further. His ears ringing, his head pounding, and his mind struggling to remain focused. He searched and stretched as far as he could. Then he retreated and climbed over Morehouse to search the other side.

Ten minutes. Twenty. The whole time resisting the pain in his ears and the circling faces that had his mind roiling. He saw the hollow-eyed faces of the ones he had failed, and they howled from the darkness of his thoughts. And when he drew back on his haunches, they laughed at his luckless search.

He stood and breathed deeply to calm himself, and the deep breaths hurt into his head. He extended his left arm and walked straight ahead. When he reached the wall, he set his back against it and sidestepped till he toed Rumley's body. He stepped over it and kept on. He reached the closed wooden door and pushed on it, but it did not budge. He guessed the length of four-by-four had been jammed against it. His hands shook. He drew another deep breath to steady himself. Then another. He aimed the shotgun where he calculated the four-by-four was jammed. He fired.

It felt as though his eardrums had imploded into his brain and expanded to press against the inside of his skull. He threw himself against the splintered door and out into the freezing rain. He dropped to his knees and cradled his pounding head against the tortured ringing in his ears. His mouth filled with a silent scream.

● ● ●

He spent a long time kneeling in the rain. Then he gathered himself, retrieved the shotgun, and in the light from the open door found his cell phone. He called Bernie and reported the bodies in the bungalow and in the powder magazine. He told her what Turtle and Dink had told him, about Sammy O getting even and Blackwood giving it the okay. He knew she was responding on the other end but could not make out what she was saying for the ringing in his ears. He knew by her intonations that she was asking questions that he did not answer. He figured one of them had to be what he intended to do next. He didn't tell her. He wanted no one getting in the way of what he had to do.

CHAPTER
FORTY-ONE

There was no love lost for Sammy O'Brien, not among the dealers and street jugglers, not among the pipeheads and clowns and ten-a-day tokers. So Peterson didn't have far to go to find someone Sammy had juiced, someone willing to point the way. And that someone pointed to a rabbit warren of brick-faced row houses in the same neighbourhood as The Tower, where Morehouse and Cassie had holed up with Morehouse's sister, where Peterson had met Benny Stokes.

The complex drove cops crazy, chasing bad guys every which way, never knowing where they were or where the hell they were going. The units on the main drag had their front doors and front windows at sidewalk level. And this was good and bad for overweight Sammy O. It was good because there were no stairs for him to climb, front or back, and because he could stand inside and watch the action on the street, which he liked to do, especially in winter with all the snow and freezing rain.

It was bad for Sammy O for all the same reasons. Someone wanting inside in a hurry had no stairs to negotiate, and from the sidewalk they could see anybody inside watching them.

Peterson found Benny half a block from Sammy's row house, near the smoked meat sandwich joint, doing what Benny did, begging change from the educated do-gooders and silver-spoon socialists, a Tim Hortons coffee cup in his hand and "Have a nice day" on his lips. One look at Peterson and Benny offered him the cup.

"Someone throw you under a bus?" Benny jived.

The ringing was still too loud for Peterson to hear, and he was too over the top to smile. He chinned at the row house. "Sammy post guards front and back?"

"Don't know. Don't care. Neither should you."

Peterson understood half of what Benny had said. He pointed to his ears and shook his head. He asked Benny to repeat it and to say it slow.

Benny exaggerated the shape of the words he'd just spoken, then he asked, "What's going on?"

"He has a girl in there I want to get out," Peterson said.

"He has a lot of girls in there," Benny raised his voice. "They're coming and going all the time, man. She the same girl you were looking for, the one running with that Morehouse dude?"

Peterson nodded.

Benny nodded. "Sammy went inside an hour ago," he gestured for emphasis. "His boys are in and out like they got something to do. Right now, Sammy's on his own."

Benny held out the cup again, and Peterson stuffed in a ten spot.

"What's with the ears?" Benny asked.

"Loud noise."

• • •

Peterson returned to the Cherokee, parked a couple of doors beyond the row house, and came out with the sawed-off tight against his right leg. No skulking behind parked cars. No ducking from the fat man in the picture window. And no worries that it was supper hour. He knew Sammy, like most big-time dealers, would have double deadbolts on the door and a sliding steel bar on the inside. So he came up on the sidewalk and shattered the picture window with the shotgun's barrel and poked the muzzle through. He took a bead on Sammy who was on his back on the floor after ducking the flying glass.

"Move and I waste your ass," Peterson said.

Sammy shouted something.

Peterson could not make out what it was, but by the way Sammy was squirming on the floor, he knew it had to do with the fat man being scared.

"Talk loud and talk slow. You understand?"

Sammy nodded. Jowls flapping. Eyes like saucers.

"Cassie Colpitts in here?" Peterson said.

Sammy shook his head.

"Did you kill her?"

Again Sammy shook his head.

"Then where is she?"

Sammy licked his lips. Said nothing.

Peterson raised the shotgun.

Sammy started back-crawling through the broken glass.

"Talk or you get more than a load up your ass," Peterson said.

"Blackwood's got her," Sammy mumbled.

"Loud and slow," Peterson ordered.

"Blackwood's got her," Sammy repeated.

"Why Blackwood?

"Payback for her fucking mouth. His own doing, drag-assing her wherever he went. But she'll pay, man. Needle does his thing, fucking right she'll scream."

From the corner of his eye, Peterson caught Benny on the sidewalk whirling his index finger above his head. He understood the signal and walked out on the fat man. He crossed the street to the Cherokee, pulled from the curb, and rounded the corner just as two cop cars screamed to a stop in front of Sammy O's row house.

CHAPTER
FORTY-TWO

"Same feeling, same disappointments," Peterson said into the phone he was cradling on the steering wheel. He was on the winding road along the eastern shore. The rain had stopped. The temperature was now above freezing, but the pavement was still slick.

He was hearing better now, sounds less muffled, though the ringing in his ears persisted. Not that it mattered much for a Skype call from his daughter. However, now he had a sudden need to tell her what he was feeling.

"You think I don't feel it too," he said. "I want there to be something. I want to say it to you, to talk to you—"

Before he had said what he wanted to say, the screen went white, and he stared at it. Looked up halfway into a sharp turn. He stomped on the brakes and sidewound toward a ditch, spun the steering wheel to pull from the skid, catching gravel and coming to a stop.

• • •

By the light of a sixty-watt bulb, Leroy Nolan sat on an overturned wooden tub in the fish shack at the end of the dock, baiting a trawl line with chunks of mackerel. Leroy had been a fisherman. His father had been one. So had his grandfather, and now Leroy's son was a fisherman too. His son was the one who owned the trawl Nolan was baiting.

Through the shack's open door, Peterson saw Nolan's old hands shake while he reached for the next chunk but fall quiet when he set a three-inch hook into it. He coiled the snood lines and the trawl into another wooden tub.

Peterson entered the fish shack and nodded. "Leroy," he said by way of greeting.

"Peterson," Nolan replied, as he baited another hook and coiled the snood and trawl. "It's been a while. I got used to those summers with you coming here. I should've known you'd come now after I seen that cop friend of yours."

"What friend is that?"

"The old one. Years back, the two of you here together when your grandfather took sick."

That caught Peterson off guard.

"Tell me about him," Peterson said.

"He stopped in to say hello. Said he was going over to the island."

Peterson walked outside and looked over at the forty-acre island with the big house that had spotlights playing the shoreline. Nolan was saying something, a muffled sound that brought Peterson back into the shack.

"What was that?" he said.

"A lot going on over there," Nolan said. "A car and a half-ton back and forth 'cross the causeway. Makes up for all the time nothing moves on that island. You here with a badge, or you just visiting?"

"Not a cop anymore, Leroy. That makes me a visitor."

"You and that old friend of yours. You going over there too?"

Peterson looked out the grungy window, the clock in his head timing the sweep of one of the lights.

"It must be something big going on over there," Nolan said. "It can't be a social call, not with you and that Blackwood, not a chance. Don't think I don't know about you throwing him down a flight of stairs. I know a lot more than I let on." He baited another hook.

Peterson smiled. "What is it people say around here? If you want to know something in this village, ask Leroy."

Nolan grinned as he coiled the line.

"So I'm asking. Did they take a young girl into that house?"

Nolan looked up. "Kicking and screaming. She something to you?"

"Sort of."

"Are you alone?"

Peterson nodded and angled to see out the window, watching the light beam.

"He throws a lot of money around here," Nolan said. "You won't get much help."

"I'm not looking for any." He turned toward Nolan. "Pass me that knife."

Nolan gave it up, and Peterson used it to cut a few lengths off a coil of blue-and-white cord stored on a shelf behind him. He folded them into his jacket pocket and handed back the knife.

"How many in the house?"

Nolan grabbed another chunk of mackerel. "Two of them brought the girl. I don't know how many more are inside. There's another in the truck that cruises between the house and the gate, but mostly he sits in his truck and sleeps. If you want to go in private, I got a dinghy could take you to the lee side."

Peterson shook his head. "I never was much of a back-door man."

CHAPTER
FORTY-THREE

He walked down the road past a slew of lobster traps stacked for winter, past Lenny Deveau's dock and his fish shack, its red paint peeling, and past an open-front shed stuffed with bright orange buoys. He carried the SIG in one hand, the sawed-off in the other. The Kevlar vest he had left in the back seat of the Cherokee, which he had parked by Nolan's place, knowing what Cotter would say to him if he ended up with his guts blown out between his shoulder blades. Knowing he wouldn't hear a word of what Cotter said and wondering if it mattered. Wondering if anything did.

He turned onto the short, iced-over causeway to the island. A raw breeze blew a slight chop on the water, and the white crests flashed in the sweep of the searchlight's beam.

The red F-150 pickup was parked with the engine running inside the wrought-iron gate, and just as Nolan had predicted, the guard was inside it asleep. Peterson tucked the SIG into his waistband, then he crept forward and came up on the truck unnoticed. He flung open the driver's side door and clocked the guard with the barrel of the shotgun. He pulled the bloody-faced, unconscious guard from the truck, gagged him with an oily rag he found behind the front seat, and tied him to the gatepost with a length of cord. It was a hundred metres to the house, and he drove it, using the guard's pickup as a Trojan Horse.

The house was a timber frame two-storey, with a one-storey addition on the back. The main house was at least four thousand square feet, and the addition tacked on a few hundred more. There was a log outbuilding about twenty metres away from the house.

Peterson remembered the firepit where the house was now. The pit had overlooked the harbour, and teens would gather there at night drinking, smoking dope, and poking holes in their arms. Blackwood had bought the island and built his house on top of the firepit. Peterson wondered if it was Blackwood's monument to his start in the drug business, because back in the 1980s he had supplied the eastern shore. He was Mr. Goodbar, feeding teens from his tap into Carlisle Martin's supply in the city.

Peterson climbed the steps to the front porch and peeked through a window into a room that ran the width of the house. Cathedral ceiling, mortise and tenon joinery between posts and beams. An open stairway led up to a gallery where the bedrooms were. The interior was as rustic as luxury gets, with a floor-to-ceiling fieldstone fireplace and wood-frame furniture straight from some cottage life magazine.

There was a fire in the fireplace, and behind a screen it was sparking from the moisture in the wood. Blackwood was standing there, one elbow on the thick oak mantel and holding a whisky-filled glass tumbler. The glow from the fire lit the right side of his acne-scarred face and glinted off the gold chain around his neck. Fastened to the chain was the six-inch, large-eyed needle that gave him his nickname. The scene could have been a Norman Rockwell if it hadn't been for Blackwood's stringy grey hair, black biker vest, and the stabbing gestures he was making with the glass tumbler. The two goons on either side of Blackwood did not add any homey warmth either. Peterson recognized them both. One was Cameron, the guy Turtle called "Come On" — a V-shaped six-footer with a .357 S&W hanging at his side in his right hand. The other was known around the city as Pinch. He wore a leather welder's cap, and was re-crossing his arms at his chest after cuffing Robbie Yorke with a backhand and smashing the old man's head against the wood frame of the couch Yorke was sitting on.

Peterson couldn't make out what Blackwood was saying, but he could tell by his smirk and the sharp way he was shaking his drink at Yorke that it was none too pleasant. Peterson judged the situation for what he thought it was. Yorke must have barrel-assed in and tried living up to his own reputation. Now Willie Blackwood was getting even.

Cassie was nowhere to be seen.

He slipped from the porch and around the side of the house to look through windows into two back rooms. One was the kitchen, with stacked dishes and stainless steel everywhere, including a hanging ceiling of pots and pans. The other room was a den crammed with oversized black leather furniture and cluttered with beer bottles and snack trays. The TV was tuned to a hockey game.

He made for the log outbuilding. Ten feet away from it, and even with the ringing in his ears, he could hear a woman crying and begging someone to stop, and that someone telling her to shut up or he'd beat the hell out of her.

He had only heard her say two words when he tried to rescue her from the crack house, but those two words were enough for him to know the female voice inside that log building belonged to Cassie Colpitts.

He clicked off the safety on the shotgun. Rounded to the front of the building. No window peek to size up the room. Just balls and a willingness to let whatever was going to happen happen. He reared back and shouldered through the front door.

Cassie was naked on the floor, and some goon was bare ass on top of her. He turned quick toward Peterson and caught a mouthful of muzzle. Swallowed teeth and blood. Choked.

Peterson shifted his feet, cocked his shoulder, and drove the gunstock into the side of the goon's head, knocking him to the floor. He stood over him and pressed the muzzle to the goon's chest. His finger was eager on the trigger, and he felt the urge to squeeze one off.

Then Cassie squealed. She was squirming away from the bloodied goon on the floor and from Peterson standing over him. Her face was rigid with pain and fear. Her right eye was closed and leaking a clear, viscous liquid. The eyelid had been pierced and her eye was bulging. There was a thin streak of dried blood down her cheek.

Peterson gasped. His senses were driven by what he

now knew the Needle had done to her. He lowered the gun, fighting back the rage he felt, and crouched so as not to appear so big and threatening. He softened his face.

"Remember me?" he said, and set the shotgun aside. "Your mother sent me to help you, to get you out of here."

Her open eye was hollow with incomprehension; her mouth had fallen to a silent cry.

He sensed the pain she was feeling. He gathered her jeans and blue cotton shirt from the floor.

"I know it hurts," he said, "but you have to get dressed. We need to go." He passed the clothes to her.

Maybe it was her desperate urge to grab for whatever or whoever offered hope, or maybe she remembered him from trying to help her that night in the crack house, but she hurried into her clothes and took his hand when he offered it.

He led her from the outbuilding to the truck.

"Can you see enough to drive?" he asked. "Can you do that?"

She mumbled something he could not make out. It took a moment for it to sink in that she had said she did not know how to drive. He helped her into the passenger's seat, got in the driver's side, and slowly backed the pickup away from the house. The gate guard was still gagged and tied to the post. Peterson fished the key to the gate from the guard's pants pocket and opened it. He drove to Nolan's bungalow a short distance from his fish shack.

Nolan met the truck halfway up the driveway.

"He's a friend," Peterson told her. Then he climbed down from the truck and said to Nolan, "Get your son's wife to take her to a doctor. The Needle did a number on her eye. And they raped her."

"What about you?" Nolan asked.

Peterson hesitated, then reached for the shotgun in the truck. "The old man is still there."

He poked his head back into the cab and said to Cassie, "Leroy and his family will take care of you. You'll be all right. I promise."

He retraced his steps along the causeway to the big house on the island. He climbed to the porch and checked through the window to see where the players were now positioned. Blackwood was still standing in the glow of the fire. Cameron still stood at Blackwood's left. And Pinch had a thrashing, yelling Robbie Yorke bent backward over the arm of the couch. Then Blackwood unhooked the needle from the chain and stepped forward.

Peterson pressed his back to the wall beside the door. He had no plan, just the realization that once he blew through the front door he would take out Cameron with the twelve-gauge. After that it was a matter of who did what.

He tried the door handle. Felt it click open. Then he drew a deep breath to settle his nerves, which were singing like hot wires. He had a stony taste in his mouth from the adrenalin rush and from summoning up the courage to overcome his fear.

The taste provoked a flashback, from the time at the north-end container terminal, when he and a jughead had faced off in the shadows between tall stacks of shipping con-tainers. Six feet apart and the jughead not backing down, pointing his .38 Smith at Peterson's head. And Peterson holding the same position, with his 9mm aimed between the jughead's eyes. He had urged the guy to drop his piece, begged him for Christ's sake, and the jughead had refused to give an inch. Then Danny's voice had blasted over the radio, "Where the fuck are you?" And the jughead's eyes had gone wild, blinking a mile a minute.

As fast as that memory had popped into his head, it popped out when Robbie Yorke screamed. Peterson stiffened, drew a deep breath, and slowly let it out. And just as slowly, he opened the door, the sawed-off waist high, and walked in, speed-scanning one player to the next.

Cameron raised his .357. Arm shaking. The suddenness of it and the grit of facing down a twelve-gauge and a man with a death-mask face had Cameron wide-eyed in confusion. One beat. Two. Finger on the trigger, but not squeezing. The gun weighing heavy in his hand. Three. Four.

Yorke was still screaming. Blackwood struck motionless. Pinch in a sudden daze. And Peterson kept walking forward. His fear buried deep under his indifference to dying.

Then Cameron fired and missed.

Peterson raised and levelled the shotgun and blasted Cameron full bore. He fell backward onto the hearth, knocking the screen aside, his left hand flying back over his head and into the fire.

Blackwood stepped aside as Pinch released Yorke and went behind his back for the gun in his belt. He came around too slow. Peterson pumped the sawed-off and blew a table lamp that froze Pinch just long enough for Peterson to chamber another round. Before Pinch could raise the 9mm Browning, Peterson fired. Pinch went backward, and the 9 flew forward. It landed at Blackwood's feet.

Blackwood eyed the gun on the floor. Peterson pumped

again. He could feel it, taste it, the gush of killing, the stupor that drove soldiers to do what their whole being told them not to do.

Blackwood saw it on Peterson's face. He looked at Yorke on the couch, at his squinting eye and his jaw locked in shock and anger. Then he looked at Cameron dead on the hearth and at Pinch gut-shot on the floor.

"Drop the needle," Peterson said.

Blackwood dropped it, and Yorke picked it up, along with the 9mm. He played the pistol on Blackwood. His look dared the dope trafficker to make a wrong move.

Peterson gestured with the shotgun at Cameron's body. "Pull his hand from the fire," he said to Yorke.

Yorke did as told.

Peterson turned on Blackwood. His blood still up and nerves in a knot. "You took her eye," he seethed.

Blackwood was impassive. "So what?"

Peterson rammed the muzzle of the shotgun into Blackwood's ribs.

"A fifteen-year-old kid," he fumed. "Fourteen when you got your hands on her."

"Old enough to stab," Blackwood blustered.

"She had your kid, goddamn it!"

Blackwood dialled up an attitude. "What do you want, man? A chick comes on, juking her ass, and I'm all up. Seventeen again. And she's slick, you know what I'm saying? I took what was on the table."

"You used her up and tossed her."

"She didn't go empty-handed. Had an armload. But she got up on herself, you hear what I'm saying? Talking about what she knew."

"About the stash or the cap on Vernon Rumley?"

"He got what losers get. Writing notes and threatening me. Me! Like I'm some gutter chump." Blackwood pointed to his forehead. "I said right here, between his fucking eyes, so he sees it coming."

"And Morehouse did the shooting," Peterson said.

"You want losers? Count that fucker in. Thinks I don't know the street. Bust my hole like he did. You know how long? Two hours and I had him here, on his knees begging. So yeah, I got even, only this time I didn't use no needle. I put a gun in Morehouse's hand. I said kill Rumley and you walk. Nothing comes back, not on me."

Blackwood folded his arms. Standing tall.

"I wouldn't be here if nothing came back," Peterson said. "Cassie walked and Cassie talked."

Blackwood flashed a dismissive smile. "So did that whore you tore some off. A smackhead with a big fucking mouth."

Peterson shoved the shotgun in hard, and Blackwood groaned. "A mouth you shut tight."

Blackwood straightened. "Cameron set that up."

"Easy to say now."

"Clean hands," Blackwood said, holding them out like he was on stage, some big performance. "I don't even own a gun. Not even the one I took from him." He gestured to Yorke. "He comes here all balls and big ass. Thirty years he thinks I keep a gun with a toe tag. What am I, a fucking lunatic? Wrapped in his own fucking guilt for being on my payroll. It wasn't the gun that kept him there. Ask him!"

Peterson held his eyes on Blackwood. "Robbie?"

Yorke didn't answer.

Blackwood jutted his jaw. "Look around, motherfucker.

I got all this and a hundred times more than what you see. I fucked over more than my share of cops and politicians to get it."

Peterson tensed. He wanted to ram the shotgun butt into Blackwood's mouth, but didn't. Instead, he opened his hand and slapped the drug slinger in the face.

Blackwood's cheeks blanched. He clenched his fists. Peterson slapped him again. Then again. Then he drew a deep breath and felt his edge grind down. He looked at Yorke.

"The cops have a witness and enough documents to put this shit and his friends away," Peterson said. "That scores it even."

"You go too," Blackwood said. "Body count's on your head. And me and you got a history of you getting too rough. I'm unarmed and you bust in and shoot the ass off my associates. Who's going to say different? Him? A retired cop who was on the take? I doubt it. Self-defence won't cut it, and manslaughter puts you inside. Hard time for a cop. Inmates all wanting a piece of you. But me? There's no stash here. Possession, maybe. But, hey, I got lawyers that'll chisel that down to a slap on the wrist. I'm easy with that. How about you?"

Peterson had the shotgun still dug into Blackwood's ribs and his finger tight on the trigger. Easy to squeeze off another. But the adrenalin was gone from Peterson's blood. The flash had faded. And the reality of what had just happened had a hopeless look about it. Two dead and two badly beaten up.

Blackwood was all teeth. "The way I see it, you're fucked no matter what you do."

Yorke rose up, swung the Browning, and cracked

Blackwood across the side of his head. Blackwood buckled and hit the floor.

Yorke turned on Peterson. "I want you out of here," he said. His bad eye was twitching, the eyelid scratched but not pierced.

"You want what?"

"I have work to do," Yorke said. "So leave the SIG and shotgun here and get on your horse and go."

"I can't let you—"

"Yes you can. If anyone has to pay for what happened here, it's me."

Yorke had the needle in one hand and waved the Browning in the other. "I saw what he did to that girl. She screamed like I heard that kid scream thirty years ago. Jesus Christ, he's no fucking good! Laughing like that. Then passing her over to one of them. They got what they deserved, and you know it. Now go! It's my play. Mine! And it's not for you I'm doing it. It's for me."

● ● ●

Peterson was halfway across the causeway when he heard Blackwood scream, and keep screaming. And then there was a shotgun blast, and Blackwood stopped screaming. And then there was the bark of gunfire inside the house from more than one calibre, followed by a long pause and then a single pistol shot. Then there was silence.

Peterson walked past Nolan's white bungalow to where he had parked the Cherokee. He was shaking and he was crying, and he was wondering if being born was worth the cost of living.

CHAPTER
FORTY-FOUR

Bernie let herself in, switched on the overhead in the front hall, and found him in the den sitting on the loveseat in the dark, wrestling with temptation. He had not slept in days, and it showed. She turned on a table lamp and looked around the room. The seven paintings of men's faces on the wall behind the recliner caught her attention. Then she saw the full bottle of Johnnie Walker set on the floor in the middle of the room, and the way Peterson was staring at it, pretending that she wasn't there. She sat down in the recliner.

"You don't lock your doors," she said.

Peterson looked at her. Then he looked past her, through the living room to the front door.

"He's not coming," Bernie said. "He's spinning plates and complaining about how much paperwork you've caused. It's a good thing the Mounties took the files from Dr. Connors off our hands, or I'd never hear the end of it. They're investigating Angelina Sampson."

Peterson's face was blank.

"We're up to our eyeballs, more than enough with the eight bodies," she said. "Still waiting on a full report from forensics, but we think we have it figured out." She counted on her fingers. "We have Morehouse down for Rumley. A preliminary from Janet has the .38 on the floor in the powder magazine matching the bullet in Rumley's head. The gun had Morehouse's prints.

"Then we have Sammy O and his boys for killing Pike, Morehouse, and the Brick. We put Sammy in the box and he was talkative from the get go, pointing fingers at everyone but himself."

Peterson still showed no expression. He hardly blinked.

"But the four out on the island?" she said. "That's something else. Blackwood and Yorke and two of Blackwood's boys dead inside the house. The two we picked up outside, the ones with sore heads, don't know what hit them. And Danny's not buying the way it looks, Yorke coming off as a superhero. He thinks what happened out there was a wax job; that someone in the know made it look like a seventy-year-old was a one-man army. He told me to say that to you, about it being a wax job. He said you'd know what he meant."

Peterson got up to retrieve the bottle of whisky. "You want a drink?"

"No."

He put the bottle down and sat back on the loveseat. He closed his eyes. "That night in the container terminal, the night I shot the jughead, I was a basket case. Danny showed up. I had the gun in my hand, and the jughead was on the ground with a bullet hole in his head. I couldn't move. I couldn't do nothing. The guy's gun was clean. So Danny fired the dead man's gun so it looked right. He called it waxing a crime scene."

He met her eyes. "Robbie Yorke didn't do anything different than what Danny did that time. You tell him that. And tell him whatever happened on that island, I'm the one who has to live with the hell of it all."

Bernie got up and stepped around the recliner to look at the paintings on the wall. The men's faces stood out against their dark backgrounds. All of them were staring inward as though fathoming a question of conscience.

"A friend is an artist," Peterson said. "He drinks off my cuff at The Office and pays me back with those. He thinks faces tell the whole story."

"What do you think?"

"I think the ones inside my head have a lot more to say. And they keep coming back to say it. Making the rounds."

"What about that priest I told you about, the one who helped me?"

Peterson turned and looked up at the paintings and then at Bernie. He drew a deep breath and slowly released it. "What can he do?"

"He can listen, and maybe offer forgiveness if you need it."

"Forgiveness?"

"If you need it."

He looked at the paintings. Then he looked at Bernie. "Who doesn't need forgiveness?"

CHAPTER
FORTY-FIVE

The RNs and CNAs at the fifth-floor nurses' station had their heads down as the night shift reported to those clocking in for the day run. One of the nurses recognized Peterson. "She had a good night," the nurse said, "and is doing just fine."

Patty was sleeping. The light above the bed was on, a Bible beside her. It was open to Psalms. One of them was pencil marked, Psalm 102.

He watched her sleep. Then he reached for the Bible and read, until one verse struck him and he read it out loud, "For I eat ashes like bread; and my drink do I mingle with tears."

He closed the book, uncomfortable with his thoughts and feelings.

She woke to see him suffering so.

"How long have you been here?" she asked.

"Not long."

There were tears in his eyes, and when she saw them hers filled too. They held on to that moment for a long time. Then he said, "I come with a lot of baggage."

She wiped her eyes, then reached for his hand. "You're not the only one with a past."

"Mine's just one ugly day after another."

Patty waited while he gathered himself.

"I saved a girl the other night, for what, I don't know. Her life's a mess and probably always will be. I offered to help, and maybe down the road she'll let me."

He looked away and started to say something but stopped. Then he looked at her.

"I killed two men," he said. "Maybe they deserved to die, but what I did was wrong. And I'll have to live with it, the way I have to live with everything else."

Patty lay staring at him. She said, "What did they do, those men?"

He inhaled deeply. "They were drug dealers and murderers. They destroyed lives."

"Did they kill the friend you told me about?"

He nodded.

"What about the law?" she asked.

"I didn't wait for it. I couldn't wait for it. Things happened. Sometimes your brain doesn't think."

He fell silent and she let the silence have its time. Then he said, "You work the streets for years, and you think what you see every day is normal. Then you go home and what's there doesn't fit who you are anymore. So I stopped going home. The job became who I am. The street became like oxygen, and I was breathing it to stay alive. Then there was nothing to go home to. I lost my wife before she died, and my daughter long before she ran away."

He lowered his voice to barely a whisper.

"I blame myself," he said. "I see lots of faces. I can't help it, but I blame myself for all of them. And then it got to be too much. One morning, I woke up in the back seat of my car. It was six below, and I was shivering in the back seat, lying there with my hands on my chest. I had my cell phone in one hand and a loaded .38 in the other. I didn't have to sniff the barrel."

He swallowed hard and let go of her hand.

"I saw the hole in the car roof and I lay there knowing what I had done, thinking that blowing out your brains has nothing to do with guts. It has to do with a Ruger in the mouth and a moment of weakness."

His mind went away somewhere for a moment. When he came back, he was crying.

She again reached for his hand and pulled him close. "I want you to kiss me, Peterson. Don't pull away. Don't say no. My life hasn't always been by the rules, and I don't have much to hang on to either. So just do it."

ACKNOWLEDGEMENTS

Thanks to Dinah and Laura for keeping my writing on the straight and narrow, and to Corporal Mike Sims for his advice and insights.